DELETED

RUTH MITCHELL

Appropriate for Teens, Intriguing to Adults

Immortal Works LLC
1505 Glenrose Drive
Salt Lake City, Utah 84104
Tel: (385) 202-0116

Cover Art by Ashley Literski
http://strangedevotion.wixsite.com/strangedesigns

ISBN 978-1-7343866-0-8 (Paperback)
ASIN B082XHN977 (Kindle Edition)

To my mom who always believed in my writing.
I wish you could have lived to see this day.

PART 1

I went to the woods
  because I wished to live deliberately.
  Henry David Thoreau, *Walden*

CHAPTER 1

Abashed the devil stood and felt how awful goodness is
and saw Virtue in her shape how lovely: and pined his loss
John Milton, *Paradise Lost*

E very night before he goes to bed, Nick erases himself from
everyone's memory. It can be lonely having no one remember
him, but it's the only way he can accomplish his work. And...it's not a
bad life. There's incredible freedom in being anonymous. Besides,
memories and all the petty relationships people construct around
them are a total sham.

In truth, each day is like a note with the instructions, burn after
reading. Life is the burning. The best part. By the time we hit our
pillows, most of the day is obliterated. We've forgotten what we ate
for breakfast, the exact words of a conversation, the face of a stranger.
All that remains are ashes and a few random scraps that won't burn.
A look. A taste. A feeling. People hoard these scraps, piece them
together, string them into a narrative and pretend it's life. But it's not.
Life, reality—whatever you want to call it—has already gone up in
smoke.

Nick knows this. He knows that not one of the memories he scans is completely true. But they're his only chance to find her. Last night he didn't sleep. He spent the entire night searching for Lucy, the one person who remembers him, the only mind he hasn't been able to hack.

He stands in his living room, surrounded by footage of a freckled girl with messy hair. Discrete lenses in the ceiling project dozens of images on white walls. He watches without sound or context, still catching the key details. This skill is how, even as a college dropout, Nick was able to purchase this oceanfront condo before his twenty-first birthday. This morning the view's nothing more than thick fog, like the layer of clouds seen through an airplane window.

The memories of those closest to Lucy flicker on the north wall. On the opposite side flash the illicit memories of his clients. A large glass desk near the window reflects and distorts images from both sides. The rest of the room is empty except for some workout equipment: a stationary bike, a weight-lifting bench, and a treadmill, each a lonely island in a sea of gray wood flooring. Nick works out while he scans footage. He's nothing, if not efficient.

He runs on his treadmill, watching another Lucy memory, this one taken from her hot friend, Karen.

The two girls sit on a quilt on a sunny scrap of lawn outside the computer science building—waiting.

"I can't believe it's February." Lucy wears a yellow sundress. Her freckled shoulders a little pink with sunburn. "This morning my mom sent me pictures of her car buried in snow."

"I know, right? This perfect weather is freaky," answers Karen. "I don't think I'll ever get used to living without seasons. But it does help stalking."

"It's not stalking," Lucy says with a self-deprecating laugh. "It's caring."

Nick laughs. *Amen, sister!*

"Did I tell you what happened Tuesday?" Lucy is too excited to wait for an answer. "He sat at that very bench and, drum roll..." She plays air drums and hits an air cymbal. "Ding! He smiled at me!"

"How do you know he wasn't watching something funny on his Spex?"

"Give me some credit. Even if I don't use Spex, I can tell when someone is on theirs. He smiled right at me."

"Congratulations! But I still say you are doing this the hard way. Why don't you sign up for his class? That way you could gawk at him twice a week like the rest of us and get credit for it."

Nick can't see Karen in this memory. But after spending a night scanning recollections of Lucy, he has a good idea what her best friend looks like. She's short, well-built, always wears workout clothes, and her white-blonde hair is styled in a pixie cut with a blue streak.

"Can you see me in computer science?" says Lucy. I'd be the only one without Spex."

"Sweetie, you're the only one on campus without Spex."

"That's my point. I don't belong in computer science. I belong in a ratty, old armchair reading the thoughts of dead men."

"While spying on live ones?"

"Something like that."

"Lucky for you, I'm an excellent stalker and a good friend. I took some photos for you in class today. I'm sending them now with a couple shots from the beach."

Karen thinks, *Charlotte: Send Lucy photos from yesterday taken at La Jolla Shores and the ones from class today.*

"With pleasure!" A female voice with a slight Boston accent whispers in her earpiece. "Sending Lucy Campbell eleven photos."

Lucy takes her phone out of her backpack. She pauses on the picture of Marco lecturing. Karen leans over to admire it, too.

"You might be right." Lucy downloads the photos. "Maybe I should take his class."

"You have to. He's the best TA. I mean, it's not just that he's a genius and all that. His enthusiasm is contagious, and he remembers everyone by name."

"Of course he does. He made his fortune with his *Good with Names* app."

"And he's not even too old for you. He started college when he was like fifteen."

"I know. Trust me. I've Googled him plenty. What sort of stalker do you think I am?"

"We've already established that you're not a very good one. No one can truly stalk without Spex. You should try mine. They're the latest model. They have telescopic lenses."

"Cool! Maybe I will. Wait! That's him!"

Marco Han's black mop of hair emerges from the building.

Karen thinks, *Charlotte: Zoom.* Immediately in her right lens, "Zoom 2x" appears. Marco's wearing a faded blue Hawaiian shirt, khaki shorts and frayed flip-flops. Karen's left lens top corner reads, "Marco Han, 19, single, UCSD Grad Student," along with a link to his social network page. Both girls let out an audible sigh.

What do they see in this dude? thinks Nick. *Look at how he dresses! It's all because he's rich. I'm rich!*

Marco hops on his board and skates across the wide pathway to the edge of the lawn to where they are sitting.

"Hey Karen, new Spex?" He flips up his board.

"Yeah, I got them last week." Karen stands up to greet him. Lucy remains on the blanket, her eyes fixed on the ground. The afternoon sun illuminates her reddish-brown mane of hair.

Marco and Karen ooh and aah over the new Spex, Lucy sneaks a look at Marco, who is trying on the new glasses and appears ridiculous in the retro frames with rhinestones in the winged tips. She stifles a laugh. He looks her way.

"No Spex, huh?"

She tries to play it cool. "Not my thing."

"Seriously? I don't think I've ever met anyone over eight without a mindseye."

"Tell me about it!" Nick hollers at the screen. *What is wrong with this girl? If she wore Spex, I'd have found her by now.*

"I'm Marco, by the way." He returns Karen's Spex and sits down next to Lucy.

"Lucy."

"Right, I see you all the time."

"I bet you do." Karen snickers. Nick laughs too.

"So, why no Spex?" he asks.

She takes a steadying breath before answering. "I like to see the world through my own eyes. I don't want to be distracted."

"That's ludicrous," says Marco. "That's like going around with your eyes closed so you're not distracted by the clouds and the trees and meeting new people." He talks with his hands, pointing to the clouds and trees as he mentions them.

"My eyes are wide open and I just met you." She smiles big. "You're new."

"Sure, but you're closed to another layer of reality." He waves a hand in front of her face. "Spex bring the whole world to you." He pops the iridescent earpiece out of his ear. "This baby can hold every recording in the last century as well as every movie made in my lifetime. Why wouldn't you want one?"

"I have funny ideas..."

"She wants to keep her mind *pure*."

"I just don't think it's that big of a leap from our thoughts controlling Spex to Spex controlling our thoughts."

Marco laughs outright. "We lost that battle long ago. All media directs our thoughts, be it a book or a movie. It doesn't matter if you see that movie in a theater or watch it while you're walking to class. Or in class, like some of my students..."

She interrupts, "'It's the movies that have been really running things in America.'"

"Nice! Andy Warhol!" He points at her. "I love that quote. And it proves my argument."

"Nah, it proves mine. It's harder to separate your thoughts from others' when you hear their ideas in your own head."

"You're hearing my arguments in your head right now. Your brain's translating the sound waves picked up by your ears. What's the difference?"

"He's right," says Karen.

"The difference is that the businesses who own apps and search engines want to suck up as much of my time as they can. To make money, they need my attention. If I take too much time to think for myself, they don't make money. I don't want Spex to crowd out my own thoughts."

"Heaven forbid! It's obvious you have a fascinating mind. I appreciate your desire to protect it. But Spex, used judiciously, only amplify a great mind."

"That is..." She gives him a saucy look. "...if you don't spend your whole day, gaming or binging on TV."

"Point for Lucy," says Karen. "It's a tie: one for Marco and one for you."

"What I want to know is how you manage your classes without Spex," he asks.

"I remember things."

"I bet you do. But you'd have to remember a lot. What was once called cheating is now applied knowledge."

"When I don't know something, I look it up—the old-fashioned way."

"You don't have...?"

She pulls her iPhone out of her backpack. "Yep, vintage."

"Can I see it? Everything still works?"

"Pretty much. Whenever something breaks, my sister fixes it." She hands him the phone. "She's a computer genius. She used to hack for the government."

"Hey! 2048!" He fiddles with the phone with childish delight.

"I used to play that on my dad's phone on my way to preschool. Can I play it on yours? It's not the same on Spex."

"So, you concede? Spex are not superior in all ways?"

"Only if you let me play 2048!" He's engrossed by the phone. "Hey, nice photo. You're cute in a swimsuit."

"Don't go through my photos!" Lucy grabs her phone.

He gives it back to her with a smirk. "You know, if you wanted my picture you could have Googled me."

Lucy doesn't answer. She stands up, turns around and runs.

Marco chases after her. Karen laughs; so does Nick. And then he deletes the memory.

CHAPTER 2

Only that day dawns
 to which we are awake.
 Henry David Thoreau, *Walden*

A face haunts Marco's mind. A girl with freckles and ponderous eyes. She must have been in his dream. He considers the face. Why's it so familiar? He sits up in bed, running his hand across the star-patterned quilt. The pastel stars are made of an assortment of cutesy prints. Where did he get this blanket? It doesn't look like something his mom would pick out. Her style is more modern than country cottage. It's not his style, either. Not that Marco has much of a style. His apartment is decorated sparsely with hand-me-downs from his parents, all sleek lines and neutral shades. The multi-color quilt does not belong, but he likes it. It makes him feel...well...like that dream. He pictures that face again. Who was she? And then he remembers: Karen's friend. Karen's a whip-smart sophomore in his Tuesday/Thursday class. He's always bumping into Karen on campus, always with her pretty friend who doesn't wear Spex. What's her name?

He retrieves his mindseye and Spex from his nightstand and puts them on.

Morning, Steve.

The computer-generated voice replies, "Good morning, Marco. It's Thursday, March thirty-first. It is fifty-seven degrees with thick fog. The marine layer should burn off by ten." Out the window the morning mist drifts through the trees. White clouds envelop the neighboring apartment building until it's no more than a faint brown rectangle.

Hey, Steve, I need to find someone.

This is an easy puzzle for Marco, who works as a grad student in the department of artificial intelligence. As a college freshman, he perfected a facial recognition program to help people remember names. His app links names with the faces of people you meet. When you meet someone new, you think into your Spex, *Name please.* In a moment a voice in the earpiece whispers back the individual's name and a tag to remind you how you know this person. The tag could be formal like the company the person works for or casual like "Joe's friend." The newest version of the app keeps track of more details about the person such as birthdays and anniversaries. It also gives a small-talk prompt, "Recently returned from a trip to Spain," or important reminders such as "Owes you fifty dollars."

If he had a picture of the girl from his dream, he could find her in real-time as long as she was in the line of vision of someone wearing Spex. Some day, the image in his head might be enough to search for her, but right now the communication between the brain and Spex is not that advanced. Marco doesn't know anyone who's found a way to send mental images to a computer.

What do you have on Karen Burns?

"Karen Burns, sophomore at UCSD?"

Exactly!

Still lounging in bed, Marco scans through Karen's pictures on her social networking page. Ahah! He's found the girl from his dream: Lucy Campbell from Beaver Falls, Pennsylvania. He browses through her social network page. Her family seems to have visited every national park. He recognizes many of them. His dad likes national parks too. There she is as a young girl wearing a pink skirt and a bulky life jacket canoeing in the Everglades, at nine waiting for Old Faithful in Yellowstone, and as a teenager hiking the Appalachian Trail. Marco can't name the color of her hair: reddish, golden-brown, maybe? In most of the photos her hair is flying wild. In most of the photos she's wearing a dress. In all of the photos she is beautiful.

There are lots of photos of her with an older sister. The sister has sleek red hair with straight cut bangs, usually up in a ponytail. The sister's married (Lucy looks about thirteen in the wedding photos) and has a baby. There's a picture of Lucy and the baby together on a blanket. Marco takes another look at the photo. The blanket has stars on it. He zooms in. The print on the blue star is the same as the print on the blue star of the quilt on top of him. It's kind of a weird print with miniature ducks wearing sailor hats. What are the chances?

He sits up and examines the quilt. He turns over a corner and finds an embroidered label.

To Lucy on your 18th Birthday
Made with love, Mom

He drops the corner, bewildered. Taking the quilt back up, he rubs his finger along the bumpy embroidery. A happy thought comes to him: He has to return it.

He decides to message this girl. And if that doesn't work, he'll search his database after class. He begins a friend request. *Hey, you don't know me but... Scratch that. This is sort of random, but I have something of yours.* No, it has to be perfect. He'll worry about the message later. Time to get ready for the day. He removes his Spex as he dresses but leaves his mindseye in. He brushes his teeth and makes his bed. His hand lingers on the soft cotton of the quilt.

"Twenty minutes till class," warns Steve.

Marco puts on his Spex. On the screen of his right lens is a social network page. It looks like he was making a friend request. Who was he requesting? Lucy Campbell? He sees a photo of a freckled girl with reddish-gold hair. She seems kind of familiar. But why is he sending her a request? He doesn't have time to worry about it. He puts on his flip-flops by the door. As he hurries down the steps he thinks, *Steve: lock the door and turn off the lights.* He hops on his long board. *Steve, the usual at the Campus Café.*

"A breakfast club with avocado and jalapenos," Steve replies. "Ready in seven minutes. What should I do about this request to Lucy Campbell?"

Lucy Campbell?

"Yes, you have an unfinished friend request."

Lucy Campbell? Never heard of her... Must be a mistake. As Marco's speed increases, the trees, the people, the buildings all blur together in the fog and Lucy Campbell is wiped from his memory again.

CHAPTER 3

Could a greater miracle take place
    than for us to look through each other's eyes for an instant?
    Henry David Thoreau, *Walden*

So far, it's been easy enough to keep Lucy's family from thinking of her. Forgetting is the natural course. Forgetting is like falling. A person must try to remember. Nick doesn't destroy memories; he isolates them. Memories are linked moment to moment in a delicate web. To make someone forget, break a strand—send an electrical signal—and the web unravels.

The only difficulty has been Marco. He keeps searching for a Lucy Campbell. This morning, he recognized the quilt on his bed on her social networking page. Nick considers taking the page down. He hasn't yet, because he doesn't want to erase Lucy out of everyone's mind. He only wants to keep them from thinking about her for a little while—long enough for him to find her.

He takes down the photo of the quilt. As he does so, he notes the discrepancy between the pictures of Lucy and the memories of her. She's sort of pretty in a wholesome way. Solid seven. But he's made men forget more attractive women. Why won't Marco forget? He must have dreamed about her. Wretched dreams! They're too fleeting. They rarely surface into a client's conscious memory long enough to be erased. But they keep returning, buzzing back like a fly you cannot kill.

In the last few months, Nick's work has become totally consuming. He no longer has time to experiment, to see what other parts of the brain he can infiltrate. He's too busy taking care of clients and protecting himself. The burden of success. Maybe he's losing sight of his ultimate goal. At times he's overwhelmed by the vastness of his ambition. He rests his forehead on the cool glass of the window. Below him gray mists swirl over the metallic Pacific. She has to be out there somewhere.

He studies another memory, one of her sister's. Mollie has a stellar mind. Good thing he had time to record her memories before he sabotaged them.

Mollie's in the kitchen, gathering ingredients for mac and cheese with butternut squash and bacon. The recipe runs in a small font across the right lens of her Spex. Lucy sits on a kitchen stool, her hands over her face. Nick says out loud, "Screen eleven, sound on." Lucy's voice pipes through his ear bud sweet and low.

"Why did I run? Finally, finally I have the chance to talk to him and I blow it. Aarrgh!" She vents her frustration into a hot pad.

Her sister mixes flour into melted butter and onions. Mollie is attractive in a boring way. Nick cannot see her right now. The memory's all from her point of view, but he has seen enough of her in other memories to know her well. Her home, her clothes, her furniture all have this mainstream sheen as if they belong in a commercial for laundry detergent.

"Him? Who's him?" Mollie asks.

"Marco!"

Mollie speaks with disbelief. "Marco Han?"

Really? thinks Nick. *Why does everyone make such a fuss about that kid?*

Lucy squeaks out a pathetic, "I know."

"The Good-with-Names-app Marco Han? The graduated-from-high-school-at-fifteen?" Mollie's on a roll. "Introduced-his-best-selling-app-at-seventeen, finished-Stanford-at-eighteen, runs-his-own-company-while-working-on-his-PhD Marco Han? You talked to him?"

Lucy nods and can't help but smile, revealing a dimple.

Okay, maybe she's an eight.

"There's no justice in the world. My little sister the technophobe, who won't even wear Spex, met Marco Han. It should have been me!"

"Hello? You're married and way older."

"I'm not interested in him like that. Seriously? Do you even think he's cute?"

Have to side with the sister there.

"Doesn't everybody?"

"He's a tad nerdy."

Yeah, does the guy even work out?

"Says the woman who married Phil."

Mollie ignores that comment. "I wish I'd been there. What's he like? I bet he's fascinating. I hear he's sooo down to earth."

"He was adorkable and charming..."

Adorkable? Honestly?

"And then I had to ruin everything..." Lucy facepalms again. "I looked like such an idiot. What's my problem? All I had to do was laugh it off. Worst case, he thinks I'm a stalker. But he'd still be flattered. Best case, he asks me out. We could be getting boba right now."

Mollie says some comforting words while she shreds cheese. Nick already knows that Mollie is twelve years older than her sister and that Lucy chose UCSD so she could be closer to her only sister.

Lucy gets off the stool and starts to help with dinner. As she rinses the colander of beans, she lets out a long, defeated sigh. "Do you ever wish you could edit your life?"

"I can," answers Mollie.

"Yeah, I know all your self-improvement mumbo jumbo. Anyone can change, break a bad habit, paint a room or sew a new curtain." Lucy points to the navy-checked flounce above the kitchen window. Mollie sewed this as well as the rest of the curtains in the house.

"I don't mean self-improvement," says Mollie as she stirs shredded cheese into the white sauce. "I mean like delete a memory."

"What do you mean?"

"What I said. I can erase memories."

"That's impossible."

"Well...then...I can do the impossible."

Nick cannot see Mollie's face but he knows the expression. He's worn it himself.

"What?" Lucy's face is wary.

"I've been dying to tell someone. You see, I did something that was...well...less than perfect. Phil was pretty upset with me, and I wished I could..."

"What was it?"

"I ran into a concrete pillar in a parking garage—a couple times, actually. I hit it once and then again two days after we repaired it. Phil couldn't stop bringing it up."

I bet he did. Woman drivers.

"...and how much it cost, and really...I did it to improve my marriage."

"Did it? Did what?"

"Tidied up his memory."

"What does that mean—exactly?"

"I erased his memory; actually, several memories. He has no recollection of my hitting that pillar—either time. I've had all this free time, you know while Porter naps, and I had a hunch that you could hack a person's memory through their Spex. The brain is amazingly organized. It's like a network of city streets folded over and over itself like a croissant. I've actually become pretty good at finding memories."

"You've done this more than once?!"

"Don't sound so shocked. It's a good thing, actually. Think of it as strengthening my marriage."

I like how this lady thinks even if she can't drive.

"Or lying?"

"What did we talk about on February eighth?"

"I don't know; I might have mentioned Marco. Like I'd remember."

"That's just it. You don't remember. Every moment we're forgetting. It's not lying; it's helping him forget something he'd rather forget."

Booyah! She gets it.

Mollie puts the mac and cheese into the oven. Still wearing her frilly apron, she walks to the living room with Lucy trailing behind. She sits down at her desk and places her hand on a glass sphere the size of a softball. The ball lights up; her hand glows pink. A virtual screen hovers above it. At the same time a keyboard projects on the desk.

"What time did you to talk to Marco?"

"About three. Why?"

"Some people organize their memories by time, others by location..."

"No, no, no, no, no! Don't go messing with his mind!"

"Just one peek. Come on! You've got to be curious." Mollie types something.

"I'm not helping you with this. Hacking your husband's mind is one thing. I mean you're married and one in purpose, or at least you file taxes jointly. But Marco! You've never even met him. You can't go rifling through his thoughts!"

This girl is kinda cute when she's angry.

"Don't be ridiculous; you're the one who wanted to edit your life."

"Only because I didn't think it was possible! It's a terrible idea. And probably against the law."

"What law? Nobody believes it's possible. You can't make laws against the impossible."

A baby cries; the memory fades. Nick turns off the treadmill. He can't help but shake his head. Back when he worked in the lab, he was driven by the fear that someone else might discover how to access memories. He never considered that his first real competition would be a bad-driving, redheaded housewife. But this Mollie, she gets it. And Lucy...she's a fool. Running from him, hiding, for what? A few worthless, fleeting, transitory memories?

A dozen Lucys flash on the wall. He's running a constant search of her face through his database. If anyone wearing Spex sees her, he'll know in minutes. But he's found no matches so far. Where is she? She might be hiding with someone who doesn't wear Spex—if another such pathetic person exists. Or she could be alone, hiding outdoors. What was she wearing? He scrolls through the sister's memories. That's right, a white cotton sundress. Not the outfit for sleeping outside. Sooner or later, she'll need food and warmer clothes. Chances are she'll sneak back to her sister's. That's why he hacked the camera in Mollie's computer. He also hacked Marco's and Karen's computers and Spex. He's set up a data source aggregator to compile these live feeds with his program searching memories and other digital data. Wherever she goes, he'll find her.

CHAPTER 4

Follow your genius closely enough
  and it will not fail to show you a fresh prospect every hour.
  Henry David Thoreau, *Walden*

March 31st, 2044
      To anyone who might find this book,
You should know that minds can be hacked by Spex. Memories erased. Lives rewritten.
      To my future self,
If you don't remember kissing Marco, the mayor's memory, or running to the woods, someone has deleted your memory. Read this. This is what really happened.
      It all started the day after the whole Marco Fiasco (Sorry, I'm not writing that bit down—no one needs to remember that. Suffice it to say, I embarrassed myself in front of Marco Han.) I received a text from my sister: Come over immediately! You'll be glad you did. :)
      I had a few free hours, so I hopped on my bike and rode to Mollie's. When I arrived she was ironing sheets. Seriously? I don't even iron

my dresses for church, and she irons sheets. I forgot for a moment to be mad at her and wondered if ironed sheets were nicer to sleep on.

Mollie greeted Lucy with, "Have you seen Marco since..."

"I made a complete and utter fool of myself? No, I've been avoiding him. One good thing about stalking someone is you know their schedule so it's easy to avoid them."

"Stop avoiding him. I did some research and..."

"You hacked his brain!"

"I was curious... He has a beautiful mind."

"I told you not to!"

Mollie wouldn't look at Lucy. She returned to her ironing and kept talking. "Well-organized, almost no filth, his memories are sorted by location—just as I suspected. And he's so generous. His sister's birthday is coming up, and he's planning on buying her a car."

"I can't believe you did this! How? It's wrong in so many ways."

Mollie made smooth, deliberate strokes with her iron. "I'll tell you if you stop your high and mighty rant. I think you'll be interested in what I found."

"What?"

Mollie enjoyed the moment. She sprayed the sheet and ironed two strokes before she said, "He has a crush on you."

"No! What? Wait! How can you tell?"

"Memories become stronger the more we choose to repeat them. Judging by the depth of his file on you, he's thought about you quite a bit."

"Are you making this up? Some colossal practical joke by a bored housewife."

"I don't have that good of an imagination." Mollie turned off the iron and walked toward the desk. Lucy pulled a chair next to her. Her sister said, "Show me Marco Han's file on Lucy." For a moment the computer projected nothing more than swirling fog. The mists cleared, revealing Karen and Lucy lounging on the lawn opposite the computer science building. Lucy was lying on the quilt writing in her notebook, occasionally twisting a lock of hair. Everything else, including Karen, was a bit out of focus. Soft jazz music played in the background.

"What's that music?"

"Marco's always listening to music. His taste is all over. I'm not sure what this piece is, but it's nice."

"I look kind of nice, too."

"You do in all of his memories. Remember memory is not an exact reproduction of reality. You don't look *that* good all the time."

"Thanks."

"But to Marco you always look good. Memories are tainted by feelings. And it's obvious he's partial to you."

"What about when I ran off?"

"That's one of his favorites. It would be difficult to delete even if I tried. But I doubt you want me to erase it."

"I didn't want you to do any of this!"

"But aren't you just a little, itty bit glad or happy or excited?"

"Of course." Lucy couldn't help but let out a happy giggle. "But will you please get out of his mind and never ever go back in?"

"I promise."

Mollie put her hands in the screen and made a gesture as if she were closing a book. The music disappeared. The images returned to fog.

"You're absolutely brilliant! You know that?"

"Yeah, but it's nice to hear someone else say so. Let's celebrate!" Mollie returned to the kitchen and took a pint of chocolate chunk ice cream out of the freezer.

Lucy grabbed two spoons and joined her at the table.

"It's such a relief to tell someone." Mollie dug a particularly large bit of chocolate. "I can't tell anyone else."

"Why not?"

"Can you imagine if this gets into the wrong hands?"

"Like criminals?"

"Or the government. I didn't quit my work just to spend more time with Porter."

"Really? What..."

"I already said too much."

"Fine, just tell me how you figured out how to hack people's minds."

"Well, after I smashed up the car again, I wanted Phil to forget the whole episode, and I realized I was perfectly situated to solve this problem. You know my work was hacking terrorist information systems."

"I did *not* know that. You always said it was top secret."

Mollie ignored the comment and continued talking. "And you know about Phil's work on mapping human thought. So, first I broke into his work computer. After I had the general layout of the brain, it was a cakewalk getting into his memory. Mind you, it took a few months. Good thing Porter takes long naps and for a couple of weeks we ate nothing but cereal for dinner."

"Tsk, tsk."

"I know, right?"

"I can't believe you... No, actually, I can. You feel worse about not making dinner than hacking your husband's brain?"

"I have my priorities."

"Don't you see the problem with this?"

"Of course I do. That's why I haven't told anyone. I could make a fortune off this. But...I can't, that wouldn't be right. All I do is delete memories of minor indiscretions. Mainly crashing my car into inanimate objects. Oh, and I deleted that stupid joke Phil always tells about the admiral."

"The one with the message in the locket?" Lucy let out a sympathetic groan.

"Yeah, that one."

"That was a benevolent act."

"I know! But if this gets into the wrong hands, one could easily cover up much worse."

"Won't someone else figure it out?"

"Yes, eventually. Maybe someone already has."

"But you still wear Spex?"

"There's no such thing as a secret. Nothing is totally secure. That's the world we live in. Everything you buy, every call you make, every website you look at—there's a record of it. We've traded privacy for convenience... I'm at peace with that."

"I'm not. It's terrifying."

"Oh Lucy! What secrets do you have? That you like Marco? No one needs to hack your brain to figure that out. You're an open book. Trust me, he knows. Or he did, till you ran off. Now help the poor guy out and stop avoiding him!"

Later that day, Lucy biked back to campus. She figured she had about fifteen minutes until Marco left his building. She waited on his bench. What would she say to him? This was all a terrible idea. She got up to leave, but right then, he walked out of the building.

"Lucy!" He hurried over. "I've been looking for you."

"And I've been avoiding you." She could feel her face turn red but kept smiling. "I'm so embarrassed. I can't believe I ran off."

"It was hilarious." He laughed, raking his fingers through his hair. "And it gave me a reason to talk to you. I have something of yours."

"My quilt?"

"Yes, I'll give it back to you on one condition. Dinner with me —tonight?"

CHAPTER 5

It would be well perhaps if we were to spend more of our days and nights

without any obstruction between us and the celestial bodies.
Henry David Thoreau, *Walden*

I *was excited about my date with Marco, but I was also nervous. So often my crushes are all in my head. The individual I'm obsessing over is a product of my imagination, bearing almost no resemblance to the person in real life. What if Marco wasn't all I'd imagined him to be? And worse (and more likely) what if I wasn't the person he hoped I'd be? In the end, all of my worrying was needless. I don't know if I met his expectations; but he exceeded mine.*

They ate spring rolls and chicken satay on top of a cliff overlooking the Pacific. They took a long time to eat because they had so much to say.

"So, you're majoring in philosophy?" Marco asked. "What's the point of that? Are there a lot of jobs for philosophers?"

"No, not really. That's what everybody asks, especially my dad. He wants me to teach like he does. And eventually I'll have to come up with some way to make money, but right now I want to answer the age-old question: how should one live one's life?"

"And how do you want to live yours?"

"I don't know." A line of pelicans flew in the golden haze above the water. "Deliberately, I want to live deliberately."

When Lucy was younger, living deliberately meant having a distinctive wardrobe. She had a weakness for anything vintage, sparkly or uber-feminine. Her closet could have been confused for a costume rack. Among other items, it held go-go boots, a flapper dress, a poodle skirt (complete with a full petticoat), a fake fur coat and a tiara.

"Most things I wore because I thought they were pretty. But when my mom would disapprove of my outfits, she'd gently remind me that no one wears kid gloves in the year 2040—well that just stiffened my resolve. I was not going to bow down to the tyranny of public opinion."

"No, of course not."

"She was also always telling me to straighten my hair and maybe dye it, make it a normal color."

"What?" He reached for a lock and played with it in his hand. "I like your hair."

Shocked with joy, Lucy couldn't speak for a moment. She simply nodded.

"Don't ever dye it... I mean, do whatever you want, but I like it... like this."

"Thank you." She kept her eyes on the ocean. She didn't dare look at him; as if one look at her face and he'd know how ridiculously excited she was about him touching her hair. The sun, nearing the horizon, left a widening wake of gold scales on the water.

"I want so badly to live my life. Not the life everyone else thinks I should live. I mean it seems like everyone just does stuff because that's what you do. They're following the people in front of them.

Like Spex, no one even stops to find out whether it's good or not to be connected all the time."

"Easy there; Spex are paying for these spring rolls." Lucy couldn't help but watch the movement of his lips as he spoke. By covering his eyes, Spex accentuated the lower half of his face. Again, she felt unaccountably shy and looked back at the sun's trail on the ocean.

"And if I weren't wearing Spex," he said. "I wouldn't be able to take pictures of you."

She almost choked on her last bite of spring roll. "You're taking my picture?"

"Just a few, I don't want to forget tonight. Besides, it's only fair," he said with an arch smile. "You already have photos of me."

"You knew, didn't you?"

"Knew what?"

"That I'd been spying on you, that there was probably a picture of you on my phone. That's why you came over in the first place. You flirted with me just to get a hold of my phone."

"Maybe I flirted with you because you're pretty."

"I'm right. I know it. You didn't really want to look at Karen's Spex. I bet you got the new model as soon as it came out."

"I had the beta model a year ago." He tapped his Spex. He had a trying-not-to-gloat face. Or maybe it was straight-up gloating. Lucky for him his gloating face was super-endearing. "This is next year's model. It's so awesome. It has rear view cameras over the ear rests."

"You have eyes in the back of your head?"

He tried not to smirk but wasn't successful. "Yeah, I've seen you checking me out plenty. I noticed you weeks ago always studying on that blanket. I came up with bogus reasons to come outside and sit on that bench."

He took her hand as the sun sank into the water. Holding Marco Han's hand, watching the ocean, Lucy thought how both had a similar pull on her. She couldn't stop looking at him or the water— both so beautiful and unknowable. But she was also a little afraid of them both. There was so much she couldn't see, couldn't know, so much beneath the surface.

In the residual light they followed a zig-zagging trail. He asked who her favorite philosopher was.

"Oh, that's easy, Thoreau."

"Not Jesus? I thought you were Christian. You wear a cross." He looked over at the silver cross lying on her freckled chest.

"Yeah, definitely, but to me Jesus is the Son of God, not a philosopher. What about you? Are you religious?" There, she'd said it. She hated bringing up religion, but it was such a big part of her. It would feel like a lie not to mention it. Her parents taught at a Christian college. Her dad taught music and her mom theology. She grew up in a home where they prayed over meals, read from the Bible and went to church most Sundays. A little old school, yes, but it was a huge part of her. Would he get that? He seemed to.

"My mom's Catholic, and my dad's Buddhist," he explained. "And I'm pretty much in a state of wonder." A ground squirrel scurried across the trail. "I'm fairly sure there's something out there bigger than me, a higher power, I suppose. When I'm surfing, I have this sense of awe of the ocean, and I don't know." He fell silent. His gaze turned toward the last remnant of day hovering on the horizon, an arc of creamy light. The rest of the sky was a bruised blue.

Soon there was no path. They weaved through formations of sandstone. In the waning light some of the rocks looked like giant faceless men. She held tighter to Marco's hand. He looked at her reassuringly. "You're going to love this."

They continued through a maze of rocks. Lucy kept looking over at him, trying to squelch her childhood fears of being outside at night, trying not to think of what else might be lurking in the dark wide open. They arrived at a rock alcove with slabs of sandstone placed to form furniture: two armchairs and a love seat.

"Excellent, we have the place to ourselves. What would you say to a movie?"

They sat in the love seat. Marco must have thought a command because without saying anything an image flashed up on the rock wall in front of them. He pulled out extra ear buds for Lucy. "You're okay with wireless earbuds, right?" He said with a tease. "No danger of tainting your mind?"

"Of course; give me those."

He pulled her quilt out of his backpack along with packs of chocolate and licorice. The rock seat was warm, radiating heat absorbed all day from the sun.

They watched *2001: A Space Odyssey*, one of Marco's favorites. She'd never seen it before. She liked the beginning with the men in ape suits and the momentous music but she soon fell asleep, her head on his shoulder. She'd wake up from time to time to see another bizarre image. It was hard to separate her dreams from the images on the screen.

They walked back through the sandstone formations in the moonlight. Marco asked how she liked the movie.

"I fell asleep," she confessed sheepishly. "So it was kind of confusing."

"It's confusing if you stay awake. That's why I like it. It's full of unanswered questions. I prefer questions to answers."

"Then you'd like philosophy."

"Hmm, maybe. I also like how slow the movie moves. It gives you time to think."

"Or fall asleep."

"Too bad you missed the part about the computer turning evil. I thought you'd enjoy that. Sometimes I think just for fun I'll change my mindseye's name to Hal."

"I'll need to watch the movie again to get that joke."

"Sure, but next time you should choose the movie." *Next time, he said next time.*

They retraced their steps along the cliff above the ocean. Marco told her how his mother whistles whenever she loses her keys or wallet, whistles as if they'd come to her.

"So, I made her Spex that whistle back."

"If I wore Spex, I'd definitely need that."

"Really? I can't imagine ever taking mine off long enough to lose them." They walked on a narrow path, Marco in front. He paused to look back at her. "You know, I kinda like that you don't wear Spex. I mean, for one thing, I like seeing your whole face. I wouldn't want to change that. That must be why I noticed you in the first place."

"And I thought it was my stunning looks."

"That too. But have you ever considered one of the mindseye wristwatches?"

"No, never! It's not just Spex obscuring my view that bothers me —though that would drive me crazy. It's the earpiece connected to my mind that freaks me out. My sister says, almost brags, that her mindseye can read her mind. If she's out shopping and suddenly realizes she's hungry, without her asking, her mindseye will tell her of a promo at a local sandwich shop."

"They all do that! It's awesome. But it's not really reading my mind, though it feels like that. Those ads are based on past behavior. Most people are hungry at about the same time, you know."

"I know. But aren't you worried that a mindseye could access your brain?"

"I don't know. Never thought about it. Anything's possible."

He was silent for a while. She considered telling him about Mollie hacking his mind but thought better of it.

They'd reached the beach. Something about the vast black waters unsettled her.

"My sister says there are no more secrets. Everything can be hacked, everything's discovered."

"She's right about that; everything can be hacked—eventually." He paused to look at the sea. "But the world still holds secrets. The real secret is the future, right? You can't hack that. No one knows what comes next."

CHAPTER 6

The heart is forever inexperienced.

Henry David Thoreau

That night I had a hard time falling asleep. At first I felt so giddy, like every atom of my being was dancing for joy. My mind raced with the possibility of Marco. But as the night wore on and I still couldn't sleep, my happiness frayed to fear. The intensity of my feelings frightened me.

Sure, I'd had a crush on Marco for months, but it was silly and casual. I never thought I'd actually talk to him and fall asleep on his shoulder and discover that he's wonderful. And now after one date, I cared so much, too much. And how did that happen so fast? How could I meet someone, spend an evening with him and suddenly he has the power to hurt me. Already, I felt this ache to be with him. I hated myself for feeling that way, but I felt it just the same.

Marco called the next morning and asked if I wanted to go mountain biking. Afterward, when we were getting pho for dinner, he mentioned how tired he was because he'd had a hard time sleeping. I said, "Me too," and blushed. He looked at me with a knowing smile.

We didn't see each other on Sunday. Marco surfed and I had church and then spent the day with my sister. But the rest of the week we spent every afternoon together. I studied on my blanket outside the computer science building, and when he was finished, Marco would join me. On Thursday he asked if I'd like to drive with him to LA for his sister's birthday party. I was surprised that he wanted me to meet his family so soon. I wasn't completely certain we were dating. We hadn't even kissed. But I agreed to go, because time with Marco, was— well—time with Marco.

The Han home appeared ordinary from the street: a tasteful brick ranch house with a circular driveway bordered by tidy shrubs. The backyard, however, was a revelation: a patio, a strip of lawn and miles of rippling waters. Only a plexiglass wall separated the suburban yard from the rest of the world. This view, explained Marco, why he dreamed so big, saw no boundaries and often had a far-off look in his eye. He grew up with the whole wide Pacific for his backyard.

Lucy loved everything about his family. His mom, Theresa, could have been intimidating. After all, she was a doctor and so beautiful. Her thick black hair, streaked silver, fell below her shoulders in gentle wide curls without a hint of frizz. She wore bright red lipstick that matched her red Spex and greeted Lucy like an old friend. She introduced Lucy to everyone as Marco's girlfriend and he didn't protest, say they were just friends or any such nonsense. He simply held her hand and kept smiling as his mom made them meet all of his extended family.

Before she met his Korean grandparents, Marco prepared a plate of food for her to take to them.

As they walked over to the white-haired couple he said, "Remind me, where did your parents go to school?"

"They met at Temple University; my dad got his PhD there, and Mom went to Yale Divinity School. Why?"

"My grandparents care about that stuff."

"So, I'm here on approval?"

"Not at all. They'll love you. I just want to help them out. I'll tell them your parents are professors and your mom went to Yale. It's crazy how much that stuff matters to them."

His grandparents sat on a bench near a jasmine bush with a view of both the ocean and the party, looking dignified. Lucy was surprised by how much she wanted to impress them. She recognized Marco's cheekbones on his grandpa's face. Marco introduced her in English, and she offered the plate of fruit, bowing slightly. Not at all sure if that was the right thing to do, she glanced over at Marco, who was smiling and relaxed. His grandparents' faces were still serious as they accepted the plate. They said something to him in Korean. He answered back in Korean. She thought she heard the word Yale. His grandpa looked at her and smiled and said something else in Korean. They talked some more. All the while she kept smiling and nodding as if she understood.

"They like you already," he said as they walked away.

"Seriously? I had no idea what you guys were talking about."

"If you had Spex, you could have used a translation app—not that those are always accurate. They miss nuances."

"Why don't your grandparents use a translation app to speak to me?"

"They understand English fine. They just don't like speaking it. They don't like to look foolish...which I do, by the way, when I speak Korean. I speak like a four-year-old."

She glanced back at the older couple. They sat in their spot, calmly taking it all in, watching the world through traditional black Spex. Mr. and Mrs. Han certainly did not look foolish. Like his parents, Marco's dad, Dan, appeared dignified. He made her think of a Korean Atticus Finch. There was something noble about the way he carried himself—until he opened his mouth.

"No Spex, huh? You know what they say about people who don't wear Spex? Always up to no good." Lucy had heard that line before, lots. But it was kind of true. Certain establishments—strip clubs, casinos and some bars—require everyone to check their Spex in at the door to protect the reputations of their clientele and avoid prosecution. Lucy had never come up with a witty reply to this jab. So, she smiled as Dan continued in good humor. "I didn't expect Marco to bring home such a wild girl, with such wild hair."

"Dad!" protested Marco's sister, Rachel, who had just joined them. "You can't say stuff like that about a woman's hair. Besides..." She turned to Lucy. "Your hair's brilliant. What color would you call it?"

"I have no idea. On my driver's license I put brown, which isn't quite true."

"It's the color of an old penny," said Marco's dad. "You don't mind my teasing, right?"

"About my hair? Not at all. There's so much of it to tease."

"Pun intended?" asked Dan, breaking out into a huge grin. "See, she gets me. I love a good pun... I call them pun-ishment." Marco and his sister groaned in unison.

"You don't have to laugh," said Rachel.

"I dare you not to," said Dan. "I know the secret to saving a bad joke. If no one laughs, you just repeat it. If you repeat a joke enough, eventually someone will laugh. See, Lucy's laughing now."

"Yeah, but she's laughing at you, Dad, not with you."

"Fine with me. All I want is for people to laugh." Dan, who came to the U.S. from Korea as a high school freshman, spoke a very precise English with just the faintest accent. Just enough to be sexy, according to Theresa, who spoke perfect Spanish and English. She was also fluent in Korean and studying Mandarin. Maybe, she was a bit intimidating.

Marco returned carrying a cake with fluffy white frosting. In front of him walked a short woman holding a bouquet of orange, yellow, and pink roses. He introduced her with a flourish worthy of the queen of England. "And this is Abuelita!"

She handed the flowers to her granddaughter. After smothering Rachel with hugs and kisses, Abuelita turned to Lucy. "Who's this?"

Lucy immediately knew where Marco got his keen eyes, so bright, so expressive, so kind. Perhaps the kindness was even more evident in his grandma because Abuelita's eyes were not obscured by Spex.

"You told me you didn't know anyone over the age of eight without Spex," Lucy said on the drive home.

"Abuelita doesn't count."

"What? It looked to me like you all adore her."

"We do, I do. But she still doesn't count. She's not *like* everyone else. She doesn't do anything normal. She's *like* you."

"You know that could be taken the wrong way. She's not normal, she's like you."

Marco took his eyes off the road for a moment and looked right at Lucy. "I was never interested in normal."

The quiet electric car, a hand-me-down from his parents, was a bit outdated and worn out. The vehicle had autopark but no autodrive. The windshield had a crack on the passenger side, and while generally neat and bereft of clutter, the entire car was covered with a fine sheen of sand.

Lucy had met so many people; she was trying hard to remember all their names.

"Is your cousin Lorenzo or is that his dad's name?"

"Sí."

"What?"

"It's Spanish for yes."

"I know what *sí* means! Which one's Lorenzo?"

"They both are. Bet you're wishing you had my *Good with Names* app right now."

"Shut up."

Marco laughed to himself and tapped a happy beat on the steering wheel. "They really liked you, you know."

"Even though I don't wear Spex?"

"Especially since you don't wear Spex. They love the irony. Mr. Technology falls for a Luddite." She didn't protest that he called her a Luddite. She simply relished the words "falls for."

The night was dark but the heads-up display on the windshield illuminated his face with cool blue light. Marco drove without Spex, his mindseye communicating with the dashboard. His music played through the speakers while all calls and messages appeared on the display that flashed across the lower part of the windshield. This car trip was Lucy's first time seeing him without Spex. She liked it. There was something intimate about watching his naked face. She found herself wanting to trace his cheekbones with her fingers.

The jazz music stopped playing mid-song. Marco's mindseye spoke through the car's speakers, "Call from Pete Marsdon, accept or later."

"Later." Intent on thought, he didn't say anything for a moment. "So, Ms. Philosophy, what would you do if someone offered you a killer deal on a car, but you suspected it was stolen?"

"I'd make sure it wasn't."

"Everything seems legit. I've looked up the car's VIN number. Everything checks out. But I have an uneasy feeling about this guy."

She smiled to herself. Even in the dark, Marco noticed.

"Why are you smiling?"

"Can't a girl smile? I'm having a good time."

"Yeah, but that's not a having-a-good-time smile. It meant something. It was a sneaky smile."

"A sneaky smile?"

"Yeah, a sneaky smile—out with it."

"Wow! You're good. Maybe it was a sneaky smile."

"And..."

"And...I'll just keep my sneaky smile to myself. Thank you. I'm a woman of mystery."

"No, you're not. You're honest as the day is long. Out with it."

"Okay. I just realized... I know how you can find out."

"You do? How?"

"I can't tell you. I promised I wouldn't."

"Tell me?"

"Tell anyone."

"Promised who? Tell what?"

They drove near the coast and though they couldn't see the ocean, they could sense it was close, by the looming absence of city lights to the west.

"Why do you drive such an old car?"

"You're changing the subject."

"Yeah, but why? If you can afford to buy your sister a new car for her birthday, why don't you buy yourself one?"

"Because this one works fine. Rachel just turned sixteen and doesn't have one so it seemed like a good idea. Wait! How did you know I was going to buy her a car?"

"You told me."

"I did not. I didn't tell anyone. I spent a couple afternoons researching cars for her and then decided not to—not yet. How did you know?"

"Lucky guess. It seems like you."

"That was not a lucky guess. You hacked my mindseye, didn't you?" He didn't sound angry. He sounded impressed.

"I didn't. I promise. It was my sister. And she didn't hack your mindseye, not exactly." Sometimes driving in the dark you say things you wouldn't say in the light of day. "Remember how my sister worked for the government hacking computers?"

"Yeah?"

She told him everything.

Marco didn't speak for a while. *This is it, the end to our eight-day romance.*

Finally, he said, "You're kidding, right?"

"No," she laughed uncomfortably. "I wish."

"Seriously? She hacked my brain. That's...wow! Could she show me?"

"You're not upset?"

"Should I be? Did she find any deep, dark secrets?"

"She said she thought you might be partial to me."

"I was, I am."

"She said you had a file on me."

"Of course I do. Wow! Can you imagine what we can do if we can access people's brains? I can't believe it. Hacking minds. We could do so much—so much good."

"Some people could do so much not good."

"I suppose so." Marco slapped his hand on the steering wheel. "You hacked my brain!"

"Not me, my sister."

"When do I meet her? Tomorrow?"

"I guess so. I always go over for Sunday dinner. You could come with me. They'd love that. But she won't be able to talk about hacking because her husband will be there and he doesn't know."

"She's made the most important technological breakthrough of the decade—no, of the century—and she hasn't told her husband?"

"Well, yeah, because she hacks his memories—all the time."

"Seriously?"

"That way she can be the perfect wife."

"And I was worried what you'd think of my family."

"I know. She's a bit of perfectionist. But you'll like her."

"Whoa, then I guess I'd better watch my thoughts."

"No, she promised to never hack your mind again. I'm sorry she did at all."

Marco pulled into an exit lane. "Don't worry about it, really." He looked over at Lucy with his own sneaky smile. "Now there's something I want to show you."

They took a short side road to a public beach and parked in the deserted parking lot. *This might be it, he might kiss me. Oh, please don't put your Spex on. Please don't put your Spex on.* He turned off the car and stepped out, leaving his Spex safe in the glove compartment.

CHAPTER 7

Direct your eyesight inward,
    and you'll find a thousand regions in your mind.
    Henry David Thoreau, *Walden*

Nick's reflection pleases him. He shaves by hand; no electric razor. A drop of shaving cream lands on the stainless steel counter. He grabs a fluffy white hand towel and wipes it up, then returns to shaving, all the while admiring his reflection. He's six-feet-two and built like a Norse god with sandy blond hair and a gold goatee. His goatee is sophisticated, not shaggy. He did not grow it to cover a deficit. His jaw is as square as any comic book hero's. Likewise, the rest of his features are even and perfect. He sets the razor down and smiles his smile—a smile so beautiful you cannot trust it, so beautiful that you lie to yourself and say you do.

His reflection assures him. Yep, definitely the good guy. He thinks of Marco. Why can't he make him forget? One month—they were dating for a measly month. How many girls have forgotten Nick? Some after a couple months of dating. To be honest, he rarely keeps a girlfriend for longer than that. Occupational hazard. It's too risky to be in too many people's memories. He tries to be in no one's. Still, it would be cool if one of his many girls fought to remember him. How could they forget someone so beautiful? It's almost as if they want to forget.

He wipes off the last residue of shaving cream. There's one girl who remembers him. He's probably all she thinks about. He returns to his living room and scans the north wall, the wall of Lucy. He zeroes in on another one of Mollie's memories. This recollection is of special interest because both Marco and Lucy are in it. They are eating Sunday dinner.

"The famous Marco Han at my dinner table," Phil says, stroking his light brown beard. "Truly an honor."

"I wouldn't say famous." Marco gives an embarrassed laugh.

"Young Innovator of the Year? The Wunderkind?" Mollie sets chicken pot pie on the table.

Seriously! Why does everyone make such a fuss about this kid?

"It's all nonsense. I'm nothing special. Right place, right time. That's all. I launched my app just as privacy laws were being loosened."

"Not every seventeen-year-old has an app ready to launch," says Mollie.

"And it's brilliant," adds Phil as he passes Lucy the basket of rolls. "It works so much smoother than other apps like it. I had a bootlegged one before yours came out. Half the time it would mistake my sister for my brother."

"I hope you didn't need to be reminded of their names," chides Lucy.

Nick laughs out loud. *My thoughts exactly.*

"The obnoxious thing was so annoying telling me everyone's name whether I asked or not. It was like having the world's worst name-dropper in my head."

"Wasn't that the name of it: Name-dropper?" asks Mollie, who's serving the toddler in his high chair.

"Something like that. All I know is the thing drove me crazy. It went nuts in crowds. I went to a Padres game and the stupid thing listed off names left and right. I deleted it after that. It was such a relief when your app came out, and it actually worked."

"You haven't tried Marco's app, have you?" Mollie asks Lucy. "You have no idea how marvelous it is. I went from dreading Phil's work parties to looking forward to them. It's not only that I have the app and remember everyone's name, it's that everyone else has it and they remember a little something about me. Now we don't have to repeat the same dull conversation every six months. Seriously, you should be in line for the Nobel Peace Prize."

"That's carrying it a bit far," says Marco.

I'd say!

"What are you working on now?" asks Phil.

Marco explains his current work, developing a program with law enforcement to do mass searches for individuals in real-time.

Ha! I can already do that. Who's the real wunderkind?

"That could be amazing!" says Mollie. "It could be used to find criminals or missing persons. How close are you?"

"It works great now. We just have some legal and PR hurdles to get through."

Legal schmegal!

"I understand you're involved in some groundbreaking work of your own." Nick can tell Marco intends this question for Mollie. And Lucy's not happy that he asked it. She's shaking her head frantically. But Marco doesn't notice, and Mollie doesn't seem to either. She probably assumes, as Phil does, that the question is for her husband.

He jumps right in, "Yeah, it's as exciting as space exploration and more practical, no MREs or diapers. I'm working on the Human Mind Project, specifically mapping memory—but you're probably familiar with the Mind Project."

Nick knows the Mind Project well. He's been a fan since he was a freshman in high school. The nerdy professor Phil just became the most interesting person in the room.

"We thought we could do it in a decade, but the human brain is much more expansive than imagined, especially in the case of memory. New memories are formed all the time. It's like mapping an intricate ever-expanding universe." Phil is smiling ear to ear, an infectious dorky smile. "We're getting close. The problem is with each discovery we find more to uncover. We're not only making a map of a brain but a working explanation of how the brain's hundred-billion plus neurons interact."

"But you've basically got it mapped out now, haven't you?" asks Mollie.

"Practically speaking, we do. But memories are like a dense, fast-growing forest. New vines or connections are being formed every day while old ones, the ones you never use, wither and die."

"I thought you said it was an expanding universe," points out Lucy.

Nick chuckles and says out loud, "That's right darling. He's mixing metaphors. But we'll forgive him because he works for the Mind Project."

"What exactly is a memory?" asks Lucy. "Is it chemical or electrical?"

Phil's eyes light up even more. "Now these are the questions I live for!" He explains how a memory is the reconstruction of synapses: an electrical charge that sets off a chemical alteration. After a memory is formed there's a period when it's extremely vulnerable. "This is why you might remember what you ate for lunch yesterday but not a month ago."

A sudden rush of longing comes over Nick. He wants to sit at this table and talk with these people about neurons and memories.

"Let me get this straight." Lucy sounds indignant.

The Lucy in Mollie's memories looks a few years younger than in reality. There are almost as many variations of Lucy as there are people with memories of her. Which memory is the closest to the truth?

"So, our memories are a mix of electrical impulses and chemical reactions?" she clarifies. The others nod. "That's terrifying! My sense of who I am, who you are... Doesn't it bother you to know that your perception of the world is based on nothing more than chemicals?"

"Why should it?" asks Mollie "So much of who you are is the result of chemicals. Your DNA determines much of your appearance, your personality, your intelligence..."

"I know all that! But memories, well, that's life isn't it? My sense of myself, my place in the world, all my relationships. They all depend on my memories, which it turns out are nothing more than chemicals and electrons?"

It's true, darling. Got to get over it.

"And they are not that reliable, either," says Phil. "We all take artistic license with our memories. Lots of studies show that people remember things that never happened."

Exactly! Lucy, you were there. You heard him. Most memories are corrupted. Why are you going to such lengths to save yours? Foolish girl.

"Honey, if they wanted a lecture, they could take your class. This is why we don't usually talk about Phil's work. Once he starts, you can't get him to stop."

"I so relate," says Marco. "Besides, it's fascinating. But I was wondering. If we have all types of memories, would it be difficult to erase one?"

"We don't erase memories. We just fail to consolidate them," says Phil. "Consolidating is moving a memory from short-term to long-term. The memory actually moves from the hippocampus to another part of the brain."

"Okay, so we fail to *consolidate* a memory." Lucy makes quotation marks as she says "consolidate." "But theoretically speaking"—she looks directly at her sister—"could someone make a person fail to consolidate a specific memory?"

"No one has yet," says Phil.

That's what you think, buddy. Your own wife has. Nick wishes he could see Mollie's expression at this comment. But he can see Lucy and she looks like she's suppressing a laugh.

"But we keep trying. It seems a great way to deal with PTSD. There's a pill that prevents people from forming memories for a period of time, like the last twenty-four hours. But it's not specific to a memory. It makes you forget the entire day. You can see the obvious drawbacks." He takes a bite of his chicken pot pie and doesn't completely finish swallowing before he continues. "No one's figured out how to locate and isolate a single memory. Whoever figures that out *will* deserve a Nobel Prize."

Why, thanks, Phil! It's good to know someone values my work.

Nick moves on to another memory. In this one Lucy looks a little frightened. He turns the sound on.

"You told him?" Mollie's voice is the on the verge of screaming. "I haven't even told Phil! How long have you known this guy?"

Marco, who seems to have tagged along on Lucy's laundry night, smiles weakly.

"I've known about him since last fall, when *you* sent me that article about him on Wired. How long have we actually been talking to each other? Umm...two weeks—today."

"And the first thing you told him is: my sister can hack into people's memories?"

"You hacked *his* brain. He deserved to know."

Mollie glances at Marco. He's sitting at the table eating one of the brownies she baked. The brownies are fudgy with melted chocolate and chunks of nuts.

"For the record, I'm totally cool with you hacking my brain. I'm way impressed."

"You should be."

"And these brownies are insane!"

"Don't flatter me."

Lucy starts talking fast. She tells Mollie about the antique car Marco wanted to buy his sister and his misgivings about the seller. Mollie softens a little when he shows her a picture of the pale pink sedan.

"That *is* a fabulous car! You've got good taste. Hmm...what's this guy's name?"

"Pete Marsdon."

"Fine, and you've already accessed his Spex?" asks Mollie. "Nothing there?"

"Um... Well, no! That's umm...illegal," says Marco.

"Technically, I believe it is. Anyhow, it's not that useful." Mollie gets up from the table and heads to her computer in the living room. She raises her voice so they can hear her. "That would only give you access in real time. Ninety percent of most lives—even bad guys' lives—are boring. You'd tune out before you found anything interesting. Memories are much better; they're like watching the highlights. You'll see."

The two follow her and pull up chairs next to her desk.

"I adore that car," Mollie says to Marco. "But does it still use gas?"

"I was planning on getting it retrofitted, and you can't beat that price."

"Are you seriously concerned about cost? Aren't you a gazillionaire or something?"

"I'm not that rich."

"Marco, I had no qualms about hacking into your brain. Do you really think I'd hesitate to take a peek at your bank account?"

I like how this lady thinks.

"You didn't!" Lucy's face is a strange mix of horror and disbelief. "What else did you look up on him?"

"I didn't quite do a full background check. I already knew a lot of stuff from looking into his head. Don't be so judgy. Wait till you see what a rush it is to look into another's mind. As Phil says, the brain is the last frontier. And don't worry, I already promised not to hack your brain again."

"You don't want to find out what I think of you?" suggests Marco.

"No, I already know you think I'm brilliant, or you will now," Mollie says with a flourish. "Behold, Pete Marsdon's brain!"

A three-dimensional image of a brain hovers above the desk. The organ is larger than life, approximately the size of a basketball and pulsing with psychedelic hues of red, green, yellow, orange and blue.

"Whoa! Excellent!" Marco gazes, mouth slightly open.

Nick's own expression mimics Marco's. Sure, he already knows how to hack memories. But this...this is exquisite and so unnecessary. Why did she even bother to create such a beautiful interface when she planned to be the only person to ever see the program?

"The colors reflect activity," Mollie explains. "Red is the most active, blue the least—like a weather map."

"I've seen brain scans before," says Marco. "But with a mindseye? Who knew?"

Mollie probes into the brain. With hand gestures she peels back layers and zooms closer. "Let's see what's inside. Here's the hippocampus—most autobiographical memories are stored here. Let's take a peek."

She zooms in closer and closer until the pulsing colors separate into distinct dots of color, a galaxy of thought with each star connected by a filament of light. Each time Mollie zooms in, Marco utters soft words of astonishment.

"I have to be careful not to zoom in too far. Memories are like a storm. If I zoom in too close, we could miss it all together. We're going to focus on the red areas. If he's feeling guilty about selling stolen cars, he'll be thinking about it over and over. Also, the more important a memory, the more links it will have to other memories. So we'll look for one with lots of connections."

It's hard to distinguish the different blurs of light from the entanglement of fine lines connecting and swirling around them. The bursts of light dart swiftly and erratically like sunshine on water. Mollie tries to catch a few with her index finger and thumb.

"How do you even catch one?" asks Lucy.

"Memories take a little patience, like catching fireflies in your hands. Thoughts, now, those are so fast they are like trying to catch lightning."

"You explore the brain like my dad grocery shops," says Marco. "Completely random."

"I should come up with something better. I've been meaning to make a search engine. But this works for now. I have a mother's instinct for finding stuff."

"I'm sure you do; but I can improve your program, as awesome as it is. And it is truly awesome. If we add a search engine, we could speed things up significantly."

Nick agrees with Marco. As pretty as Mollie's program might be, it would be tiresome to work with. Still, maybe he could do something to spiff up his interface.

"Ah! Here's a good one." She extracts the largest red point enmeshed in thousands of thin lines. "Voila!"

With a twist of her wrist, the zoomed-in brain fades.

They can hear a man's heavy breathing. Pete runs by the bay. The evening sky has the same pearl-like sheen as the water.

A call comes through on his Spex. Pete stops running.

"Hey, Jason!"

"I need the money."

"Fine, fine, I've got a customer. I just need to close. I promise by tomorrow..."

"I don't care about tomorrow. Saturday, Saturday or..."

"Or what?"

Short pause.

"I'll turn you in...my hands are tied."

"Wait...wait!"

The call ends.

Marco and Lucy look at Mollie with beaming faces.

"I feel like Nancy Drew," says Mollie, pinching a slightly larger red blur. "Let's check this one. It's linked to the Mission Bay memory."

Another window, another view, this time Pete is in his kitchen, buttering toast. He makes a phone call. "Marco."

"That's me! He's calling me. He called me this morning! He tried to sell me the car again at a deeper discount." Marco strokes his chin. "The car's stolen; I'd bet my life on it. But who's Jason?"

The conversation ends abruptly when Phil comes home from work. Mollie greets him. He tells her about his day. But she's not listening. She's watching Marco and Lucy, heads together, laughing over some private joke. He's touching her face. Mollie's view returns to Phil. Nick watches a little longer, hoping to catch another glimpse of Marco and Lucy. But no luck.

Nick takes a moment to check all his other searches. In addition to keeping tabs on Marco, Mollie and Karen, he is also scanning for anyone who has a memory of him. His search comes up empty, the desired outcome. Still, he feels a twinge of disappointment.

Total anonymity is the goal. But whenever he discovers someone with a memory of him, Nick feels a bit of a rush. Right now the only person aware of his existence is Lucy, wherever she may be. After studying so many memories of her, his best guess is that she'll go back to her sister's. He inspects the feed from Mollie's computer. It looks like she is about to go somewhere. She's carrying the little boy and a yoga mat. Nick smiles to himself. Mollie's Friday yoga class would be the perfect opportunity for Lucy to sneak back in the house. He grabs his keys and puts his shoes on.

CHAPTER 8

> The intellect is a cleaver;
>> it discerns and rifts its way into the secret of things.
>> Henry David Thoreau, *Walden*

While Marco built a search engine for Mollie's program, I hung out at his apartment. I liked watching him work, so focused and determined. Nestled on his couch, I half-heartedly finished an essay. He sat nearby hunched over his desk, stacking virtual cubes in columns and rows, completely absorbed in coding. The nearness of him was enough.

From time to time, he would look up from his task and ask, "You okay?"

"I'm killing it," said Lucy, "And you?"

"Same. I hope you don't mind this—my ignoring you and all that. I love having you here."

"I know." She savored his Spexless smile. It was nice to see his eyes smile, too. When she finished her essay, she opened her paperback copy of *Walden*. She had read it so many times that she could open to any page and start reading. A soft breeze blew in from the open sliding door. On the patio a couple of his surfboards leaned against the wall. Towels and a wet suit were draped on the railing.

Occasionally she would read a line out loud to Marco. "Listen to this: 'Our inventions are wont to be pretty toys which distract our attention from serious things.'"

"Serious things," he said, looking over at her with that smile that made her toes wiggle. "Like paying attention to you?"

"That's not why I read it. Just some lines are so great I can't keep them to myself. You can see why I like this guy?"

"Sure—maybe you'll let me borrow that book."

"Like that quilt of mine you never gave back."

"You noticed? I can get it now. Do you want it?"

"No, not yet. It's my security blanket. It always gives me another excuse to see you again."

He came over and gave her a kiss. "And again, and again."

While they ate pizza, cross-legged on the living room floor, Marco talked about the difficulty of searching memories.

"There's different types of memories, you know. Semantic memories, facts and figures, the stuff you learn at school. And there's also spatial memories, like the route you walked to school. But what we are especially interested in are episodic memories. The stuff that happens to us in school."

"Like laughing milk out your nose."

"I did that! True story! And it was chocolate milk."

"I wish I could see that!"

"I bet it was pretty funny. But how did I file that memory? By word: chocolate milk, by image: milk coming out of my nose. I never saw it but I can imagine what it looked like. Maybe by location: the school cafeteria?"

"That would mean there's some overlap of the different types of memories? Wouldn't that make it hard to completely delete a memory?"

"The best way to describe what your sister does is disconnecting memories. But you're right, there's a lot of overlap. And I haven't even gotten into physical or emotional memories. Like a child can remember a mother's touch. I've decided to focus on keywords and images. The same way my facial recognition software works. And while I'm at it, I'm going to see if I can search the memories of lots of people simultaneously."

Impressed as she was, Lucy thought there might be a simpler way to find the guy from Pete Marsdon's memory. After dinner when Marco returned to writing code, she looked up Pete on her tablet. She searched for him on a social network page and then zeroed in on his list of friends named Jason. The third one down was the guy from the memory. She recognized his face: Jason Murdock. She clicked on his page.

"Hah! He works for the police department and he likes to take photos of his car. I'm not an expert; but it doesn't look cheap."

Marco joined her on the couch. "That's a Maserati! Is he an officer?"

"No, some sort of administrative clerk. Oh! Oh! Oh!" In a rush she had an idea so big and complete it made her head hurt. "He's altering the VIN numbers on the stolen car reports he submits."

She was right. By searching the clerk's memory, Marco and Mollie confirmed Lucy's theory. Two weeks later both Pete and Jason had been arrested as well as four other people involved in the stolen car ring.

They watched a news account of the bust at Mollie's, sitting on the couch in the living room, Marco put his arm around Lucy as she curled up next to him. Porter stacked virtual blocks on the ground in front of them. He played with the baby computer Mollie designed for him. The images projected from a red rubber ball the size of an apple. He could barely talk but could code a program that made holographic farm animals dance.

"I feel like a superhero," said Mollie, who sat in a comfortable armchair nearby.

They discussed what other wrongs they could right. Marco had already used mind hacking to catch cheating students. Lucy wondered if they could use it to help Karen with an investigative story she was working on.

Mollie shut her down. "You can't tell Karen about this," she said. "Ever! No one can know."

Marco agreed. Both said that until they found a reliable way to prevent mind-hacking (other than Lucy's suggestion of not using Spex, which they laughed at) the knowledge that minds could be accessed via Spex was too dangerous to share. Lucy felt a little uneasy with this plan, but only a little. They were all so intoxicated with their success.

"What if we investigate my mechanic?" said Mollie. "Every time I take my car in, he has me do a long list of necessary repairs. I've hacked into his mind but it's such a mess, I can't tell if he's lying or not."

"Maybe my search engine will help," said Marco.

"You finished it?"

"That's how I caught the cheaters."

"So, it works?" asked Mollie.

"Yeah, it was easy enough. Once I knew they copied someone else's work, I confronted them. Before I said anything else, they started sniveling and confessed the whole thing. No one has bothered to ask how I knew."

"That's fabulous!" she said. "I hate cheaters."

Marco and Mollie went to her desk while Lucy stayed on the couch watching the news. There was a short piece about how the mayor was suing a local tabloid for libel. The paper alleged that he was taking money from a drug cartel. She called their attention to the newscast. The two turned to watch the last bit of the story on the mayor.

When the clip finished Marco said, "I've got this!"

It took a couple hours to break into the mayor's mindseye. He had much better security than most. However, his brain was wide open.

Again, they sat around Mollie's desk, staring at the colorful image of a tie-dyed brain, the colors ebbing and flowing like flames on hot embers.

Marco typed in the search bar: drug cartel. Rows and rows of random numbers replaced the colorful brain. The numbers formed a cube, the digits shifting constantly in a motion like running water.

"As I said, not as pretty as your program, but it works. The most important memory should be at the top."

"It's my turn to be impressed," said Mollie. "You did all this in a couple weeks?"

Marco shrugged. "I didn't sleep much, but it was worth it to get those cheaters. And now we can search multiple minds at once."

He pulled a long row of numbers from the top of the cube. With his fingers he stretched the numbers until the projection became a window full of food, a table in a restaurant laden with corn and flour tortillas, fried shredded pork, avocados, tomatoes, onions and cilantro. The image was so realistic Lucy felt like she could reach in and grab a chip. The mayor sat at this table in the back of a Mexican restaurant with two men.

"It's all in Spanish; I can't understand," said Mollie. "Do you speak Spanish?"

"Not really, but I understand it." Marco listened for a moment. "He's guilty, definitely guilty. They just offered him mucho dinero, and he asked for more."

"What's our next step?" asked Lucy.

"Dinner," he said. "I'm starving. Carne asada fries would hit the spot."

While they gorged on fries with grilled steak chunks smothered with guacamole, sour cream and cheese, Phil came home from his lecture. Mollie still hadn't told him about her new hacking hobby, so they talked of everything else but what they were most interested in. Mainly they ate and politely listened to Phil. "I heard the funniest joke today. There was this admiral..."

"Not this joke again," said Mollie.

"What, you've heard it? Why didn't you tell me? You've been holding out on me."

Lucy caught Mollie's eye. Marco saw her suppressing a laugh and smiled too.

"What's going on?" asked Phil. "What are you three laughing about?"

"Nothing." Lucy stood up and left to change her laundry.

Marco volunteered to help. Once safe in the laundry room he asked, "So what were you two cracking up about?"

"That joke about the admiral. Phil says it so much she deleted it from his memory."

"Seriously?"

"Yes, and now he knows it again. Maybe it's futile to delete memories of anything we really love."

"Could be," he said. "My mom always says, 'The things we love most always come back to us.'"

CHAPTER 9

Knowledge forbidden?
   ...Can it be a sin to know?
Can it be death?
John Milton, *Paradise Lost*

Marco fell asleep while I finished folding laundry. I watched him sleep. He snored slightly. I thought it was adorable. Mollie and Phil had also gone to bed. After playing the mayor's memory, the computer's projection had reverted to a rotating cube of random numbers. The numbers seemed to ripple and shift. Perhaps the memories were changing order as one became more important than another. I sat down at the desk and pulled at the top memory, like pulling a loose thread on a sweater.

The projection opened to a parking garage. The mayor's footsteps echoed in the concrete building. The memory was tinged with a creepy light. Lucy felt certain the mayor was afraid. She was a little frightened herself. He flinched when he saw a man waiting for him.

The mayor wore night vision Spex and had a clear view of the stranger. A young man in a charcoal suit. He was not Lucy's type but so forcefully attractive, she felt herself blush. He spoke and his words reverberated across the concrete walls.

"If you do something wrong and no one remembers, did it really happen?"

He leaned against a pillar, riffling through a copy of *Paradise Lost*, the fluorescent lights gleaming off his golden hair.

Dolly, ID this man. Start recording. A video camera icon with the word "ON" appeared on his left lens. Out loud the mayor said, "What do you want from me?"

"An answer."

"What the..."

"If you do something wrong...maybe even evil "—he stroked his neatly trimmed goatee—"and no one remembers, does it really matter?"

"What are you getting at?"

"I think you know."

A computer-generated voice with a slight southern accent spoke in the mayor's ear, "His face has no matches, Mr. Mayor—most unusual."

Dolly, call the police.

The stranger closed his book. "I wouldn't do that." He took a couple steps forward, standing between the mayor and his black sports car.

"Do what?"

"Call the police?"

"I didn't say anything about the police."

"Yes, but you thought it. You asked your mindseye to call the police. Tell her not to. You don't want the police sniffing into your business, do you?"

Dolly, cancel the call.

The stranger continues speaking with a persuasive almost sexy whisper. "You're armed. I only brought my book. I'm not here to cause trouble. I'm here to help you."

The mayor relaxed a little. Lucy could tell because the memory became brighter.

"So, you read minds?"

"In a way. The important part is: I know."

"Know what?"

"Your secrets."

"I have no idea what you're talking about." The mayor took a gun out of its holster and waved it in front of him. "Step aside!"

The guy with the goatee answered with a smirk. "You never load it."

"Want to find out?"

"Shoot away. It's not loaded. No matter what you told Celia."

The mayor lowered his gun. "How do you know? What do you know?"

"Everything." The man took off his Spex and smiled. "Everything worth knowing."

"Celia?"

"Celia and Gladys, and the deal with the drug cartel."

The mayor studied the stranger's eyes.

"I thought the devil would be shorter."

The guy with the goatee let out an unkind laugh, really the only unattractive thing about him.

"Quite the opposite. I'm your savior. I'm offering you redemption."

"How?"

"Wire me a quarter million, to this account." The numbers appeared on the top corner of the mayor's right lens. "And in the morning, your wife, the pesky reporter, the auditor, your secretary, the cleaning lady. They'll all forget—everything."

"My kids?"

"Your kids, your brother, a dozen others. You were not discreet, my friend. As soon as I get the money, even you won't remember. It will be like none of it ever happened."

"How's that possible? Are you going to kill me?"

Again, he let out his ugly laugh. "What good would it do to kill my most frequent customer?"

Lucy woke Marco.

The second viewing was less threatening than the first. The man in the suit was more charming, younger, not the least bit threatening; even his laugh was pleasant. His book no longer had a visible title. The mayor was already altering this memory.

This guy said the mayor was his most frequent customer. How many customers did he have? How many memories had he erased? Marco copied his face.

"Did you get that account number? I'm going to search this dude. See if I can get a name or a pseudonym. And get your sister."

"Wake her up? It's two a.m.!"

"She'll want to see this, and this memory won't be here in the morning."

The next day the memory was gone as well as the recording on the mayor's Spex. In fact, the whole cube of drug cartel memories had become a two-dimensional square. All that was left were a few minor memories: scenes from cop shows with drug cartels and a couple news reports. As soon as Phil had left for work, they started searching. Both Marco and Lucy had decided this was important enough to skip class. They looked up the bank account. It was closed. All they had was an image: an excruciatingly handsome young man with inscrutable eyes.

After hours of searching and finding nothing, they were all getting cranky and tired. Marco offered to get some lunch. Lucy said she'd go with him.

"No, take a nap. You only got a couple hours' sleep last night. I'll be back before you know it."

She lay down gratefully on the couch. He kissed her forehead before he left. She fell fast asleep.

She woke with a start. The warm, lush light of late afternoon filled the room. Her sister was talking to Porter in the nursery. In that first haze of waking she tried to recall, *Why am I sleeping on my sister's couch in the afternoon?* Then she remembered: the mayor's memory, the man with the goatee, the entire day spent searching for him.

Why doesn't anyone remember him?

She sat upright. She knew.

Where was her phone? She looked under the couch. It had slipped in the couch cushions. Her hands shook as she called Marco.

"Hey?"

"He's cleaning up after himself. He's deleting the memories of anyone who's seen him."

"What? Who's this?"

"Lucy."

"Lucy who?"

She was too late. But she had to try.

"Lucy! Your girlfriend. Listen to me, Marco. Someone's erasing your memory through your mindseye. As soon as you get off this call, you need to take it out and wait for me."

"Is this a joke?"

"No, please, please take out your mindseye and wait for me!"

"Who's this?"

"I'll explain everything. Please take out your mindseye! Will you do that?"

"This is crazy."

"You have to trust me."

"I don't know who you are."

"Please take out your mindseye. Will you do that?"

"All right, sure."

"I'll be right there."

She hung up the phone.

Mollie was in the nursery picking Porter up from his nap. Lucy took the mindseye out of her ear.

"What…"

"Marco doesn't remember me! I need the keys to your car."

"Marco?"

"My boyfriend, your little hacking buddy; he went to get sandwiches."

"What are you talking about? Lucy, why do you look so upset?" The doorbell rang. "I need to get that."

She left the room. Lucy stood for a moment, looking at Mollie's mindseye, a translucent petal, in the palm of her hand. She could hear a man's voice. She peeked through the nursery window. Standing at the door, holding a clipboard was the man with the goatee.

In a moment she made a series of quick calculations. The man was not a threat to her sister; her memory was already erased. He had come for Lucy. She dropped her sister's mindseye on the floor and ducked into the bathroom attached to the nursery. The bathroom connected to the master bedroom. She hurried through her sister's room to emerge unseen in the family room. She grabbed her backpack resting by the couch but left her phone. Anyone able to hack memories could also track her phone. She rushed to the kitchen, took Mollie's hoodie from where it sat draped over the back of a chair and stuffed it in her backpack.

"Lucy!" Mollie used her everyday voice. She obviously didn't see the man as a threat. "This guy's selling 'No Soliciting' signs. Isn't that hilarious? Help me choose one."

"Ha ha! Sure, just a minute," Lucy hollered as she slipped out the back door. She remembered not to close the sliding door because it always screeched. She crept through the side yard and found Phil's old mountain bike. Biking was her best option even if it meant she had to leave through the front yard. A shiny silver sports car was parked in front of the house. It looked like some sort of expensive and dangerous insect, not the sort of car a door-to-door salesman could afford. The man was still in the house with Mollie. She'd made it to the front yard unseen.

The front door opened. "Lucy!" yelled Mollie. She hopped on the bike and sped away. A car engine roared to life. She didn't bother to glance back. She veered off the road across the sidewalk and into the park. Elementary kids scattered as she plowed through their soccer practice. She pedaled to the back of the park to the dirt trail leading into the canyon. No silver sports car could follow her there.

In less than fifteen minutes, she arrived outside graduate housing, sweaty and gasping for air. She stood at the edge of the parking lot, sheltered by trees. She could see across the lot into Marco's second-story apartment. Someone was with him, talking. Good. Maybe it was Henry or Cade or any one of his friends who had met her, someone who could back her story that they were dating, that Marco actually knew her. Hopeful, she left the bike at the edge of the woods and darted across the parking lot. Marco stood alone in the window. For a moment, she saw his face and he saw hers. The front door opened and out came the man with the goatee.

She ran. Clattering steps rattled down the stairs behind her. She dashed across the parking lot, jumped back on the bike and rode for her life.

She flew, moving faster than she ever had on a bike. It would have been thrilling if she weren't so terrified. Her mind screamed to use the brakes, but she didn't. She bounced down the bumpy trail, her backpack slapping against her back. She rode under a tangle of freeway ramps and then deep into thickets of live oak. Her front wheel snagged on a root and she went over the handlebars, landing in some scratchy bushes. She scraped her palm, and her wrist was already beginning to swell. Her knees and elbow were bleeding; but she felt no pain. In a moment she was back on the bike. She rode for a long time on twisty paths through sage and willow, crossing train tracks and dry riverbeds. The farther she went, the more she wondered if she'd made the right decision.

CHAPTER 10

As a single footstep will not make a path on the earth,
   so a single thought will not make a pathway in the mind.
   To make a deep physical path, we walk again and again.
   To make a deep mental path, we must think over and over
   the kind of thoughts we wish to dominate our lives.
   Henry David Thoreau, *Walden*

I am exactly the wrong sort of girl for this sort of adventure. Nothing in my 18 years of suburban life has prepared me for this. I never once snuck out at night, or toilet papered or climbed a chain link fence. I didn't take gymnastics or martial arts. All I ever did was run, go to church, do my homework, and doodle in my sketchbook. And to make things worse, I'm wearing the worst possible outfit: a sundress and sandals. Pebbles keep snagging in my shoes. And last night, the whiteness of my dress stood out in the darkness. If only I had been wearing something else, something normal like jeans and a dark t-shirt. Why do I have to be so quirky and full of contrary opinions? If I were a little more like everyone else, I'd have worn something sensible.

But this is what I had on when that guy showed up, leaving me no time to change. I barely escaped.

After leaving Phil's bike in a thicket of willows, I picked my way through the scrub oak in the dusk, trying not to make a sound. Two women were running on the trail below. I held still, bits of their conversation drifting up to me. One woman talked about her daughter in college. I thought of my own mom on the other side of the country—blissfully unaware that her youngest child was hiding in a gully.

I wanted to ask the runners for help. But I couldn't. If they were wearing Spex (which was pretty much a given) no matter how much they might have wanted to help, they would have been spying for the hacker.

After the runners' voices faded, I began again to creep along the hillside. All the locals refer to this bit of wilderness as the canyons. Like the sewers of Paris, these ravines, too steep for development, connect most of the neighborhoods in San Diego. I run here often, and know how the trails link one gully to another. Just last week I was mountain biking with Marco in an adjacent canyon. But I've never been on these trails alone. Mollie is always warning me about the dangers of the canyons. "They are crawling with homeless people. And Phil's friend once found a dead body in one."

Her words rang in my head as the woods grew darker. I had to find a place to sleep. I settled on a dirt trench, a crack in the earth, created by erosion, a good distance from the main trail and exactly big enough to sit in with my knees against my chest. I scrambled in, resting my head on my legs, for once glad that my hair was the color of dirt.

I didn't sleep much. Insects chirped. Trees rustled. Coyotes howled.

My every breath was a prayer: Please don't let me die! Please don't let him find me!

In the first morning light, I climbed out of the pit. The top half of my dress was soaked with dew, the bottom half smudged with dirt and blood. My muscles stiff and sore, the aftermath of running and *sleeping in a ditch. It felt good to stand up. Simply surviving the night gave me a sort of confidence, a reckless joy.*

Thick fog filled the canyon, allowing me to walk freely with my head up, no longer terrified about being seen. Now my white dress served as a sort of camouflage. I blended in like a ghost in the mist. Walking in the fog reminded me of something my mom used to say about mortals being time-blind. Humans experience time like we're walking in a room with the lights off, making our way by touching and identifying objects one by one. Because we can only touch one object at a time, we conceptualize the room chronologically. First, we touch the end table, next the couch, the wall, the picture and so forth. But if we were to turn on the lights and suddenly see the entire room, we might see things we never expected. Perhaps right above us hangs a crystal chandelier or in the corner crouches a giant tiger. That's how it is for God, my mom would say, He can see the past, present and future all at once. But us humans, we're all stumbling in a dark room—or a foggy canyon.

No one can really see the past, can they? Which is strange because everyone has experienced it. But for the most part the past disappears just as fast as the fog erased the trail behind me this morning. Sometimes that feels like a loss; but if a person doesn't forget some things, if I could recall every moment of my life with equal clarity, the past would overcrowd the present. In a way, forgetting propels us forward. But if I were to forget everything or if I couldn't make new memories, the present would have no context, it would become meaningless, like a one-note song. Who would I be if this guy erased my memories?

I slept in the woods last night to save my memories. But even as I write this I know that I don't remember things perfectly, that my memories, like all memories, are warped. A close sketch of reality, yes, but not the full truth. Every moment, even if I remember it exactly, which according to Phil is not likely, is still only a sliver of reality. So which reality is the closest to truth? Is there such a thing as truth? Or is life simply a series of faulty memories, a chain of random chemical and electrical impulses? I want to believe it's more than that. That's why I ran, that's why I'm writing this. I prefer a faulty record to oblivion.

Lucy closes her notebook. The sky arches blue above her. After hours of writing and waiting her hand is cramped and her bottom numb from the hard stump she's sitting on. Below her the canyon winds, a green river of sycamores, sage and willows punctuated by the occasional palm tree. The homes and trees on the other side of the canyon appear crisp and distinct in the bright light. The morning fog now seems a surreal dream. Judging from the sun's place high in the sky, her sister should be leaving for her yoga class about now. Time to go.

Yesterday Mollie's house was a second home to Lucy. But now she feels like an intruder. Each creak of the floorboard or rattle of the ice maker startles her. Her first stop is the bathroom to use a flushing toilet and wash the blood from her arms and legs. Her scrapes are superficial. She dabs antibiotic ointment on them but can't find bandages big enough. Before she leaves the bathroom, she remembers to steal a roll of toilet paper and hand sanitizer.

Next, she fills her water bottle and raids the kitchen. She snags a box of granola bars and empties the fruit bowl into her backpack. She notes the time: 12:15. Her sister should return from yoga a little before two. That doesn't leave much time.

She sits down at the desk, wishing she'd taken more interest in computers instead of always relying on Mollie. Whenever she called her sister for tech support, Mollie would answer, exasperated, "You know, no one taught me to do this."

"I know. You were just born knowing everything."

"No, I was born knowing I could solve problems. And you can, too."

Lucy tries to channel her inner Mollie as she searches the computer. She explores the desktop the same way her sister searched through Pete Marsdon's brain, randomly opening files.

She can't find a thing.

This is not a surprise. She didn't actually expect to find the program. If this guy bothered to erase her from Marco's mind, he probably cleaned Mollie's hard drive. She'll have to look for something else. Maybe Phil's work mapping the human mind is still available?

But first, she has to check something. She can't resist. She opens Marco's social network page. Research, she tells herself. But really she just needs to see his face, his smile, his black hair falling across his forehead like the waves in a Japanese print. She scrolls through his photos, stopping at a group photo from his sister's birthday party. Lucy knows she was in that photo. She remembers protesting joining the group photo because everyone else was family. But Marco's mom insisted. So she stood for the picture with his hand on her back. Now, there is no sign of her. One day. Not even twenty-four hours and someone has taken the time to Photoshop her out—and to fix the shadows. Studying the photo, Lucy begins to question if she remembers it wrong. Was she really in that picture? She almost doubts that she went to the party or dated Marco. It all seems too good to be true. She drifts to the conversation with Marco on the drive home. How ridiculous was it that he thought she could have hacked his Spex.

Hacked his Spex!

Maybe she doesn't have to figure out how to hack this guy's mind. Maybe all she needs to do is hack his Spex. Excited, she opens a new tab and starts researching hacking Spex. She begins with a how-to video. The commentator says, "Hacking Spex is as easy as remotely accessing any computer's video camera."

As easy as remotely accessing any computer's video camera. I am such an idiot!

She turns off the computer. The man who was able to erase

himself from everyone's memory could have and would have easily hacked her sister's camera. How long has she been here? He could be here any minute. She scurries to the kitchen and grabs her backpack. Out of the corner of her eye, she spots a tall figure moving across the backyard. She doesn't bother to take a closer look. She dashes to the front door.

The sliding glass door opens with a shriek.

CHAPTER 11

The swiftest traveler is
he who goes afoot.
Henry David Thoreau, *Walden*

Lucy races down the hall and out the front door. She leaps off the steps. The man's silver car is parked in front of the house. If only she had time to note the license plate, but running steps pound close behind.

Lucy can run faster than most grown men, close to a five-minute mile, but not as fast as this guy. He's gaining on her. She blocks the gate behind her with several garbage cans. This yard sits on the edge of a mesa overlooking another neighborhood. How to get to the street below? She steals a child's scooter.

Pausing at the edge of the lawn, Lucy picks out her route, a sandy path. The bluff is steeper than most black diamond slopes, and there is no snow to soften a fall. The fence rattles as the man climbs over it. Garbage cans tip over with loud thuds. Shifting her weight, she pushes off, plunging down the hill.

She's moving fast, too fast. It's impossible to steer on the loose dirt. Branches swat her face and arms. She squints and holds on tight, opening her eyes just in time to see a fast-approaching patch of cactus. Wrenching the scooter tight, she skids to a stop. She falls off, tumbling the last few yards down the hill. Her skin burns as she slides across the AstroTurf. No sign of the man on the mesa above. He must have gone back for his car. She hurries to the front yard and sprints down the street, diving into the thick undergrowth on a vacant lot. She hopes this bit of public land also connects to the canyons. Deep in the bushes she watches. She hears screeching tires followed by the silver car speeding down the hill. He drives away from her, toward the house with the fake grass. She can't see him now. But she hears a car door open. He feels dangerously close.

Lucy scampers down the ravine to a drainpipe. How long is this pipe? The smallest light, as big as an evening star, blinks at the end of the tunnel. She crawls in. With her backpack on she doesn't fit. She takes it off, pushing it ahead of her. Her head scrapes the top. Her hips graze the side. It's a tight fit, but that means the man can't follow. He's huge. How in the world can he run so fast?

Trying not to think about the wet slimy things her hands touch or the spindly creatures that occasionally crawl over her, she moves on into the darkness. How did she go from a college freshman with good grades and a boyfriend to a creature slithering through a tunnel? It's almost like she died, as if when she ran to the woods, she crossed a threshold. She no longer belongs to the real world. She's not dead, but she's forgotten. Which is worse?

To be forgotten is a sort of death. Some believe that an individual only truly dies when the last living person forgets them. Not that Lucy's completely forgotten. Just no one's worried about her or has noticed that she's missing. It was obvious from Marco's blank face yesterday that he doesn't remember her.

The pinprick of light at the tunnel's end grows. It blossoms to the size of a butterfly, then a lemon and now a dinner plate of sunshine and green grasses. She tumbles back into the world landing in a marshy, muddy alcove sheltered by willows.

She wends her way through the canyon, not sure where she's going. She slows down as she climbs a steep slope covered with wild mustard. The tall, reed-like stems grow thickly in thousands of stiff parallel lines, making it hard to pass through them. Could someone see her movement from a distance, like a snake in the grass?

She spends the night on that hillside, a canopy of yellow flowers towering above her. In the early morning light, she wakes to rain, her body covered in thousands of yellow petals.

The rain falls harder. She moves on, a damp shadow crossing a valley of silver and green. She doesn't see another living creature. All have disappeared in the canyon's secret places. She wants to find such a place for herself. Sometimes she bumps a low-hanging branch and a shower of cold water runs down her back. Wet and numb, Lucy trudges on. She crosses down the hillside toward a thicker clump of trees when she sees it.

A body.

She screams, then covers her mouth. Adrenaline surges through her.

Living or dead: both options terrify her. A few inches of face peer through the cinched opening of a mummy sleeping bag. An eye opens.

An old man, who looks a little like a mummy himself sheds the sleeping bag, smiling and chanting.

> *"Little Miss Muffet sat on her tuffet*
> *Eating her porridge and whey*
> *When along came a spider*
> *and sat down beside her*
> *and frightened Miss Muffet away."*

"Sorry...So sorry to wake you." She backs away, her eyes steady on him, afraid to make any sudden moves while in this man's sight; as if this old homeless man is some wild animal that would instinctively chase anything that runs.

He keeps glancing at her sideways and catching her eye as if they are both in on a secret. He starts singing.

> *"Three blind mice, three blind mice.*
> *See how they run. See how they run.*
> *They all ran after the farmer's wife,*
> *Who cut off their tails with a carving knife.*
> *Who? Who? Who?"*

She notices the red veins in his eyes like lightning strikes. "*He* is after you!"

CHAPTER 12

Our truest life is when
  we are in dreams awake.
  Henry David Thoreau, *Walden*

Marco walks on the top of a cliff next to a girl with hair the color of autumn light. He's dreaming. Everything's pale gold, even the sea shining in the distance. The cliffs descend forever. He cannot see the bottom. He leans down to kiss the girl. She moves closer but turns as if she hears something. She looks behind her, screams and runs. She runs to the cliff's edge and jumps with her arms outstretched in a swan dive.

He watches her swirling down, down, down and realizes she has wings, golden wings of light. As she disappears, the mist absorbs her color and hums gold. But soon the light disappears. The sky turns gray. It is not night; it is not day; it is darkness. The darkness presses all around him. He's breathing darkness, choking on darkness. It will kill him. He stumbles to the edge of the cliff. There's the smallest, faintest light in the darkening gloom. He's certain he will die without that light.

He jumps off the cliff but something, no, someone, holds him back. The hand of a man. He looks back; it is a young man with a goatee. Marco doesn't recognize him, but he knows he hates him. He hits this man. Droplets of blood stain the man's crisp, white shirt. He staggers back. Marco attacks again. His anger surprises him. He's winning the fight, and then the man's hands turn to silver claws. They gash Marco's face and cut into his heart. His attacker is no longer a man but a dragon, a snake-like silver-bearded beast, laughing at him.

"You'll never find her, and you'll never find me." The dragon leaps off the cliff. Marco stares helplessly as the creature's long tail whips above and then disappears. He's lying on the bloody ground, looking up at the darkness, hoping death will come quickly.

"Rise and shine," says Steve. "Ten a.m. meeting." Marco jerks back into reality. At first, he's relieved that he's still alive. But then he feels something. He puts his hand to his breastbone. Why does his heart ache? His cheeks are wet. Has he been crying? He feels exactly like he did when he was nine and his rat died. His chest tightens. It's difficult to breathe. He gets up, showers and dresses. Every step in his normal routine requires an unusual amount of exertion as if the pull of gravity is greater.

When he was in preschool, Marco had a lot of nightmares. One night his Grandma Han heard his screams. She turned on the light in his room, stroked his hair.

"No more bad dream. I teach you." She helped him with this for many nights. First, showing him how to focus on his breath. "You control breath. You control dream." Once he mastered that she helped him visualize his dreams.

"Dream in your head." She'd tap his forehead. "You control head."

When he'd wake screaming. She'd shuffle in his room. "Dream in your head, you control your head." And it worked.

First, he learned to change non-threatening objects in his dreams like the color of a balloon. After he could do this, he learned how to switch dreams, like switching stations on the radio. If a dream became too scary, if the pack of dogs had almost caught him, he'd switch it and he'd be surfing orange waves.

Until this morning, it had been years since he'd had a nightmare. He supposed that controlling dreams had become second nature to him. But now he wonders if he had simply outgrown nightmares. Maybe he no longer can control his dreams. If he could, he certainly would have kissed that girl. Thinking of her, his heartache lessens.

Outside it's drizzling. He searches for his jacket; it's unusually heavy. There's a book in the right pocket. A book. Who still uses paper books? It's a dog-eared copy of *Walden*. Inside the front cover in pencil and loopy script it reads, *Property of Lucy Campbell*. He finds a permanent marker in his junk drawer and scribbles the name on the palm of his hand.

He's late now. As he hurries down the front steps, the rain falls harder. His Spex begin to fog, but he thinks a quick command that turns a fan on. His lenses clear up. While he unlocks his bike, the maintenance guy drives up in his golf cart.

"Morning, Leroy."

"Marco, my man! When are you going to get me a pair of those fancy glasses?"

"You want some, I have an old pair..."

"Nah, no point in getting me a pair. My wife would be jealous."

"I could get you two."

"Nah, I'm just messing with you. I couldn't take a gift like that."

"Are you sure? I'd be happy to."

"No, no, it's too much—wouldn't feel comfortable."

"Then for Christmas, maybe?"

"Maybe...Hey, you going to meet up with that girl of yours?"

Marco is about to tell Leroy that he has him confused with someone else. But instead he looks at the name on his hand and asks, "Which girl? I mean, what does she look like?"

"There's more than one? You sly dog! This one has lots of freckles. Real cute!"

Marco runs back up the stairs into his apartment, grabs the marker from the counter, and writes on his other hand: "Call Abuelita."

CHAPTER 13

Not till we are lost, in other words, not till we have lost the world,
do we begin to find ourselves.
Henry David Thoreau, *Walden*

As the rain picks up, Lucy's need for shelter becomes more urgent. She settles on a large green shrub about the size of an elephant. The branches droop to the ground like a ruffly green skirt over which hangs the embroidery of thousands of creamy blossoms. Inside it is dark, but the ground is dry.

She sits on a bench of twisted roots and trunk, her hair dripping, her dress wet. If only she'd snagged a change of clothes and a blanket at her sister's. But still, she feels safe in this hiding place, like she did as a child when she was scared at night but snug in her bed. As long as she hid her head under the covers, as long as she couldn't see the monsters, nothing could hurt her. All the monsters that scared her back then turned out to be only in her imagination. She had hoped the same was true of the guy with the goatee. She had almost talked herself into believing that there was nothing to fear. But after yesterday she knows he is not a creature of her imagination. He's real, and he's after her.

She wakes in the middle of the night. The rain pounding, her hair damp. A train thunders through the canyon. A flash of light illuminates a silhouette outside the tree. A man is standing close. But, she's too tired to be scared, too tired to be cold. Sleep overtakes her.

Birds wake Lucy. She understands their song. *Cheep, cheep, cheep. chur, chatta chatta choo. I'm alive, I'm alive. One more day alive.* It is her first thought, the grateful prayer in her heart. "One more day alive." Bits of yellow light burst through the branches. There's a blanket on her, a thick woolen blanket that may have once been beige but now is the color of dirt. Where did it come from? She remembers the figure in the middle of the night. The blanket weighs on her, heavy and warm. The top is a little damp from rain; but the underside is warm from her body's heat. She should be scared that some stranger was so close while she slept. But she isn't. Fear feels like a waste of energy.

She unfolds the blanket, spreading it out on the floor of her shelter, a space about the size of a twin bed. She wants to lie flat on her back. She's tired of sleeping curled up like a rodent. The bursts of light grow bigger and the bird calls louder. She takes out her journal from her backpack and sketches. As she draws, the hovel of branches absorbs the sun. The warming earth smells of green things growing and from above wafts the heady scent of blossoms. Satisfied with her drawing she writes some more:

April 2, 2044

Looking up through the net of branches, my mind drifts upward. How does this shrub appear from the mesa overlooking the canyon, from an airplane flying above, from space? Does God see me?

This planet is one of billions. I am one of billions. How could it possibly matter what I remember? All of my memories, true or not, will die with me, sooner or later. Right now it feels sooner. Death feels real. The trappings of civilization create a false sense of security, superiority. We are the gods of this planet. Suddenly, removed from all that, I feel my own insignificance. I don't think I ever realized that I was mortal. I mean, I knew in theory; but now... Every day seems a miracle—and possibly my last.

Does this guy want to kill me? He probably only wants to erase my memory. Maybe I should let him. What would I lose?

The truth. (If there is such a thing?)

And—Marco.

Haven't I already lost him? He doesn't remember me. Our relationship exists entirely in my brain, in a combination of chemicals and electrons and in this book—ink on paper. I will die, these pages will disintegrate and what will it matter that I loved Marco Han?

I can't say why, but it matters.

And what about the truth? This guy's erasing people's memories. He's stealing the truth. He's altering the past, and I'm the only one who knows. What should I do with this truth? Would anyone believe me? I have no proof. And what if he found me? Is the truth worth dying for? I don't know. But I'm still hiding.

She sketches the man with the goatee. It's vague but true. She wishes he wasn't so attractive. In movies the bad guys always look scary: snake-like nostrils for a nose, a creepy tattoo on his face or at least a mask obscuring his countenance. But this guy, he would be cast as the boy next door. Make that an exceptionally good-looking boy next door. He has a sort of noble look like a young King Arthur or some Norse god. The world would be much simpler if all the bad guys looked evil.

She adds a few more lines to the drawing and then underneath scrawls a big question mark. A shadow crosses her book. She looks up.

"Old Saint Nick was a Jolly old soul, a jolly old soul was he." Standing a few feet from her is the homeless man.

He says, "He took my cat, he took my sock, he took my memory."

"You gave me the blanket?"

He nods.

"Thank you."

She offers him her last orange. He refuses. She gives it to him anyway. He takes it politely and then eats with surprising ferocity, the juice dripping onto his white beard. She's not sure of his ethnicity or his age. Is his skin golden brown or is he just very tanned? He seems to belong to no group and at the same time belong to all. He seems as old as the world.

After he wipes the juice from his face with his jacket sleeve, he points to her sketch. "Old Saint Nick was a Jolly old soul, a jolly old soul was he. He took my car, he took my girl, he took my memory."

He talks in a sing-song voice as if he's reciting nursery rhymes.

"I was a mad scientist. My mom so proud of me. I was the Mad Scientist in a lab at the universi-tee. I married Clara Lou with eyes so brown and true. She was much too young to die."

"Who died? Your mom or Clara?"

"Clara? Clara who?"

"Clara Lou, you just said..."

"Clara Lou with eyes so brown and true. And lips and hips so fine. She once was mine."

"Yes, and did she die?"

"Everyone dies. Don't believe their lies! Everyone dies—except me. I'm the Mad Scientist."

Lucy regrets giving her last orange to this man. Why did she think he might know something?

"Everybody dies—except me and Nick. Old Nick, he has no clue and now I've found you." He breaks into a wide smile showing strong white, straight teeth. She isn't sure she can trust him, but he's not wearing a mindseye, and she hasn't been getting anywhere on her own. Also, something about his face reminds her of a phrase her dad would use sometimes: "a man without guile." She once asked him what that meant and he said, "You know, the true of heart."

"And what exactly is that?"

"Someone who loves his fellowman."

"And how do you recognize that?"

"Lots of children are that way. In grown-ups it's rare. When you see someone without guile, you'll know. It's in their eyes."

She looks at the homeless man again and makes up her mind. She hands him her last granola bar.

The next day, while foraging for food with her new friend, Lucy stumbles upon a hillside covered with nasturtiums. The bright orange flowers glow in the shade of the live oak like a carpet of stars. She's seen these flowers before, when she went mountain biking with Marco. He told her the blossoms were edible, but he couldn't talk her into trying one. Now she's up for anything. She pops one in her mouth. They're not bad. They have a plant-y taste, followed by a mild burn like a radish or a pepper. They're actually pretty good, and she's hungry. She picks another flower. This one has a bee inside it. She shakes it gently, and the insect flies out.

"Go on home, bee. Go on home to all your hon-ey." One day with the Mad Scientist, and she's rhyming everything. "Buzz on home, busy bee, and make me some honey."

Honey! Somewhere in this canyon there must be honey. Lucy follows the bee down the slope. She loses this bee but finds another on a blooming sage. She follows it to the canyon floor. Now there's a steady stream of bees. She must be close to the hive. Bees swarm around what looks like a manhole: a concrete cylinder two feet off the ground with a heavy lid ajar. Buzzing all around, bees come and go from the opening in the lid. Lucy takes a few steps back, sets down her backpack and retrieves the hoodie she took from her sister. She puts the hood on and pulls the strings tight so that only her eyes peek through.

Cautiously, she approaches the manhole. The lid won't budge.

She finds a thick stick to use as a lever. The stick breaks. More and more bees stream out. A furious cloud of bees surrounds her. A few bees sneak into her hoodie. The buzzing deafens her. Spindly legs crawl on her face and neck. A sharp sting, followed by another and another. She runs from the storm of bees, flinging off her jacket but not soon enough. She's stung three times on her face and once on her neck. The pain throbs, so much more intense than a single bee sting. She can feel her face swelling. She stumbles back to her shelter and collapses on the floor.

"Lucy, Lucy likes her honey, but it makes you look funny."

She can barely open her eyes. She's not sure how long it has been since she was stung. The Mad Scientist has brought her backpack and the hoodie. He joins her inside her refuge but at a comfortable distance. While her face swells tighter, he recites a poem. Lucy recognizes it because she loves old poems, especially ones named after her. She's surprised that he memorized this poem by Wordsworth. Perhaps, she's made some mistaken assumptions about his education.

> "She dwelt among the untrodden ways
> Beside the springs of Dove,
> A Maid whom there were none to praise
> And very few to love:
> A violet by a mossy stone
> Half hidden from the eye!
> Fair as a star, when only one
> Is shining in the sky."

He skips the last stanza, the one about Lucy in her grave. Did he leave it out by chance or intentionally? She spends the rest of the day in her hiding place writing and sketching. The Mad Scientist refills her water and reads her entries. Does he understand them? He looks at her with so much empathy and insight. But the moment he opens his mouth, he babbles another incoherent poem or song. Maybe she just wants to believe he comprehends her. Still, she writes with more purpose.

If something happens to me, the Mad Scientist can keep this book safe and give it to someone, maybe my sister or Marco so they'll remember me.

It's strange, this desire to be remembered. It feels as if my life would be meaningless if I'm forgotten. I suppose that's why some people seek fame, to assure themselves that they matter. The more people who know us, the more valuable we must be. Which is silly, right? To think life's value consists in how many people remember you. I mean, some horrible people, like Hitler, are remembered while most of the good people he doomed to death are forgotten.

Most of the billions who have lived on this earth no one remembers. Why should I be any different?

The next day her face swells so much she can barely open her eyes. Her face hurts, and she feels disoriented, all buzzy inside. She remembers what her mom gave her for bee stings.

"Benadryl. I need Benadryl."

The Mad Scientist answers, "This little piggy went to the market."

"I bet I do look like a pig."

"This little piggy went to the market," he points at her. "This little piggy stayed home. This little piggy had hot dogs," he pointed at himself. "And this little piggy went wee, wee all the way home."

He's right. No facial recognition software would recognize her with her face so distorted. She has fifty dollars in cash. This is her chance to go to the store.

She stands in the checkout line with two packs of hot dogs (they were on sale two for one), a smallish watermelon, Benadryl, toothpaste, marshmallows (also on sale for two dollars a bag), hot dogs buns, two loaves of wheat bread, a bunch of bananas and a jar of peanut butter. Everyone in the store keeps looking at her. She must be a sight in her dingy dress, flyaway braids and swollen face. She smells awful, too. At first the coolness of the store was pleasant, but now she's shivering. The clerk asks if she brought her own bags right as Marco walks through the automatic doors.

CHAPTER 14

Perhaps the facts most astounding and most real
are never communicated man to man.
Henry David Thoreau, *Walden*

Marco looks distracted, like he's thinking about a complicated equation. He does not even glance her way. He walks straight to the back of the store, probably for milk or ice cream. They're the only two items he ever makes a trip to the store for. Everything else he orders online.

The checker asks Lucy again about bags. She holds up her backpack. She considers looking for Marco. But talking to him seems too risky. The man would keep close tabs on him and his memories. Lucy's face might not make any matches with face recognition, but the man would certainly notice a strange girl telling Marco to take out his mindseye. Besides, what were the chances Marco would listen? If a dirty, homeless Marco approached Lucy in the store, told her she was his girlfriend and then gave a delusional account about a mysterious man who erased him from her memory, she wouldn't follow him out of the store. She'd run the other way.

The checker asks how she wants to pay.

"Cash."

"Did you type in your number? The hot dogs are two for one."

Lucy types in her number.

It takes her some time to pack everything into her backpack, everything but the watermelon. Why did she buy a watermelon? It sounded so good. She puts on the bulging backpack and carries the heavy fruit in front of her.

She reaches the doors the same time as Marco carrying a half-gallon of mint chocolate chip. He steps to the side to let her pass. "Whoa! That's some allergic reaction. Let me guess, you bought Benadryl?"

She nods. She feels so much. It's Marco in the living flesh talking to her and...he doesn't know her. She's surprised by how substantial he is. She has thought about him so much these past few days. The memory of him has sustained her, and yet, now seeing him in person, she realizes how poorly she'd remembered him, how insufficient her memory of him was compared to the real person. He's taller and his hands are more veined, more rough, while his hair looks so soft, so wonderful. Black with a tousled curl. She wants to touch it.

"Does it hurt?" Even through his Spex she can see the concern in his brown eyes. He has so much sympathy for some random, puffed-up street waif.

She can't answer. She scurries off, embarrassed, confused, afraid. She trudges the half-mile to the canyon, lugging the watermelon, continually looking back, hoping he's following her, hoping he's not, regretting that she hadn't taken her chance and spoken to him. Who knows, maybe he would have believed her.

She catches her reflection in a black SUV parked near the canyon trail head. She stops. Who is this girl? Her hair's a disaster, her face grotesque. She looks homeless. She is homeless.

As she walks down the canyon trail, self-pitying tears roll down her swollen face. A couple mountain bikers approach her. For a second, she forgets that she's unrecognizable, that she no longer needs to hide. She plunges into the tall plants at the side of the trail, huddling on the ground, trying to calm her breathing, thinking all the while how much she wants to turn back and find Marco. The bikes pass. Sitting under the tall weeds, she rummages through her backpack and finds the Benadryl. She takes a double dose with the last of her water. Marco asked, "Does it hurt?" His eyes were so kind. She moves her hand to her chest to push back against the terrible exploding feeling in her heart. A horrible wail escapes from her mouth, startling several crows that fly up from the field. The watermelon rolls out of her lap as her face falls to the ground. She cries while crows circle and caw above her. She cries till her throat is sore, her tears mingling with the dirt.

When she wakes her face is in the mud. The plants above her create a black filigree against a lilac sky. The watermelon split on a rock with sticky juice trickling out. Ants creep to the crack in the melon. Lucy brushes the ants and dirt off the fruit. She tears off a big chunk. Juice runs down her hands. She licks the liquid running on her wrist. So sweet. She bites the melon, heedless of the stray ants scurrying on it, now on her arms.

She went to the store in the late afternoon. It's dark now, safe to walk on the main trail. No more joggers or bikers would be out this late. A young bunny hops ahead of her on the trail, darting from side to side like a pinball. Normally, Lucy loves bunnies. Every time she sees one, she points it out with delight as if God created these creatures for her personally. Mollie used to joke that if Lucy were an animal, she'd be a bunny. "You're fast like one and even have the same coloring." This is true. The fur of the wild bunnies is the same indeterminate golden-reddish brown as Lucy's hair, especially at the base of their ears. But now she sees the abundant bunnies as possible sustenance. How would she design a snare to catch rabbits? She's not sure that she could actually kill a bunny. The thought of skinning one makes her heartily grateful for the hot dogs in her backpack.

At the top of the ridge, four palm trees silhouette against a navy sky. Up ahead shine the gleaming eyes of a coyote. Another bunny hops onto the trail. In a flash the coyote chases it. He drives the bunny into the sagebrush. The coyote snarls. A man steps out of the shadows. Lucy screams.

CHAPTER 15

Our torments also may in length of time
Become our Elements.
John Milton, *Paradise Lost*

Lucy's skiing, sort of. She's hurtling down the glaring mountain, one foot attached to a ski, the other in a garbage bag and duct tape. It looks like her leg might be in a cast inside that garbage bag. For the most part she keeps the garbage bag foot off the ground, but occasionally uses it as a brake. She falls a lot. Each time, she comes up laughing. Her cheeks and nose are red, her eyes the same soft blue as the mountain sky. A water droplet hangs from her nose. Her hair's a beautiful mess.

"You're going to break your other leg," says Fred, an eighteen-year-old from Beaver Falls. This is Fred's memory. It's hard to tell exactly what Fred looks like because he looks in mirrors rarely. But Nick knows that he's tall, lanky, with a gap between his teeth and a large, perpetually sunburned nose. Fred has an extensive file on Lucy, which has proven most useful.

Lucy's brushing snow off herself. She asks Fred for a hand up. Instead he throws snow at her. She throws some back at him. She's laughing. Fred moves in closer. Lucy's face looms large. Nick sees a water droplet in her eyelashes. The pattern of her iris looks like a pale blue snowflake. She's saying something, but her voice grows blurry. Her face comes in sharp focus. Nick laughs softly to himself. Fred is going to kiss her. Fred makes his move. The screen is all lips and then a beach on a sunny day.

Why the beach image? Maybe she smells like sunscreen? Memories can be random like that. A message flashes across all screens. LUCY CAMPBELL: VON's 1032. He hurries to his desk and checks out the match. Minutes ago, someone typed Lucy's phone number into the keypad at a grocery store. He accesses the surveillance cameras in the store. He runs them through a search looking for Lucy's face. No luck. He checks the location of the store. It's only a few blocks from the canyon across from the high school. He has focused on this canyon ever since he chased her into it. But after days of searching and finding nothing, Nick assumed she moved on.

A few minutes later and another notification: Marco's searching again for a Lucy Campbell. That kid. He's obsessed. Everything reminds him of her. He's become a total waste of time. Nick has been less vigilant about disconnecting Marco's memories. Let the dude search for her. What can he find? Nearly all her digital records have been erased. Her family still remembers her. They just aren't thinking about her. It's not hard to make people forget; just distract them. Nick often feels a bit of disgust at how quickly people are able to give up loved ones: lovers, siblings, parents. It makes him think less of the human race. People say a lot about enduring love. But he has yet to see it. And Marco doesn't count because it hasn't even been a week. Besides, Marco's probably more interested in solving a puzzle than in Lucy herself.

He checks Marco's location from the GPS in his Spex. He was in the same grocery store where Lucy's number showed up. Nick searches through Marco's most recent memories. He's leaving the store and talking to an odd-looking girl with ratty braids and a funny face. "Wait a minute." Nick zooms in on the image of this girl. Closer, closer. Her left eye fills the entire screen. Her iris is a pale blue snowflake.

CHAPTER 16

You can always see a face in the fire.
   Henry David Thoreau, *Walden*

"This little piggy went wee, wee all the way home!"
   The Mad Scientist chants jubilantly.

Sure, now he's talking, thinks Lucy. *What happened to his constant recitation and muttering?* If he hadn't been so quiet in the first place, she wouldn't be hyperventilating. She can hardly breathe. She takes a moment to calm down.

"This little piggy bought hot dogs?"

She unzips her backpack and retrieves the hot dogs.

"They're better cooked but perfectly safe raw. And since we can't have a fire..."

He pulls the package out of her hands.

"My hot dog has a first name. It's fire, fire burning bright, In the forests of the night."

"Is that a good idea? Do we have anything to start a fire with?"

He hurries ahead of her, still chanting.

"What immortal hand or eye, Could frame thy fearful symmetry?"

"Wait! I wanted one of those!" Her only option is to follow. A fire glows in the distance. The wind carries loud laughter. Where is he taking her? Why is she following? She steps over logs and through the bramble toward voices and soft orange light.

In a clearing under a sprawling sycamore tree, flames burn three feet high; some leap higher. Beside the makeshift fire pit, the Mad Scientist sings, "There'll be a hot time in the old town tonight."

Sitting with him are three weather-beaten souls. All three join him on the chorus. Yelling, "Fire! Fire! Fire!"

"Friends?" Lucy asks.

He points to each of them in turn. "The butcher, the baker and the candlestick maker."

A skinny man looks up. "I guess that makes me the butcher?"

"I'm the baker," says the woman. "Did you get cookies? Tell me you got cookies."

"Have a seat," says the other man who is tall and thick with muscle. "You're the guest of honor. Did you bring beer?"

"Beer, beer, the price is dear."

"Nah, I couldn't risk being ID'd." This was true, but not the whole truth. Not a drinker herself, Lucy didn't even think to buy some.

"You don't buy it, ya fool. Ya pinch it."

"I couldn't do that—ever."

"Spend a few more days in the canyon and get back to me," says the big man. He has shoulder-length brown hair and a full, remarkably clean, beard. He looks somewhere between thirty and forty.

"So, are you the candlestick maker?" she asks.

"No, I'm Rex."

While the scientist passes out sticks and hot dogs, Rex makes introductions. "This is Weasel," he says pointing to the skinny man, who is not at all what Lucy expected a homeless man to look like. He looks more like an accountant, complete with glasses. (She makes a quick study to make sure they are not Spex and that he is not wearing a mindseye. He isn't.) His clothes aren't even that dirty. Lucy's dress is in worse shape.

"And this is Penny, but I call her something else." The woman has a square flat reptilian face. Lucy tries to imagine her young and beautiful but can't.

She asks if any of them are wearing a mindseye. Penny laughs, revealing toothless gaps. "Do pigs fly? We barely have enough to eat." Looking at Penny's ample belly, Lucy finds this last bit hard to believe. And Rex looks well-fed and gigantic. How? Lucy has only been in the woods for a week and is losing weight. She can tell because her bra is looser. Rex suggested she steal food. That option hadn't even crossed her mind. She felt guilty enough sneaking into her sister's house. But if she were going to survive, she would have to shed some of her good girl habits. That thought makes her a little sad. The main reason she ran was to preserve her identity. Yet, in order to physically survive it might be necessary to alter some fundamental aspects of herself. Would a Lucy who steals and lies still be Lucy? Of course, she's also been changing in positive ways. She can now climb fences like a champ and has completely lost her fear of the dark. What does it mean to preserve one's identity when identity is as fluid as the flames she's staring at?

"Run away?" Penny asks nodding to Lucy as if she's an expert on running away.

"Not exactly. I'm hiding from someone."

"Who?" asks Weasel.

"I don't know."

"In the canyon, in the wood, lives a girl very good." The Mad Scientist looks into the fire as he speaks.

> "In a penthouse, in the city,
> seeks a man, a girl so pretty.
> If he finds her in all her glory,

no one else will know her story."

"Is he always like this?" Lucy asks.

"We call him the Poet," answers Weasel.

"He told me he was the Mad Scientist."

"No one names themselves," says Rex.

"Except you." Penny stares Rex down.

"She needs a name," says Weasel.

"My name's Lucy."

"No," says Rex. "We'll call you Princess. So, Princess, why exactly are you here?"

"It's a long story."

"We ain't going nowhere."

"You might not believe it. You'll think I'm crazy."

"Listen here, Princess: We're all crazy." Rex spears another hot dog and puts it in the fire. "Some of us more than others. But everyone on this whole damn planet is crazy! Tell us your story; doesn't matter much if it's true."

By the time Lucy finishes, the fire has burned down to trembling coals.

"Foolish girl," says Rex. "I'd give anything to have my memories erased. I'm hiding from my memories while you're hiding to keep yours."

"But that guy might kill her," says Penny. "Besides, she wants to remember her boyfriend. No one wants to forget their first love."

"Like I said, foolish girl."

"We can get this guy," says Weasel. "We could do it, easy. Princess, you go on campus. Let a thousand Spex record where you are. The man comes. We jump him. You're free."

"I don't know if he works alone."

"The devil has legions of angels," says the Poet.

"See!" says Lucy.

"You believe his gibberish?" asks Rex.

"I kind of do. I think he might know this guy."

"What are the chances? How would he know this rich boy?"

"He says he's a scientist. Maybe this guy worked with him. Maybe he did something to mess with his mind."

"He says his hot dog has a first name." Rex takes a sip from a bottle of something more potent than beer. "He's whacked."

The Poet keeps singing, "Fire! Fire! Fire!"

Lucy asks, "Is that a real song or is he making it up?"

"You don't know it?" asks Penny "We always sang it at camp." She starts singing along. "'Late last night while I was home in bed, Miss O' Leary left her lantern in the shed.'"

Weasel and Rex join in. "The cow kicked it over and she winked her eye and said it will be a hot time in the old town tonight. Fire! Fire! Fire!"

The four of them are having a good time. They could be four friends camping. They start over and this time Lucy joins in.

"You can sing," Weasel says to her.

"Yeah, I'm in...or I was in my church choir."

"Church, huh?" asks Rex. "What do you think of God now?"

"He's all I have."

"Seriously? You spent the last of your money on hot dogs and watermelon. Your face is swollen and you're hanging out with a lunatic, a druggie, a murderer, and a whore."

Penny makes an offended noise. "I prefer to be called a *lady* of the night."

"I was all alone. Now, God gave me you."

"That's God for you—completely unreliable."

She studies the three of them. Is one of them really a murderer? Of the two men, Rex appears the more murderous. But his comments about forgetting make her think he must be the druggie.

"Sing us a song," begs Penny. "A church one."

Lucy protests.

"It'd be nice, like a lullaby," suggests Weasel.

"Sing!" yells Rex. He really does look like he could kill someone.

Lucy obeys.

She tilts her head back. The night sky is scattered with sparse stars. "'Be still...my soul. The Lord is on thy side...'" Her fragile voice is almost lost in a faint breeze. "'With patience bear thy cross of grief...and pain.'"

The Poet closes his eyes as if in meditation. He hums along.

Rex stares into the coals.

"'Leave to thy God to order and provide, In every change He faithful will remain.'"

She sings slowly and softly. As she sings, she feels a power, a strength she didn't know she had. At moments her voice feels too strong and true to be her own. She sings all the verses, not caring whether the others want to listen. She wants to hear this new voice, her voice, in the darkness.

"That was pretty," says Penny with wet eyes. The Poet and Weasel are asleep.

"I don't believe any of it," says Rex, "But I'm glad you do. You know your puffiness has gone down a lot. And when you sing...I'm beginning to think you might be pretty."

Before Lucy has the chance to reply, someone else does.

"You have no idea." A man stands across the fire from them. Even in the darkness, Lucy recognizes his goatee.

CHAPTER 17

I have found that no exertion
   of the legs can bring two minds much nearer to one another.
   Henry David Thoreau, *Walden*

The man steps out from a cluster of willows. He's wearing a suit, possibly the same one he wore in the mayor's memory. He moves toward them. He steps between Weasel at the end of a log and Penny sitting on an overturned bucket. Penny appraises the newcomer and reflexively gives him an admiring smile. He smiles back. "May I join you?" Not waiting for an answer, he sits at the other end of Weasel's log. He throws a bunch of dried weeds on the hot coals. Flames crackle to life.

"Should I take him now?" Rex whispers in Lucy's ear.

"What do you want from me?" she asks.

"Lucy, Lucy, Lucy..." He's younger than she expected, barely older than Marco. But in a weird way his youth makes him more threatening. "I'm thrilled to see you. There's been a massive misunderstanding."

"Misunderstanding? You deleted my sister's memories!"

"Only a few—a very few—she remembers you and loves you. Porter misses you."

"Because he's not even two and doesn't wear Spex yet! Everyone else has forgotten me!"

"I haven't." The flames cast light and shadows on his face. "I've been looking everywhere for you. I've watched thousands of memories of you, literally thousands. I probably know more about you than you do. I've been worried sick. Like maybe it was my fault that you've done this...run away, living in the woods."

"It is."

He shakes his head and laughs. "A massive misunderstanding. I'm not trying to hurt you. I'm not a violent person. I abhor violence. That's why I do what I do. To be honest, I've stopped my work, everything, to find you—save you."

"Yes, but first you want to erase a month from my life."

"It doesn't hurt one bit."

"Tell that to the Poet!"

"The Poet?"

The Poet's seat is empty. When did he leave? It occurs to Lucy that the guy with the goatee never seemed to recognize him. Maybe Rex is right. Maybe the Poet is simply crazy.

"I want to stay me. I'm the sum of my memories. Take them away, and who am I? Erasing my memories is erasing my life. You might as well kill me."

"It's not the same, not even. Everyone forgets something. No one knows who they are—not really. What is identity? Is it how others see us? But they never know the whole truth, do they? We hide ourselves. I know. I've looked into thousands of minds. Perhaps identity is how we see ourselves? But we never see ourselves clearly, do we? We lie, or let's say, 'spin,' to ourselves." He makes quote marks with his fingers and stands up. He speaks and carries himself like a game show host or a politician. "We hurt someone. We say things like, 'We didn't mean to,' or, 'It couldn't have hurt that much. I'm a good person, I've done nothing wrong, not much.' I know. Believe me, I know. I've peeked into loads of minds. People feel guilt, sure—but they spend more time convincing themselves that they've done nothing wrong. Some of the best people live with guilt and some of the worst have no shame. No one really knows who they are."

"God does."

He laughs his mocking laugh. "It would be nice if there were a God, very comforting. An absolute power to right all wrongs, a guarantee for a happy ending. Trust me, darling, I want to believe in God like everyone else. But if you'd seen one-thousandth of what I've seen in memories: murder, rape, incest, perversion, infidelity, cruelty, stealing, abuse, betrayal, every form of selfishness, you name it. If there were a God, he's certainly asleep at the wheel. I'd much sooner believe in the devil than in God."

Rex nods along as the man continues.

"If there's a God, where is he? Why does he let us wallow in our pain? Why do people suffer? That's where I come in. I erase pain."

"Even if it means erasing the truth?"

"Darling, there's no truth, not really. Everyone's reality is based on memory, electronic signals processed by a biased mind."

"Then why do you care so much about the memories I hold? Why should you erase my truth?"

"Is this about Marco? Because, to be honest, he doesn't remember you. It was too easy to make him forget. It was like he wanted to. You always liked him more than he liked you. People only forget what they want to forget. Trust me. It makes my job easy. You see, I'm not stealing memories. I'm erasing guilt, shame and pain. I give people a second chance. What does everyone want? To be happy, right? I make people happy. What's wrong with that?"

"You make an awful lot of money making people happy," Lucy blurts out.

"I have to. At some point I have to expand. Do you even know what percentage of the population I reach? I am not even making a dent. There's massive pain in the world, and I can do something about it. Don't you see? People talk about world peace so much that it's almost a cliché. But I can do it. It's within my reach. If I erase enough hurt, enough prejudice, there will be peace. Can't you see how important my work is?"

Rex speaks up, "Can you really erase memories?"

"He can, and he wants to erase mine."

"I want to make you happy. You can't be happy living in the woods. Come with me, Lucy. I'll erase your memory, you'll be back in school, you'll spend Thursdays with your sister, you'll see your nephew..."

"NO!" She stands up. "I don't want to forget."

"Relax. Who knows, maybe you'll meet up with Marco again. You'll fall in love all over again. Not many people get the chance to fall in love for the first time twice."

Rex interrupts, "Can you delete my memories?"

"Absolutely, if you bring Lucy."

"I'm not coming!" She walks away.

Nick grabs her wrist.

Penny pulls on his shirt. He falls off-balance and rolls back, landing partly on Penny, partly in a low-growing vine. Before he can get up, Penny bites his ankle. He howls. She whips out a knife, holding the blade to his neck.

"Don't. Make. Another. Move."

In a flash Rex joins them. He bends down to look into Nick's desperate face. "Can you really erase memories?"

"He can!" yells Lucy.

"Will you erase mine?"

"Yes! Whatever you want." Flames illuminate his face. In the light, he looks young and afraid.

"Then I won't regret doing this." Rex picks up a large rock. "I won't even remember." He throws the rock at Penny. It hits her head with a sickening crunch. She falls back, letting go of the knife. Freed, the man lunges for Lucy.

Weasel tackles him, yelling, "Run, Lucy, run!"

CHAPTER 18

We must learn to reawaken and keep ourselves awake,
    not by mechanical aid but by an infinite expectation of the
dawn.
    Henry David Thoreau, *Walden*

L ucy sits in the branches of a sycamore tree. Her feet dangle in
    the white mist below. The fog hides her, but it could also
conceal danger. She can only see faint outlines of trunks and
branches. Or is that a person? The woods are unusually hushed.

When she first ran from the campfire, she heard more screams
and fighting. And then the noises became unrecognizable. She could
not tell if they were human or animal. A part of her felt irresponsible
fleeing the fight. A greater part of her knew she had to get away as far
as possible. After running about a mile she climbed this sycamore
tree. She's not even sure how she made it up the lowest branches,
which are a good ten feet off the ground. It was all a mad blur of
distant screams, adrenaline and desperate prayer.

Now the fog seeps into the canyon until nothing's recognizable.
Fog has a strange way of distorting things. It hides and reveals and

somehow makes solid things appear to be made of nothing more than mist. What is real? Does reality even matter? The man is right. Her memories do not equal truth. Each memory is only her warped sliver of reality. And what is reality, anyway?

Sometimes, briefly, Lucy tries to imagine that there is no God. The very thought feels like standing at the edge of a tall cliff and thinking: *I could jump from this, why not?* Sitting high in this tree, forgotten by everyone, she wonders anew: *What if there is no right or wrong? What if my actions don't matter? What if I don't matter? What if nothing matters?*

She doesn't recall learning to pray. She just always has. And God has always been there for her. Growing up, few of her friends were believers. In high school she hung with an intellectual crowd. They were all too smart for God. They teased her about going to church. Said she just liked an excuse to wear a dress and to sing. That much was true, but it was more than that. She believed; and she liked believing. She liked how church made her feel.

Every week at church she was reminded that she had intrinsic worth. God loved her, so she didn't need to worry about what everyone else thought. This sense of God's love freed her from social expectations. It gave her the courage to be different. But what if she'd imagined it all? What if she loved a God who didn't exist? Or like Marco, He had completely forgotten her?

She prays all night, not a verbal prayer or even a cohesive thought, rather her whole soul yearning, reaching for something greater than herself, hoping she is not—has not always been —forsaken.

"Lucy!" A voice she does not recognize calls in a loud whisper. "You gotta get down. Cops are a coming."

Sirens wail in the distance. She scoots down to a lower branch. Weasel stands at the base of the tree. A phantom in the fog. She's touched that he remembers her real name since they all called her Princess. As she shimmies down, he tells her his plan. He'll distract the police while she escapes.

"Shouldn't we stay together?"

"There's a body. In a few minutes police will be swarming this canyon."

"A body! Whose?"

He ignores her question. "If they catch you, he'll win. You can tell your story till you're blue in the face. He'll keep on erasing memories. Eventually, he'll erase yours. You won't even know why you're in jail."

She makes the last leap to the ground, landing in the bramble. Her wrist hurts a little, but otherwise she's okay.

"Whose body?"

"Penny." His voice catches in his throat.

"The guy with the goatee?"

"No, Rex. I wanna kill him! He ran off with your guy."

"He's not *my* guy." She stands up, brushing the dirt off her hands. "Where's the Poet?"

"No idea. Maybe he called the cops."

"You can't turn yourself into the police."

"I won't. I'll just keep them busy while you get away. But it's better if they catch me than you. I belong in jail. They'll be happy to take me back."

"Wait...what for?"

"Don't you recall?"

She shakes her head.

"Rex wasn't kidding when he called me a murderer."

"Oh!" She involuntarily lets out a little gasp. "And you're guilty?"

He nods. The sirens scream louder. "You've gotta go, to your sister's or Marco's; somewhere. Just go!"

"Why are you helping me?"

"Some things are wrong. Murder is wrong even if no one remembers. Believe me. I know."

Nick's ankle burns where the psycho lady bit him. Human bites can be worse than dog bites. He knows this. But he doesn't want to go to the emergency room to treat it. Too many questions. They'd want to know about the woman who bit him. He can't very well say, "Oh, she's lying somewhere in the canyon with her head bashed in." He cringes. Rex said he didn't mean to kill her, only stop her.

Ah, the regret. He had been so close. For one moment his search was over. Lucy was within reach. He winces as he recalls the moment she recognized him, that look of disgust. Why wouldn't she listen to him? Rex listened. Rex understood. In the end, Rex saved him. The massive oaf snores on the couch. Can he trust this guy? In general, Nick doesn't trust anyone. That's why he works alone. And this dude is a bit of a loose cannon and rather violent for his taste. But he saved his life, and Nick made a promise. And he keeps his promises.

In the darkness a thick fog shrouds the ocean, the same fog that hid Lucy from him in the woods. They searched for a long time. How did she disappear like that? Nick would have kept looking, but police arrived. Who called them? He and the big guy barely escaped. On the bright side, the police search means that while Nick nurses his wounds in the comfort of his own home, more than a dozen Spex are now in the canyon, assisting his hunt for Lucy.

The smelly guy on the couch starts moving.

"Hey, what's this?" Rex stares, mouth agape at the images flashing on the walls.

"Memories."

"Whoa!" He walks around the room, taking it all in. He stops at a memory of Lucy swimming in a mountain lake. He watches for some time. Her legs and arms and back are naked in the water. The way Rex looks at her bugs Nick. It feels intrusive. "When I was a kid," says Rex, "I went to church, and they said God sees everything. I didn't think it was possible. Maybe I was wrong. Maybe you're God?"

"She must have left the woods. There's no sign of her." Nick scans the memories of the police in the canyon. A few of those searching got a glimpse of the dead woman's face. Eyes open. Mouth frozen in a scream. The image appears over and over. Nick can't look anymore.

"Where do you think she went?"

"Maybe her sister's, or her dorm room or Marco's. I'm keeping tabs on all three locations."

"Whoa! You did this all by yourself? Impressive!"

Truth be told, Nick hired out a few middle-aged hackers who live nearby, as he often does. The hackers assist him when he has to hack multiple sources in a short period of time. He pays them cash upfront and has never offered to erase any of their memories. Nick doesn't want these clever hackers to get a whiff of mind-hacking. As soon as the job is done, he erases their memories. Every time he goes into one of their minds, he learns a few new hacking techniques. So now, he pretty much *can* do this all by himself.

"Yep, all by myself. I'm always watching. Sleep is for wimps. Poor Lucy! She doesn't have a chance. I will track her down."

Marco stands on a narrow dirt path holding a girl's hand. Green leaves and orange flowers carpet the hillside. The sky above reflects the forest floor, dark green with blossoms of light. His eyes follow the hand to the girl, a strong freckled arm leading to a mane of hair the color of nutmeg, framing a vague face. A familiar laughing voice says, "Marco, take off your Spex." He obeys. Instantly, the world becomes more distinct, more full of light. Sounds seem sharper, outlines crisper. It's as if he woke up. Except he knows he's dreaming. This girl belongs to dreams. Her face has features now. He's still holding her hand, soft and firm with a quiver of warmth. She has a friendly, freckly face. It appears as if all light comes from her smile.

"Kiss me," she says.

He obeys.

All the world is a whirl. He stands on bursts of sunlight. Golden flowers bloom above him. The only constant is where their mouths meet. When the kiss is over, he reaches to put his Spex on.

"Don't! Promise me you won't!" She grabs his hand to stop him. "Don't put on your Spex!" He hesitates. But he wants a picture of her. Her face blurs as he puts on his Spex. She darts away, making an upset noise. He tries to go after her, but he can't. He can't move. He tries to call her, but he doesn't know her name. The golden flowers turn into golden trumpets with lip-shaped flutes, making a terrible noise. He covers his ears but can't escape the din.

He wakes with a start. Someone is in his room. He flips on the light. The girl from his dream stands at the foot of his bed.

CHAPTER 19

It takes two to speak the truth: one to speak, and another to hear.
    Henry David Thoreau, *Walden*

When she left Weasel, Lucy ran without thinking. She soon realized she was running to Marco's, like a horse to the stable. She never really made a decision. She wanted to be with Marco. But once on her way she came up with a few good reasons for this plan. First, his place was closest. Next, he had the ultimate search engine for faces; and finally, she didn't want to entangle her sister with this guy. Lucy couldn't put Mollie and Phil and Porter in any more danger. But now, standing in Marco's room, so close that she could reach her hand out and touch him, all her flimsy logic comes crashing down. What was she thinking? Her sister would at least recognize her. But Marco, he doesn't know her. Why would he ever listen to a dirty homeless stranger? And besides all that, he is shirtless.

"Tell me why I shouldn't call the police right now?" He rubs his eyes. His Spex sit safely on his nightstand.

"Marco, I need your help."

"I know you." He says with a hint of a question. This is more than she had hoped for. She nods. He steps closer. He looks her up and down. Marco's no body builder. But he surfs most every day and his arms and shoulders show it. Lucy tries not to stare. This feels even more awkward than their first meeting because now she cares so much more. The room is so small and Marco so real. She tries to look at anything but him. She notices her copy of *Walden* sitting on his nightstand.

"You're the girl from the grocery store." She pats down some flyaway hairs. She wishes she could have taken a shower before coming here. "You look a ton better." He remains cool and calm as if every night some strange girl bursts into his apartment.

"Yeah, the swelling's gone down." She can't think of anything else to say. She has so much to say to Marco, her Marco, the Marco that knew her and liked her. Not this skeptical, sexy stranger, eyeing her like she's a mythical creature.

"Is your name...Lucy?"

"You remember?"

"No." He looks down at his hands. He holds out his left one. *Lucy Campbell* is written on his palm. She takes his hand and traces her name. He steps toward her, crossing into her personal space. She thinks maybe he's going to kiss her. But his eyes are confused. To him she's a stranger, a messy burglar. Why would he kiss her? He turns his head slightly, and she glimpses a glint of silver. She closes the gap between them and snatches the mindseye out of his ear.

"Whoa! What the..."

"I don't have time to explain. We're in trouble. We've got to go. Now! Put on a shirt, will ya? I'll grab your keys and wallet."

"Are you kidnapping me?" He smiles a goofy smile. She feels irrationally jealous that he would be so willing to run off with a strange girl even if it that girl is her.

"I'm serious. We don't have much time. Ten minutes at most."

She opens his junk drawer in the kitchen and retrieves his wallet and keys. He returns buttoning his shirt.

"Hey! How do you know where I keep my stuff?"

"I'll explain later. We're not safe." He's carrying his Spex.

"No! Leave those. That's how he's erasing your memories." Marco hesitates, opens his hand and looks at her name. He sets them down.

As they run down the front steps, he asks where they are going.

"Abuelita's."

He pauses and looks at her. For the first time that night he seems a little freaked out. "How do you know Abuelita?"

"Marco." She takes a deep breath. "I'm your girlfriend." She's in too big of a hurry to look at his reaction. Perhaps a little scared. How would it feel to wake in the middle of the night and find out some transient is your girlfriend? She gets in his car, shuts the door and buckles her seat belt before she dares look at him.

"My girlfriend, huh?" He also seems intent on avoiding her eyes, possibly because he's backing the car up. "That explains a lot," he says with his eyes on the rear-view mirror.

"Like what?"

"I might as well tell you." His lips twitch like he's trying not to smile. "That explains why—from the moment I saw you—I wanted to kiss you."

"You remember me?"

"Not one bit." This time he looks over and smiles. That smile that makes flowers bloom and rain fall. "I just want to kiss you."

By the time they are heading north on I-5, Marco understands the basics. Lucy skips the embarrassing part of the story when she was spying on him. They don't have time for that, anyway. She tells him about learning to mind-hack from her sister and stumbling across the man with a goatee in the mayor's memories. It does not take long for Marco to connect the dots.

"He must be scanning all memories for his face. Anyone who sees him, he erases their memories. This dude must have some insane search algorithms. Consider me impressed."

"Emphasis on insane! This is the guy who chased me into the woods you are talking about. As well as erasing me from your memory."

"No doubt the guy's a creep. But a brilliant one! How long were we dating?"

"A month."

"That is a lot of memories to erase. My hat's off to him. I suppose he couldn't touch your memories because you don't wear Spex."

"Yeah, and the only other person I know who doesn't wear them is your grandma. That's why we are going to her place. He won't find us there, giving us time to find him and erase his memory."

"Love the plan, but we shouldn't have taken my car." As soon as he says it, Lucy realizes her mistake. In the rear-view mirror a string of white headlights shines behind them. Two of those bright beams could belong to the man. If he could hack into Spex and Mollie's computer, he would certainly be tracking Marco's car.

"For the first time in my life I wish I had autodrive," says Marco. "Then we could stop somewhere, get out and send the car on its way. He could follow it to Canada."

They consider the different ways they can get to Abuelita's. They can't take a bus or a train. Too many people with Spex would see them. They could rent a car at a community kiosk, but paying would leave an electronic trail. Also, they have no idea how close this guy is.

Marco slows the car down.

"What are you doing?"

"Testing the waters. I want to know what we're dealing with."

They drive just below the speed limit for about ten minutes. And then they notice it: a pair of headlights steady behind them, like coyote eyes shining in the dark. Marco speeds up, the headlights stick with them.

"We have a live one!" He looks over at her. "Apparently this guy is not a figment of your imagination."

"You thought I was crazy."

"No crazier than me—leaving my Spex behind, getting in the car with some strange girl." He pulls off the freeway and crosses under it, squealing tires as he turns. "I thought perhaps *you* were a figment of *my* imagination."

They stop at a light, planning to turn left back onto the freeway going the other direction. "What type of car does he drive?"

"I don't know...an expensive one, a shiny silver..."

"Look in the rear-view mirror."

A chrome car pulls up behind them. It's the guy. Rex is with him.

Marco runs the light and speeds onto the freeway. The shiny car follows with a screech. Marco's surges ahead. The speedometer passes 100 mph as he maneuvers between a semi-truck and a tanker. He grips the wheel, his face rigid, his eyes fierce. Lucy knows where his head is. She's run from this guy three times. During a chase the rest of the world disappears; all other thoughts and emotions evaporate. All that remains is survival. But this time she's a passenger without any direct control of her escape. And without all her energy focused on staying alive, there's a lot more room in her head for fear. Her mind veers down terrifying routes. Each car they weave past she imagines a crash, an explosion, crumpled metal, burnt limbs, her parents called to identify her body.

Lucy's not sure what upsets her more: the idea that she might die or that this guy will win. She has the luxury to wonder if there's any point in running. Even if he stops chasing them, he can easily track their car. The odds seem against them.

Marco pulls off the freeway, takes a few quick turns and parks in a multi-level parking garage. All Lucy's frantic worry stops; it's time to run.

As they dash up a flight of stairs, the chrome car peels into the garage. They run across a sky tunnel to a locked door. Two sets of pounding steps echo up the stairwell. Marco places his hand on the door pad. The door clicks open.

They slip into the building. Shots fire as the heavy door slams shut.

Marco and Lucy run.

He uses his hand print again to let them into another corridor. "That should stall them for a bit," he says as he closes the door. "Even with a gun." They slow down some, no longer moving at a dead run but still hurrying through the maze of labs and offices.

"I have access to this building because I consulted with this company's Spex designs." Marco points out the security cameras everywhere. "Soon enough he'll know we ran through this hall. But right now, he has no idea which door we're going to come out of. From that parking garage there are about seventeen different doors we could exit through."

He leads her to an underground passage connecting several buildings. In the third building he stops. She's about to protest, then realizes he's found a vending machine. They buy a couple bottles of water, a few candy bars, some mini doughnuts and a bag of chips. They stuff the supplies into her backpack and exit through a side door, rushing across the empty parking lot. They catch their breath in the woods bordering the property. The tree trunks shine silver in the night.

"Tell me everything you know about this guy." Marco says as they make their way through the trees.

"Only two people had a memory of him: you and Mollie."

"Impossible!"

"That's what Mollie said. I remember her exact words: 'Sheesh, this guy has the sort of face that the lady at the dry cleaner would remember.'"

"So, he's easy on the eyes?"

"Yes. I mean...most people would say so. He's not my type."

"Apparently, I'm your type." Marco stops for a moment. "And

you're mine..." She can't tell from his tone if this is a statement or a question, so she lets it hang in the air. They walk in silence for a bit until they come out of the trees, standing on a grassy ridge. Far below them twinkle the glittering lights of suburbia. Marco points to a dark corridor running along the base of the hill.

"Our passage to safety."

"How exactly are we getting down there?"

"Carefully. Very carefully."

He leads the way down the steep slope of rocks and dirt. Lucy follows.

"Mollie thought maybe your search didn't work. But it did. We knew it did because we searched for people who had a memory of you."

"And...?"

"Let's just say I'm not the only one who has a crush on you."

"Seriously? I've got to see this."

"You actually hated it."

"Did I?" For a moment he pays close attention to his footing, grabbing hold of sagebrush to keep steady. "You have a crush on me?"

"Obviously. I was your girlfriend."

"Was?"

"I mean...I could be...I mean it's just weird with you not remembering me. I'm not going to force you into a relationship... Ahh!" She slips on some loose dirt and slides several feet, causing a mini rockslide.

Lucy stops talking for a bit and concentrates on not dying. Her feet and calves cramp as she tries to keep balance. Several pebbles are caught in her sandals. She slips again, sending a few larger rocks down.

"This is *not* working!"

"I know!" Marco hollers back a few yards below her. "You almost killed me with that rock." He climbs back up to her and offers a hand. Scared and grumpy as she may be, she still appreciates the thrill of holding his strong hand.

"I'm sorry," she says as she takes it. "You don't deserve this."

And she means it. He's been amazing: dodging traffic on the freeway, abandoning his car in a parking garage, thinking to buy food and find an escape route, all for an unknown girl in a dingy dress.

"I'm guessing you don't deserve this, either. C'mon, we've almost made it."

At the base of the treacherous hill they trudge through a dark passage of willow and grasses. The ground becomes soft and squishy and the grasses taller. Soon cattails tower above their heads and Lucy's toes are covered with mud. They stop to take their shoes off. The tide rises fast. They won't be able to make it through without some wading.

"Why did he erase our whole relationship?" asks Marco. "Couldn't he have just erased mind-hacking?"

"I've thought about that. Maybe it was easier for him because so much of our relationship revolved around mind-hacking." Lucy straps her sandals onto her backpack. "My sister knew who I was. She just didn't know who you were."

The lagoon narrows almost to a river, flowing under the road and spilling out into the ocean. To get through, they must go into the water. Marco takes her backpack, valuable because of the food in it, and carries it above his head. She doggie paddles in the cold, dark water. Panic rises up in her as her legs churn in the bleak water. Anything could be hiding in the ocean. Everything is dark. Above is the low-hanging roof of the concrete bridge. She swims and prays and keeps her eye on Marco. As soon as her feet touch the sand, she scrambles to the empty beach.

Lucy takes a moment to calm down and take deep breaths out in the open sky. Noting that her wet dress clings to her body a bit much, she takes her hoodie out of her backpack and puts it on. It's dry and warm, but she's shivering.

"Don't worry," Marco says. "We're almost there."

They walk toward some cliffs. On their right is the expansive darkness of the ocean. Something about it scares Lucy, like it could swallow her up. To the east the sky is lightening behind a wall of familiar cliffs.

"This might be where we went on our first date."

"Could be," he says. "But for me this *is* our first date."

In some ways it feels like a first date for Lucy, too. Except this go-around she's less certain about what Marco thinks about her. She's embarrassed about her grumpy outburst on the hill. And the stakes are higher now, partly because they're running for their lives, but it's more than that. It's because they have a history together and though he can't remember it, Marco must feel it. Lucy certainly can. And then there is what he said earlier about wanting to kiss her. Every so often she remembers that comment and wonders if he meant it. Each time she glances at him in the darkness, he's already looking at her.

The water keeps rising, pushing them closer to the tall cliffs. Waves splash around their ankles and then their knees. They walk right up against the sandstone cliffs stretching several stories above them.

She raises her voice above the crashing surf. "I'm sorry to drag you into this."

"Stop apologizing. Hands down, this is the best first date ever!" They scramble up some wet rocks to higher ground. He offers her a hand. "Not every first date has a car chase."

"And gunshots."

"Yes, all first dates need gunfire."

They climb down a ledge onto soft sand. "Do you think we're safe now?"

"We won't be totally safe until we erase his memory," says Marco. "But I'm confident we've lost them for a bit and I know a place where we can rest. I can see it now."

The beach stretches for miles, lined with cliffs and grassy bluffs.

"You don't see it, do you?" He stands behind her and puts his arms around her pointing to the cliff. He pauses and turns to her, their faces inches apart.

"Whoa! That was weird!" He pulls back a little. "I just had the strangest case of déjà vu. Like I've said all of that to you before and we were standing on a beach just like this."

She knows what he's referring to. Marco said those exact words, "You don't see it, do you?" when he showed her red tide on the night of their first kiss. She tells him so, except she doesn't mention the kiss part. That would be awkward with his face so close to hers. Instead, she asks if he remembers anything else.

"No, that's it. It was just a flash, but kinda cool. Maybe more memories will return." He points again to the cliff and directs her eyes to a white adobe house, two-thirds up the sheer face, lodged in the sandstone like a giant barnacle.

They climb the switchback trail leading to the cliff house. Lucy ran cross-country and track and knows how to push through exhaustion, a skill that has come in handy this past week. But after living in the woods with little food, water, or sleep, she's hit her limit. Her legs shake and her stomach knots. She's cold, too. She's so miserable it's hard to pinpoint all the sources of her discomfort. But more than anything, she's tired. As fast as it came, her adrenaline dissipates. All she wants is to curl up in a ball and sleep. But she must keep moving. And this is not a path Marco can carry her on. In some places it's no more than foot ledges and hand holds. He keeps giving her a hand and gentle words of encouragement. The cliff, the color and texture of pie crust, crumbles in her grip, leaving her hands covered with fine grains of sand. Rocks slip below her feet and tumble to the beach below, landing with the sound of a startled breath.

When they reach the abandoned house, the sky's a shadowy blue. Only a few stars still shine. Marco opens the door and calls to see if anyone's there. His voice echoes in the empty house. While he checks each room to make sure the place is vacant, Lucy lies down on the cool tile floor. Before she knows it, she's escaped reality.

"Good morning, sleepyhead."

Lucy sits up and stretches. She feels good, so good.

"Where are we?"

"I told you last night. Abuelita's dream house. She keeps trying to buy it. I don't know why they won't sell it. Probably hoping zoning laws will change and they can build a hotel here."

"It's unbelievable!" The entire west wall is, or at least had once been, windows. Two panels are boarded up, but it's still a stunning view. The ocean, so menacing last night, now sparkles a cheerful blue.

Marco rummages through the backpack. "Every time Abuelita comes to see me she stops by this place. She's tried to buy it so many times, she feels responsible for it. She cleans it up or whatever. I don't know exactly. But she's planning to visit me tomorrow. She should stop here first. All we need to do is stay put." He hands Lucy breakfast: a water bottle and a pack of mini doughnuts.

She leans up against the wall beside him and eats her doughnuts, their shoulders not quite touching.

"And you're really my girlfriend?"

She nods.

"It's hard to believe. Not that I wouldn't want to date you. I mean obviously I did...and I do." He steals one of her doughnuts. "So, we've kissed and stuff?"

"Um... Yeah. I mean, we've kissed. We've only dated a little over a month." She keeps her eyes down. Many of the terra-cotta floor tiles are cracked. "This must be so weird for you."

Marco also talks with his eyes on the floor. "I dreamed about you. That must be how your name ended up on my hand."

"Really?"

"I was dreaming about you last night. And then there you were, in my bedroom."

"Really! What did you dream?"

He takes the last doughnut in the package. He examines his hands. He opens and closes the one that has her name on it. "We were somewhere in the canyon." He takes a bite; he clears his throat. "I was kissing you. I know it was you; you had all those freckles." He puts his hand to her cheek. In a softer voice he says, "You got some powdered sugar on your face." He wipes it off near the corner of her mouth. This time she's certain he's going to kiss her. She leans toward him and the front door bangs open.

CHAPTER 20

Nick sleeps late. He wasted a couple hours last night circling the office complex arguing with Rex. The big guy wanted to split up to corner Marco and Lucy. This plan made sense, but after Rex pulled out that gun, Nick didn't trust him. What if he shot Lucy? If he'd known Rex was going to retrieve a gun, Nick would have never agreed to that random errand on the way to Marco's apartment. He's done with Rex. He smells bad and is so condescending. Who is he to tell Nick about reconnaissance? Just because he's fought overseas. Nick's whole life is reconnaissance. He can't wait to erase Rex's memories. But until then he's stuck with him.

Now there's a more pressing matter to consider. Marco and Lucy are reunited. Hours of meticulous editing undone. True, it simplifies things to have only one target. Tactically speaking it's easier if they are together. Still, Nick feels like he has lost something valuable. He checks the location of Marco's car. It's in the same spot in the parking garage where they left it. They must be on foot. He studies a map of the area. Where did they go? How far could they walk? They can't hide for long. He has access to the memories of everyone wearing Spex, but he wants a more educated guess. He looks for another Lucy memory, one he's already seen but discounted.

She's at a party; Marco's there. This is a copied memory from Marco's sister. When he has time. Nick copies memories before he isolates them.

The sister is talking to Lucy. Rachel is tall with an athletic build, a serious face and long thick, straight hair. *Solid eight.* She favors her father more than her mom. Like most teen girls, she wears trendy, oversized Spex. Hers are aquamarine with pink pinstripes. She shows Lucy a mini-fridge tucked in the corner on the patio. Inside are jars of pale green fleshy objects packed in red brine. "What's this?" asks Lucy.

"The kimchi fridge. Ever tried it?"

"I don't think so. What is it?"

"Spicy pickled cabbage. Appetizing, huh? I actually love the stuff if it's my grandma's recipe. I can't stand it from the store. But Dad loves it, so does Marco. He eats it with everything, including mac and cheese."

"Appetizing."

"Mom complains that it makes the whole house stink, so we keep it out here. She won't kiss my dad if he has kimchi breath. Keep an eye on Marco. He normally pounds the stuff with carne asada. But he hasn't had any tonight." Rachel's comment makes Lucy blush right as Abuelita joins them.

"Hey Abby, I'm showing Lucy the kimchi fridge."

"Are you a fan of kimchi, Lucy?"

"Haven't tried it."

"You should. It's muy bueno...and spicy. You can never have too spicy. Verdad, sí?... So Lucy, I see you don't wear Spex. Why not?"

"I like to see the world through my own eyes."

Abuelita looks heavenward. "Praise the saints, at last someone who sees. I'm glad Marco recognizes your worth even if he's enamored with those dumb glasses."

"Those dumb glasses are paying for my trip to Belize this summer," says Rachel. "And didn't he offer to buy you a new house?"

"Verdad, sí, he's very good and generous, as a brother should be. But I don't need my grandson's charity. There's only one house I'll ever let him buy me."

"You haven't given up on that?" asks Rachel.

"I don't give up—especially on my daydreams. Someday I'll live in that house, but until then I prefer mi own casa!"

"With gang members for next-door neighbors."

"Frankie takes out my garbage every week."

"Ah, Frankie's okay. He's not in a gang. Or is he?" The sister prattles on. Nick rubs his goatee and walks to his desk. He taps on the glass top and a keyboard appears. He types in the grandma's name: Esperanza Florez. A picture appears. He uses her photo to search through Marco's family's more recent memories. He replaces his wall of sex and crime with memories of Marco's grandma. In so many of them she's cooking or offering people food. Nick feels some admiration for the old lady. He considers himself a bit of a foodie and must admit she has some talent. The breadth of her repertoire is impressive. She's not limited to traditional Mexican food. One day she makes sushi, the next, French macarons, the next a Swedish princess cake. Nick's stomach rumbles. He goes to the kitchen for a snack and returns with salsa and corn chips.

Rex takes a chip out of the bowl. "What's this? The Food Channel?"

"I'm searching memories of Marco's grandma. I have a hunch."

On one screen Abuelita stirs posole, on another she bakes cookies. On another she rolls out tortillas. The tortilla one is recent. She's in the kitchen at Marco's parents' home. There's worry on her face. Nick checks the memory. It belongs to Marco's mom. He turns on the sound.

"I'm going to visit Marco and Lucy this week," says Abuelita.

"Lucy?"

"Sí, Lucy, Marco's girlfriend. You know, I have a good feeling about that girl."

"Marco's girlfriend?"

"Sí, Lucy. I'm the one who's supposed to be forgetting things."

"Mom, Marco doesn't have a girlfriend. I'd know. I live for that stuff."

"Apparently not. You met Lucy! She came to Rachel's party. Fun hair, no Spex. You've got to remember." Abuelita turns and wipes excess flour on her apron.

"Is this some joke?" asks Theresa. "Because it's not funny."

Abuelita looks up from the counter, her face obviously perplexed. She looks at her daughter, who is even more confused.

"You don't remember Lucy?"

"Mom, I'm worried, I think maybe..."

"I see..." A flicker of understanding passes the older woman's face. "I must have just dreamed it..."

Nick registers the look on Grandma's face. Maybe he's paranoid. (Fine, he erases himself from everyone's memory. He's definitely paranoid.) Still, something about the expression on this old lady's face makes him nervous. She suspects. The memory is from yesterday.

He turns to Rex. "You need a bath, now."

"Why, we going somewhere?"

"Time to visit Grandma."

CHAPTER 21

No method nor discipline can supersede
   the necessity of being forever on the alert.
   Henry David Thoreau, *Walden*

"**P**raise the Holy Virgin Mother of Jesus! Lucy! You're alive."
Lucy is engulfed in the lavender-scented arms of Abuelita. "It's
a miracle!" Marco's grandma wipes tears from her dark eyes.

"What are you doing here?" he asks.

"I could ask you the same question, mijo. This is my place; I
always come here."

"I thought you were coming tomorrow."

"Sí, verdad, that's the miracle. Hurry, I won't feel safe till we're
back home." They gather their stuff and follow her out the front door
and up a narrow trail. "I was at church last night, praying for Lucy,
and something clicked. I decided to come a day early. I see you've
given up your Spex. Bueno."

"Praying for Lucy? How did you know she was in danger?"

"I didn't—I was very uncomfortable for her. No one seemed to
remember her. Yesterday, I was talking to your mom and mentioned

how much I like Lucy but she had no idea who I was talking about. My daughter told *me* I was going senile. Imagine that! So, I came a day early."

"Why didn't you call me?" asks Marco.

"I tried. Last night. Remember?"

"That's right! Sorry, I forgot to call back."

"You called back, all right. We had a fight grande, I told you to stop wearing your mindseye, and you said I was crazy. Imagine my delight when I went to your place this morning and saw your Spex sitting on the kitchen counter."

"How did you know where to find us?"

"That's the miracle. I didn't. I mean, I hoped you and Lucy were together and that you were hiding some place safe from Spex. Who exactly is erasing your memory? Is it the government?"

"I don't think so," says Lucy. "Just some guy who makes his living erasing people's memories. I'll tell you on the way."

They drive north on I-5 toward Abuelita's home in San Pedro. Marco and Lucy sit low in the backseat, hoping no one on the freeway can see them. Abuelita wants to know everything, especially about where Lucy has been hiding. She recounts as much as she can, shouting a little from the back seat. She tells them about the bee stings and the Poet, and about the terrible night hiding in the tree. How she felt completely alone. "And now both you and Marco are helping me. I can't believe it. It feels like a miracle."

"Funny thing about miracles," says Abuelita, "They seem impossible until they happen, and then they feel perfectly reasonable, the inevitable outcome. We have to remember the darkest moment to appreciate the miracle."

They park in front of a faded pink stucco house with an orange tiled roof and blue metal bars over the windows. The yards surrounding it overflow with weeds, old furniture, and car parts. An overgrown bougainvillea shades Abuelita's doorway. Warm hued flowers carpet the yard.

Even when Marco's mom was a little girl, this was considered a sketchy neighborhood, and in the past fifty years it has only gotten worse. When Marco was twelve, his mom bought his grandma a house in an acceptable neighborhood. Grandma said thank you very much but never moved in. She kept saying one more month. My flowers need one more month. After a year she sold the new, better house. This was during a housing boom. She made a tidy profit. She wasn't leaving the barrio.

Every day after school a bunch of neighbor kids would gather in her yard to play, eat a snack, and talk to the bright-eyed, silver-haired woman. Many of the kids who played in her yard became teachers, business owners, nurses and police officers. Most of them left the neighborhood, but a few climbed a different ladder. They joined gangs and quickly rose to the top. Several gang leaders made it clear that no one should mess with Abuelita. Her neighbor Frankie Valdez kept a close eye on her. He took out her garbage, changed her oil and scared off any troublemakers, all in exchange for the occasional fresh tortilla with butter.

As Abuelita unlocks the turquoise door, Frankie peeks out through the window next door. Marco waves. They played together as boys. Inside, Abuelita goes straight to the kitchen, promising food. All Lucy wants is a shower. Marco helps her find a towel and some clean clothes.

As hot water streams over her she sits for a long time on the shower floor. The water washes away the dirt from the past week. She discovers scratches and bruises on her legs and arms. After showering, she wipes off a section of the fogged mirror. She looks much the same as ever. She can almost imagine she hasn't been sleeping in the woods. This can't be the girl who ran all night, the girl who heard a woman die in the canyon. Something like that leaves a mark, doesn't it? But here she is freshly showered, looking the same as she has on so many benign school mornings, except maybe a bit of puffiness on her right cheek, a reminder of the bee stings.

Lucy finds Marco and his grandma in the kitchen. She's rolling out tortillas, and he's frying eggs and sausage. It's mid-afternoon but breakfast sounds right.

"Looking sexy!" Marco says as soon as he notices she's in the room. He's mocking her outfit. Abeulita's purple velour nightdress hangs on Lucy like a tent but is almost a foot too short. "Can I touch it?" He pats her arm. "Ooh, fuzzy. Fun to snuggle." Abuelita shoots him a warning glance, and he takes a hand off Lucy.

"Mija, try this." She offers Lucy a warm tortilla smothered in butter and sprinkled with cinnamon sugar. They eat at a small red table by an open window, looking out on the back yard. Through blue twisted security bars, they can see three fruit trees and a hazy sky. The table is spread with fresh squeezed orange juice, eggs, chorizo, and Abuelita's delectable tortillas. Lucy thinks she'll be just fine hiding out here for a while.

"I spent most of last night thinking about accessing memories," says Marco. "And I think I know where to start. But first I need a new computer. Your vintage Airbook won't cut it, Abuelita."

His grandma offers to buy a portable computer that afternoon. Lucy likes this plan. A few minutes alone with Marco without constant chaperoning would be nice. She keeps thinking back to this morning and their almost-kiss.

Marco writes his grandma a detailed list of what computer equipment to buy. She in turn gives them clear instructions of what to do while she's away.

"Don't open the door for anyone." Right then there's a knock. "That'll be Frankie," she says. "I saw him when I was picking the oranges and told him I was making tortillas. He'll want one. You two can hide in my bedroom while I get the door. It's best if no one sees you, even if it's Frankie."

She starts toward the door.

"Wait...stop!" Marco calls her back with a whisper. "Was Frankie wearing Spex when you saw him?"

There's another knock, much louder and more insistent, followed by an explosion of glass.

They escape out the kitchen door, Abuelita leading them.

"This way!" She points to a paint-splattered ladder leaning against the side of the house. The three climb up the ladder, pulling it up after them. The roof is flat with a knee-high wall around its perimeter. The wall is part of a false roof covered with ceramic orange tiles. In a few places there's a drain for rainwater, nothing more than a hole with wire netting over the top. Through the drain they can see large boots tramping on gravel. A dog barks, tools clank, followed by a low, guttural cursing.

Lucy scoots across the roof to the front of the house and peeks over. A gleaming sports car waits on the street. The guy with the goatee strolls in the front courtyard. He's still dressed impeccably, as he was when she saw him by the campfire, but he seems slightly off. His eyes are red rimmed, his left eye bruised.

He picks up a shard of glass from the window Rex broke. Blood wells up on his finger. He curses and drops the glass. He walks to the fountain in the center of the courtyard and rinses the blood off his hand. He turns his gaze toward the house. Lucy ducks. Shots ring out.

"Just wasting bullets," says Abuelita. "He only has three left and then he'll have to reload. Not sure why he's using a .38 special. Still, keep your heads down."

They both look at his grandma in disbelief. How does she know so much about guns?

Below running steps and another voice, a harsh whisper.

"Don't shoot. Just get them!" Soon there's a scraping noise as if some big objects are being dragged to the side of the house.

"He's coming up!" Marco says a bit panicked.

"Then push him down," says his grandma.

"He has a gun."

"So do I." Abuelita starts rummaging through her humongous leather purse. "I just can't find it...stall him."

They search the rooftop for a weapon. Lucy finds a broken tile. She tosses it down. It glances of Rex's shoulder. Marco rips off another one and hurls it at him. The tile strikes above Rex's left eye. He wobbles and curses but keeps climbing, a trickle of blood streams down his cheek.

Marco peers over the edge, ready to throw another tile at Rex. A voice yells his name. "Marco! Down!" More shots ring through the air.

CHAPTER 22

All is not lost, the unconquerable will, and study of revenge,
immortal hate, and the courage never to submit or yield.
John Milton, *Paradise Lost*

The neighbor kid shot Rex in the back. The large man toppled
backward from the stack of buckets he was standing on. Nick
ran to him, checked his pulse. Dead.

There was no avoiding Rex's blank stare, but Nick tried. He fled
to his car and drove off. Rex's empty eyes stayed with him. He had
asked him to erase his memories. Nick hopes the homeless man has
finally escaped whatever demons had been tormenting him. Those
dead eyes; they were haunted.

Why did he grab the gun? Nick eyes the weapon sitting on his
desk. *Another person is dead.* He can't think about that. He's still
looking for Marco and Lucy. They were recently spotted with
Abuelita at a marina in Dana Point. Several people remember
them. A forty-five-year-old man ogling Lucy doesn't even notice the
other two. *Creep!* Another is a teenage girl at the dock who's
checking out Marco. *Honestly, what do they see in him?* This girl

watches him help his grandma as she crosses the wobbly docks. The last memory belongs to a retired lawyer who has returned from an afternoon of fishing. This dude actually recognizes Marco Han. He's cleaning his fish at the cleaning station as he sees the famous techie walk by. No one seems to have seen or noted which boat the three boarded.

Nick gazes out his window, a handful of boats, dark smudges on the dazzling water. If they made it out onto the Pacific, they are safe from Spex and from him. The odds of finding them feels daunting.

After running five miles and doing twenty pull-ups, Nick's ready to check his traps. Certainly, someone saw something more of Marco or his grandma, maybe even Lucy.

He has a match.

He takes a towel and wipes the sweat off his forehead. He commands screen ten to magnify and turns on the sound.

"I got my boys to take care of the body."

So, they didn't call the police. For a moment he feels a wave of relief, and then not. The police might not know, but Rex is still dead.

On the screen, Marco asks if there's any identification on the body. Frankie shakes his head. "Who are these guys, and why are they chasing a college professor and his grandma?"

"I'm a grad student," corrects Marco. "I don't know who this guy is, but he can erase people's memories."

Frankie instantly sees all the advantages to this skill. He leans in closer to Marco, his elbow and half his body on the table. "Can *you* do that?"

"I think maybe...apparently, I used to know how before this guy deleted my memories. I hope they'll be easy to restore. Then we can erase his memory of us and this whole nightmare will be over."

"I'm surprised," Frankie says while taking the last tortilla, "that such law-abiding citizens as you three wouldn't immediately go to the police." Somehow, he made law-abiding sound like an insult.

"Police wear Spex," says Lucy, who's all cleaned up now but wearing the silliest fuzzy purple nightgown thingy. *But she's still kinda cute.* "And I don't want to live in a world where law enforcement has access to the public's memories."

"What's the plan?" asks Frankie.

"I've got a friend," said Marco.

"Joe?" asks Abuelita.

Marco nods. He invites Frankie to come with them, but Frankie won't hear of living on a boat.

"Fine, then you must promise to keep your Spex off for at least a week," says Marco.

"You're kidding right?"

"No," says Marco. "The moment you put them on, you give this guy access to all your memories. Not just what's happening at the moment."

"Do you know how much work I'd miss in three days?"

"Oh, shame! Some starlet will have to go without her fix."

"Marco, have some respect. This is Frankie's income," says Abuelita. "Frankie, I know this is hard for you but our lives are on the line. Please, for me?"

"I'll throw in five hundred dollars in cash," adds Marco, slapping a wad of money on the table.

"Not enough." Frankie puts his hand on the cash.

"That's all I have. We left in a hurry."

"I'll throw in another three hundred dollars." Abuelita sets more money down.

"Fine." Frankie takes it. "No Spex for three days. It'll be a vacation." He leans back in his chair and puts his feet on the table.

Nick laughs. "You barely made it three hours." What was it that made Frankie cave in? He checks his recent memories. Frankie put his mindseye on to order a pizza: supreme with anchovies.

Nick searches for the boat's owner, the Joe mentioned in Frankie's memory.

Even though he no longer has access to Marco's mind, he can still search most of his digital data. He finds three Joes in Marco's contacts. He surveys the memories of two of them—useless. The third is a blank slate, completely offline. This man doesn't even have a working phone number or an address. He does find a social security number and his wife's obituary from two years ago.

> Sarah Jones Hoffman, 67, died after a courageous two-year battle with cancer.
>
> Even as a child growing up in Boise, Idaho, Sarah had an unusual love for numbers. In high school, she helped her school take state in the Mathlete competition. She majored in math at Boise State. Upon graduation she taught math to middle-schoolers. For twenty years her passion was helping adolescents love math.
>
> Always generous and self-sacrificing, Sarah moved to Southern California to care for a dying aunt. With this move she decided to take up surfing, which is how she met the love of her life, Joe Hoffman. After a whirlwind courtship, they were married on the beach where they first met.
>
> They enjoyed nearly ten years of boating off the coast of California. The fairy tale came to an abrupt end two years ago when Sarah was diagnosed with lung cancer. She never smoked a cigarette.
>
> All who watched her face death were inspired by her unending cheerfulness, compassion and courage. In addition to her heart-broken husband, she leaves behind a brother, Matt Jones (Lily) and three beloved nieces: Mary, Sarah and Jill.

Along with the obituary is a picture of a man and a woman cheek-to-cheek. The picture is taken on a boat, water and horizon in the background. The woman has a round face and sparkling eyes. Her shabby gray hair is up in a messy ponytail. The man has white hair and a droopy walrus mustache. He's wearing a Hawaiian shirt.

Nick traces Joe to the registration of a small yacht and dock rental in Dana Point. But he'd like to link him with Marco. He searches for memories with images of Marco and the man from the obit photo. *Bingo! He's found him!*

The first memory he finds is a good one. It's the memory of a high school buddy of Marco's. A kid named Derek, but everyone calls him Turtle.

The three are in the ocean on a clear June morning, waiting for a wave. Marco catches one. Nick grudgingly admits that he's a decent surfer. Marco kicks out when Turtle sees something moving towards Joe. Turtle hollers, "Shark!" Joe starts paddling away slowly. The shark fin follows him. Turtle's freaking out. "Shark! Shark!" Marco returns. He's paddling furiously straight toward the fin. The shark head pops out of the water, mouth open with all his terrible teeth.

CHAPTER 23

God himself culminates in the present moment,
   and never will be more divine in the lapse of ages.
   Henry David Thoreau, *Walden*

"It was just a fin," says Marco. "It's not like I was paddling into a shark's open jaws. Every time Turtle tells the story, the shark gets bigger and I get closer. He swears the shark bit my surfboard. It didn't. I still use that board." Marco takes another bite of his grilled cheese sandwich.

The four sit on the deck in soft evening light. Joe wants to tell all his Marco stories. The two met when twelve-year-old Marco started surfing at Joe's favorite beach. Since he left for college, Marco hasn't seen or talked to his old surf buddy. Joe isn't the sort for computers or Spex or even old-fashioned phone calls. It was difficult to stay in touch. But Marco knew Joe could be trusted and would help, no questions asked. And so it was.

When they showed up this afternoon Joe greeted him with a casual smile and nod as if they'd been surfing that morning. In fact, Marco could swear Joe was wearing that same shirt when he last saw him five years ago. Joe's boat also hasn't changed. The vessel is so old, its décor and fixtures long ago graduated from "outdated" to "classic." The only alteration is a red X painted across the name on the bow: Happily Ever After. Marco suspects Joe made that striking modification when his wife died three years ago. He heard about her death from a friend. He couldn't make the funeral but sent flowers and a note. The only difference he sees in his old friend is that his smile doesn't quite reach his eyes.

At first, all Joe seemed interested in was how much Marco had grown—not that some strange guy was chasing them.

"And have you been working out? You must have gained, what? Fifty pounds? Can't believe you're taller than me! Look at you!"

They were headed out to sea before Marco could fully explain their situation. Now, after traveling north several hours, they all felt safe enough to stop for dinner.

"Well," asks Lucy, "what happened with the shark?"

"A wave came," says Marco. "An epic wave. We could all see it coming. We looked at each other, nodded and dropped in. I had to hustle a bit. We rode it cautiously at first and then...had some fun."

"The best ride I ever had," says Joe with a wistful look.

"Me too."

"And the shark?" asks Abuelita.

"He's still out there somewhere." Marco points to the sea. "We could see his fin from the shore. We didn't go back in—not that day, not that week."

After dinner Joe returns up top, and Abuelita clears the dishes. Lucy and Marco offer to help, but she refuses.

"There's no room in that galley for anyone but me. You two should catch up, enjoy the evening."

They move to the back, sitting on a bench that runs the width of the boat. A dozen or so dolphins play in the wake. Under the netted pattern of sunlight on water, the animals swim, gray backs, white bellies. The dolphins with their permanent smiles follow them for a long time. Lucy rests her elbows on the back of the boat with her chin in her hands.

"Maybe we should sail around the world and never return."

"Yeah." He scoots closer. "We could live on a deserted island, build a tree house like the Swiss Family Robinson."

"Are there any deserted islands left?" she asks.

"I think so. The world's a big place." To their left is the faint line of the coast, almost an illusion. To the right sits the endless, shining sphere of the Pacific, water and light broken up by an occasional leaping dolphin.

"You know dolphins have amazing memories," she says. "They've done studies and a dolphin will recognize the call of another dolphin it hasn't seen for as long as twenty years. They actually get all excited about hearing a long-lost friend."

"I believe that." Marco thinks, *Steve, search dolphin social memories.* Then he realizes his mistake. He slaps his forehead and tells Lucy.

"Do you miss Steve?"

"It's an adjustment."

"I'm an adjustment, too."

"Nah, being with you feels right. I'd say normal but so much better than normal, normal on a higher plane of existence." The setting sun glints off her hair. "Is this how it felt when we first met?"

"I don't know how you felt, but I couldn't stop smiling for days."

She tells him about their first meeting. This takes a while because he asks a lot of questions. As the sun approaches the horizon, the ragged clouds turn a fiery pink. The water beneath them mirrors the shades of the sky, surrounding them with sunset. Yet they are only vaguely aware of the beauty around them. They're much more aware of the wonder of each other. They talk as the gold on the horizon burns out. The sky turns pale blue, dark blue, then black. Thick clusters of stars appear and the air becomes chilly. But they talk on, impervious to the cold, unmoved by the starlight.

"You never did tell me about our first kiss."

Lucy turns her face from him. "It's embarrassing."

"What? Did I miss or something?"

"No, it's just embarrassing to talk about it with you looking at me like that."

"Tell me! It's my life. This guy stole my memories. I want them back."

"Fine." Even in the half-light he can see her turn red. "We were driving home from your sister's birthday party and you said you had something to show me. I was hoping this meant you were going to kiss me."

"How long had we been dating?"

"Eight days—not that I'd been counting. We stopped at a beach and you told me to look at the crashing waves. As far as I could tell they were just waves. But you seemed so excited."

"Red tide, huh?"

"You remember?"

"You're not the first girl I've shown red tide to."

Lucy gives a sort of hurt laugh. "I see, and I thought it was so romantic."

"Ah, but you're the only girl I've abandoned my home, my work and my family for."

"When you put it like that, I feel horrid."

Marco puts his arm around her. Her bare arms are cold to the touch. "None of this is your fault. You hear me? None of it."

"But what are you doing about work?"

"It'll be fine. So what if I lose my job?" He shrugs. "No big deal. Things will work out. When you do the right thing, things always work out. Right?"

"I don't know. Penny defended me and now she's dead. Weasel helped me and now he's back in jail, probably."

"I know. I know. But I have to believe things are going to be okay." He pulls her in closer. "Finish your story. I want to hear how it ends."

"If you took all the girls to see red tide, you know it by heart."

"Yes, but I want to hear how you remember it." He lifts his free hand up to tuck a hair behind her ear. "Every detail."

"Well...okay...this is silly you know."

"Go on."

"So, I couldn't see it. Remember last night, or I guess it was this morning, when you were showing me the house on the cliff and you had your arms around me and you had this moment of a déjà vu. Well, that's because that's exactly how we were standing."

"Cool!"

"You pointed to the wave, and I saw it: the water flashed a pale green as if there was a glowing serpent inside the wave." As she talks, he slowly traces the contours of her face. "Then you showed me how if we rubbed our feet in the wet sand it would leave a green afterglow. We wrote our names on the beach, watched them glimmer and disappear. I was so excited about the glowing water and sand I forgot about my hoped-for kiss." She inadvertently glances at him when she says "kiss." Marco, too, stops his gentle finger tracing and turns his face toward her.

"And I kissed you."

Her reply is a whisper. "You remember?"

He answers with a gentle kiss.

The only sound is the hum of the engine and water slapping against the boat. Above them the sky is a torrent of stars, reflecting in the water below. It's as if the little white boat is the center of the universe, completely surrounded by stars. As they kiss, unknown creatures swim in the dark depths beneath them.

CHAPTER 24

So shall the world go on,
    To good malignant, to bad men benign,
    Under her own weight groaning.
    John Milton, *Paradise Lost*

"You don't look like a computer guy." The girl speaking has reddish-brown hair and lots of freckles. Sadly, her eyes are not blue. But her eye color is not readily apparent since she's wearing plum-colored Spex. She's sitting across the table from a wickedly handsome young man—even with his goatee. When she met him this morning at the farmer's market, he told her his name was Hans. He had approached her with a bouquet of blue delphiniums.

"Forgive me, I don't normally do this. But you're so beautiful, I had to buy you these."

He walked with her through the market. They sampled honey and cheese and shared a loaf of crusty bread studded with raisins. He asked her to dinner. She spent the afternoon buying a new dress, shoes, and jewelry. He knows this because he spent a few minutes hacking her memory finding her taste in music, movies and books.

Nick also spent a little time rearranging his apartment to appear more traditional. He switched off all the screens. The computer on his desk will continue to searching for the faces of Marco, Lucy, Abuelita and Joe. He set an alarm so that if a match were found, he'd be notified at once.

He crowded his weights, bike and treadmill into an empty room he uses for storage. He moved the couch, normally crammed against the wall, back into the room, now facing the windows so two could sit and watch the sunset. He put out a coffee table and a Zen sand garden, checked his wine stock, and changed the sheets on his bed. He didn't put much thought into his preparations. Getting ready for a date was as routine as brushing his teeth. This was not the first girl he'd met at the farmer's market. This is how he celebrates closing a deal.

Nick loves first dates, when the person you're with is brim with possibilities. "Dating," his father once told him, "is like chewing gum. When you first unwrap a stick and put it in your mouth, it's fresh and flavorful. But when it loses its taste, it's time for another piece." A strange bit of advice to give a six-year-old, but totally valid in Nick's experience.

The deal Nick settled this morning was, to be honest, rather small. He erased the memory of a minor embezzler, but it was his first bit of business since he'd started searching for Lucy more than a week ago. He's still searching. He just needed a break, a chance to remember what he's fighting for. It's such a rush, that moment when his client switches from dreading him to loving him. Lucy's charming —hiding out in the woods for her convictions—but she's mistaken. He's the good guy. His customers need him. He makes people happy. What could be wrong with that? What did it matter what Lucy thought when he could so easily find someone like Margie, this eager young woman sitting across from him?

"I mean you dress better than most computer guys." She fiddles with her bracelet.

"Haven't you've heard of geek chic?"

"You definitely have style and...what is it you said you did?"

"I have my own consulting company. It's insane how much people pay me. But for my clients I'm quite indispensable."

"I imagine. Do you have any hobbies? You look very..." Her eyes glanced at his forearms which, even under his suit coat, she could see bulge. "...very athletic."

"I work out some. I got used to working out every day when I spent my summers fighting wildfires." He's read enough women's minds to know that they have a weakness for firemen. Nick's not sure why he doesn't just say he's a fireman, why he keeps telling the girls he meets that he works with computers. But he does. Probably because he's naturally honest.

He pauses as their meals are served. She's ordered seafood risotto. He's ordered steak, rare. Nick cuts his steak as he talks.

"Nothing's as terrifyingly beautiful as a forest fire." Blood trickles on his plate. The blood reminds him of Rex, shot in the back, lying on Abuelita's back patio. The woman in the woods, her head bleeding, her mouth open, eyes vacant. If only someone would erase his memory.

"You okay?" his date asks. "You went quiet."

"I was thinking of the fires. I saw some terrible things."

"I imagine..." The girl keeps talking; he does not hear her. He can't look at his plate. Out the window people mill on the street in the twilight. A face appears, a ghost from his past wearing a shaggy white beard. Now alert, even a little frightened, Nick scans the crowd again. The familiar face is gone, possibly a trick of his imagination. He turns his attention once more on Margie but before he can answer her question, a message appears on his Spex: Marco's friend Joe has been sighted in an electronics store in Oxnard.

CHAPTER 25

To love or not in this we stand or fall.
John Milton, *Paradise Lost*

April 7, 2044

It's crazy how happy I feel right now hiding on a boat in the Pacific, hiding from a stranger who wants to take everything precious from me. But I am happy.

I had no idea I could ever be so happy, that anyone could be. When I'm with Marco, I feel so much overflowing joy and contentment that it feels like I must emit some sort of glow, a cloudburst of light visible to all, even in the bright sun. Abuelita and Joe certainly can see something. Every time they see us together, they smile knowing smiles.

Yesterday we headed north all morning, a white dot on the shimmering blue. Joe went into Oxnard with a long list of computer supplies from Marco and a grocery list from Abuelita. Two hours later we were back on the water, headed south, and Marco set to work. First, he set up some fancy non-traceable data connection. After that he asked me a lot of questions about Mollie's program. I tried to help, but within a few minutes his best guesses surpassed all of my *knowledge. I stayed nearby in case he came across a problem that my memory could assist with. He worked late into the night. I went to bed before he did, and when I woke the next morning, he was still working. He said he slept some, but he doesn't look like it. He's still working, and I'm sitting beside him, reveling in the fact that we are together and this whole ordeal is almost over. Watching him, I catch my breath. Marco's here. Marco found me. I think back to the night I spent in the tree. How I feared God had forgotten me. How I couldn't imagine any more happiness. And now Marco's here I never thought...*

"What are you writing about?"

Lucy snaps her journal shut.

"You."

"Can I read it?"

"Maybe—someday. This has an account of our first kiss too. I should have just had you read it in here."

"But I like how you told it. A book doesn't blush or argue with me."

"Or kiss back."

"A definite drawback. What else is in there?" He reaches for the book.

"No!" she pulls the book up to her chest, wrapping her arms around it. "You can't go flipping through it willy-nilly. It's full of embarrassing stuff."

"Now I *have* to read it."

"No, really, it's boring. Just my thoughts and sketches and favorite quotes."

"Then I'll only read the parts about me. Those won't be boring."

"Those are the most embarrassing. While I was in the woods I had too much free time and I thought about you way too much." She looks for a safe page to show him, a detailed pencil drawing of the undulating canyon.

Marco scoots in closer to survey the sketch. "This is good. You're an artist! Why aren't you studying art?"

"Fewer job prospects than philosophy majors."

"Are you sure about that?" He reaches to turn the page.

Lucy clamps her hand down on his. "Nuh, uh, uh!"

"Fine." Somehow, he takes her hand and casually entwines it with his. He's adjusted fast to this whole boyfriend thing. "I only wanted to see more of your sketches." He pats the book. "This is awesome. I wish I had a book like this."

"You do—or at least you did. The first time you saw my journal, you said the same thing, so I gave you one."

"I wonder what I did with it. I wonder if the man erased that, too. I hate these gaps."

"We all forget, don't we?"

Marco doesn't answer. He returns to his portable computer. It's sort of a shame to be stuck inside the boat on such a beautiful day. But the computer's holographic projections are much easier to work with in indoor light. He works late into the night again. Lucy bows out at about two a.m. to get some sleep.

The next morning, when she enters the galley, Marco watches an image of Abuelita's house. The view seems to be from Frankie's window.

"You did it?"

He smiles a flabbergasted smile. "I'm not exactly sure how." He replays the memory. They are looking through a barred window at a silver car parked in front of Abuelita's house. Marco's decade-old car is parked behind it.

"It was easier than it should have been." He runs his hands through his hair, which now rivals Einstein's in awesomeness. How he can have bedhead without ever sleeping? "The hardest part was making sure my activity can't be traced. But writing the mind-hacking program was so natural, like riding a bike. I don't think he wiped that from my memory. I suspect he only erased my knowledge that it can be done. Whoa! That's not how it was!"

The computer displays Abuelita's pink house, bougainvillea and bullets flying fast as confetti.

"We were on the roof during that?"

"Obviously this memory is exaggerated. I don't remember that many bullets. And my car doesn't look that junky, does it?"

She decides it would be politest not to answer the last question.

Over dinner Marco brings everyone up to date on their friends and family. He spent the afternoon accessing memories, their safest connection to the outside world.

"Mom's trying to reach you, Abuelita. She's getting annoyed."

"But not worried?"

"Not yet. Don't be hurt; she hasn't even noticed I'm missing, and I'm her son."

"Ay, but Theresa calls me every day. How often do you call home?"

Abuelita passes around her homemade corn tortillas. She made fish tacos with a red rock cod Joe caught that afternoon. They eat out on the deck.

"At least once a week. But it's been three days. You'd think she'd notice."

"I've been gone for more than a week," says Lucy. "No one's noticed."

"Not true," says Marco. "I noticed in a way, and that was with this guy altering my memories." He puts cabbage on his tacos, then douses them with hot sauce. "But I don't think he's doing that anymore. Your sister keeps thinking about you and calling you. She's getting worried. Something's changing."

Joe wipes some sauce off his mustache. "No one would notice if I went missing," They all protest. "No, it's true. Don't lie to protect my feelings. I've always kept to myself and even more so lately. The only person who'd miss me is dead."

"I'm so sorry." As soon as she says them, Lucy's words feel inadequate.

"Don't be. I'm not asking for pity. I'm saying what's what. I don't feel sorry for myself. I feel lucky. Something happened when Sarah died. Something beautiful. Those last weeks as I watched her... I can't explain it." Marco puts down his taco. No one else is eating.

"I had no idea anyone could love someone that much. Sitting by her deathbed, her eyes shining, her breath rattling. The whole room charged with something holy. Somehow in losing her I realized what I had, and it was..." His eyes rest on the horizon, but he seems to be looking at something else, something beyond sight. "It was everything." He takes a long drink. "So maybe it hurt like hell and maybe it still does. But I'd rather hurt than not remember."

Abuelita picks up her taco and takes a big bite. After she finishes chewing, she says, "Love is pain."

"Always so positive, Grandma."

"It's not negative, Marco, it's the truth. You have to be brave to truly love. You must open your heart to pain. Always be wary of those trying to eliminate pain. That's what's wrong with this guy." She looks at each of them. "Verdad, si? Love and pain are two sides of the same coin. Who loved us the most? Christ Jesus? Si? He loved so much he bled from every pore. To go through life without pain is to go through life without love. That's how it is."

"Grandma, you know Joe's Jewish, right?"

"It's okay," says Joe. "She can talk about her Jesus all she wants as long as she doesn't cook bacon in my kitchen."

The next morning Abuelita rolls dough out for cinnamon rolls using a wine bottle as a rolling pin. The pots and pans in the boat's kitchen rattle in the cupboards. The sea is rough today. But Marco's oblivious to his grandma's intricate performance of skill and balance and sheer determination. He has been on his portable, searching memories since daybreak. Lucy, who is chopping nuts for Abuelita, calculates how much sleep he's had in the last three days. It can't be more than a few hours.

He looks up from the display. "Change of plans!"

"What? What did you find?" Lucy sets down her knife for a minute, the boat sways and the knife slides off the table, clanking on the floor.

"He's clever..." Marco shakes his head in disbelief. He races through several memories, all the while running his fingers through his hair. From where Lucy stands, the computer graphics are hard to recognize. They appear like ghosts or wisps of smoke.

"What?" Lucy places the recently retrieved chopping knife in the sink before sitting down next to him for a better view.

"I don't know what he did, but they remember you now. They're searching for you."

Across from them, Abuelita rubs butter on the dough with her hands. "Smart of him, actually," she says. "Now he has the whole world looking for you."

"And me too," says Marco. "I'm the main suspect."

"What?"

"It's Karen's memory. The police just interviewed her. They asked about me. She doesn't remember that you and I dated. But something's linked us together."

"We can't use you as bait anymore, can we?" says Abuelita.

"No, if I go out in public the police will find me first. That's his plan."

"But would he risk that?" asks Lucy. "Couldn't you tell the police about him?"

"Sure, and he'd delete their memories. I'd have to convince them to remove their Spex. Police would be more likely to remove their guns."

"But you could show them. You could hack someone's memory and then they'd believe you."

"We don't know for sure that this guy isn't working with the government. And even if he's not, we can't tell the police about mind-hacking, not yet," says Abuelita. "I'll be the bait."

CHAPTER 26

Farewell happy fields,
    Where joy forever dwells:
    Hail, horrors, hail.
    John Milton, *Paradise Lost*

April 9, 2044

We just dropped off Joe and Abuelita. Marco's driving the boat and I'm sitting next to him, writing in this book. I've been writing so much it's hard to imagine stopping. I suppose I'll write one more entry when it's all over. It'll be nice to have this behind us.

All in all, we have a solid plan. Joe and Abuelita hope to draw this guy to Abuelita's house. Her neighbor Frankie and Joe will tackle him down. Abuelita will give him a heavy dose of insulin. As his blood sugar drops, this guy will find it harder to resist. They'll put Frankie's mindseye on him and Marco will erase his memories. Abuelita can monitor his condition. If he gets too sick, they'll drop him off at the hospital. With any luck he'll be sick for several days, giving Marco plenty of time to delete memories. When he recovers, he'll have no memory of his sickness or of anything else.

What I'm most worried about is the initial confrontation and that Frankie won't be available to help. But Abuelita reminded us she'll be packing her own gun. Marco wishes he could be there in person. But knows that he can't. Being on a most-wanted list is a liability. We all agree that we don't want the police involved. We spent a long time discussing this. Abuelita summed it up best when she said, "This is more technology than our society has the wisdom to use."

So now we wait. Marco thinks it could be as long as a couple days before the man finds Joe and Abuelita. (A couple days on a boat with Marco— I could think of worse fates.) But knowing this guy it will be sooner. He always turns up when you least expect.

He can't take his eyes off her. Nick has watched so many memories of Lucy, her face in all its expressions has flickered on his living room walls, become so familiar to him that even when he closes his eyes he sees her. So now being so close, seeing her in person, he feels the same thrill one might feel when spotting a movie star in real life.

She tucks her hair, the color of cinnamon, behind her ear. She's writing in a notebook. Marco's next to her, driving out to sea. Nick snuck onto the boat a few minutes ago when Joe and Abuelita went on shore. He will wait until they're a safe distance from land. In his right hand he holds Rex's gun like a dead rat. He prays he doesn't have to use it.

As they pass the buoy that marks the wakeless zone, Marco increases the speed. Every ripple of water catches a glint of gold as the sun dips toward the horizon.

"Get up, Marco, or I'll kill you both."

Marco stands.

"Put your hands up." He obeys. "Good. Now, I don't want to hurt anyone—truly. If you both do what I say, everyone will be okay." Nick points his gun toward Lucy. "Keep driving. The moment the engine stops, I'll shoot him. I will." He nods his head at Marco. "Lead the way to the lower deck. We need to talk."

Marco walks down the steps with his hands up. The two men disappear for a moment. Then Lucy sees them on the bow, Marco with his hands up while Nick aims the gun at him. She can't hear them. Perhaps they aren't saying anything. Marco stands with his back to the ocean facing Nick, who still has the gun pointed at him. The whole scene is backlit by the sun's wide glare on the ocean. There might be a small boat nearby, but the sunlight is blinding. Nick raises a hand to shield his eyes from the sun. Marco leaps forward and tackles him, knocking over a bucket of bait. Hundreds of anchovies scatter across the deck.

Lucy can't just watch.

She has to help. Leaving the engine on, she bounds down the steps. She hears the thuds and grunts of a fight. As she comes out on the bow, Nick hits Marco. He jerks backward with his hands above his head and falls into the ocean.

"Nooooo!" Lucy runs past screaming, slipping on the fish on the deck. At the boat's edge, she searches the water below. Where is Marco? She climbs the boat's railing and jumps.

Under water, everything blurs. Near by, dark hair sways and a large hand floats, not moving. She reaches for the hand but it slips from her. She screams, swallowing salt water that burns her lungs. She struggles to the surface. Coughing and gasping, she gulps in air. The sun's unbearably bright. Her head hurts, her lungs hurt, her heart hurts. She sinks into the darkness.

PART 2

I sung of Chaos and Eternal Night,
   Taught by the heav'nly Muse to venture down
   The dark descent, and up to reascend...
   — John Milton, *Paradise Lost*

CHAPTER 27

Our vision does not penetrate the surface of things.
We think that *is* which *appears* to be.
Henry David Thoreau, *Walden*

First light, then pain. That's how the world returns to Lucy.

The room is so bright, too bright. Is she dead? No, she hurts too much to be dead. Her lungs burn.

As her eyes adjust, the room comes into focus: a window (the source of all that glaring light) medical monitors, a couple empty chairs by the door. Something tickles her face. She pulls a plastic tube out of her nose. A nurse makes *tsk*ing noises and returns the tubing.

"Sorry that bothers you, hon, but you need it."

"Why am I here?" The last thing she remembers is studying on a blanket outside the computer science building, waiting for something or someone. It feels like moments ago and, then again, like an eternity.

"Boating accident. You almost drowned. Salt water does bad things to the lungs. Lucky there was someone to save you." The nurse gives her a carton of apple juice and some graham crackers. Lucy is starving. When did she last eat?

"The police have been waiting for you and your parents—such nice people."

"The police?"

"And then there's the hero, Nick. He swam more than a mile carrying you. Imagine that. I thought at first he was your boyfriend, but no, just a Good Samaritan. You could have been saved by an old tuna fisherman, but instead you get Mr. Underwear Model. You totally scored...except, of course, for that creep trying to kill you."

Lucy chokes on her juice. When she coughs, the pain in her chest makes her eyes tear.

"Kill me?"

"Oh no, I've said too much. I shouldn't be the one telling you. You don't remember?"

"Who was trying to kill me? Why would anyone want to kill me?"

"I'll find your parents." The nurse starts to leave. "Let you calm down."

"No, don't go! Who tried to kill me?"

The nurse lets out a resigned sigh. "A creepy cyber-stalker. The police searched his apartment and found all this stuff, computer records. You know how they can do that. This guy was obsessed with you. Every spare minute he was searching for you. And he had some of your things in his apartment. He's actually kind of famous: that tech guru Marco Han. You must remember him?"

"Marco Han?" Of course, she remembers Marco Han. But there's no way he was stalking her. He doesn't even know she exists. Everything is backward. She's the one who stalks him. And then a memory bobs to the surface.

She's standing near Marco Han outside the computer science building. He's wearing a blue Hawaiian shirt and holds a skateboard. He stands so close she can see a bit of plant fluff caught in his hair.

And that's it. Did he talk to her? Did she finally meet him? It seems like the sort of thing she wouldn't forget, so probably nothing happened. But it's weird how she can recall every detail like it was yesterday and then the memory ends abruptly like the power went out.

If he had talked to her, she would have written about it. She needs her notebook. Or maybe she should ask Karen or Marco.

"Where's Marco Han?" she asks the nurse. "I need to talk to him. He'll be able to explain everything."

"Oh, honey, you can't. He's dead."

She sets her half eaten graham cracker down.

"Oh no, don't cry. I've said too much. You don't need to cry." The nurse puts her arm around Lucy, awkwardly because she is sitting in a hospital bed with tubes attached to her. "He's just assumed dead. They haven't found his body yet."

Lucy cries harder. Her sobs turn to coughing, with each cough her lungs burn more. Now she's crying because of the pain.

"It's fine, dear, everything's fine now." The nurse hands her a tissue.

"I don't know why I'm crying. I didn't even know him." As she wipes her eyes and nose, Lucy notices her hospital wristband with her name, age and admittance date. She double-takes at the admittance date: April 10, 2044.

"Is it really April?" She was just sitting outside the computer science building. It was the end of February. She knows because she was studying for a test in her ancient philosophy course scheduled for March first.

"Today's the eleventh," answers the nurse.

Lucy stares out the window.

"You okay, hon?"

Minutes pass, and she doesn't answer. Puffy clouds float in the sky. Golfers amble on the rolling lawn under eucalyptus trees. Beyond them rests a serene ocean. She can't answer. She's too busy trying to recapture the last month of her life.

Her parents both look older than they did at Christmas. Maybe they are simply tired. As soon as her mom releases her from a tight hug, Lucy asks, "Can you get me my notebook?"

"You're alive." Her mom wipes a few tears. "If you asked me to paint myself purple, I'd find a way to do it."

"Good, because I need that notebook. I have to know what happened."

"We all want to know what happened." Something about the way her dad said this makes Lucy think maybe he doesn't, not really. Does she actually want to know everything? Maybe as one doctor suggested, the memory loss is protective. Perhaps what she experienced in the week she went missing is so traumatic, a part of her wants to keep it forgotten. Yet, other than her damaged lungs, the doctors have only found a few minor scrapes, bruises and a small rash from poison oak—nothing to make them think she was physically or sexually assaulted. What does she want to forget? And why can't she remember the last six weeks? She was only missing for a week.

Mollie barges in. "Can I hug you, or are you hurt?"

"A little hurt from Mom's hug."

"Mom let me in just for a minute. I just want to touch you and know that this is real." Her sister maneuvers to the spot closest to Lucy. More hugs, more tears. Mollie steps back, so her mom can return to her post by Lucy's side.

"And you're really okay?" Mollie asks, still wiping tears. Lucy can't recall ever seeing Mollie cry before. When her sister was married five years ago, Phil, her big teddy bear of a husband, couldn't stop blubbering with joy, but Mollie remained placid and gorgeous as always, not a hair out of place.

"Fine. I mean, my lungs hurt and I'm exhausted and I can't remember a thing."

"Oh, I forgot." Mollie holds up a brown paper bag with a promising grease stain. "I brought food."

"Bless you! I'm starving."

Lucy unwraps a fish taco, inhaling the scent of fried fish, shredded cabbage and lime. An eerie feeling washes over her. She's done this all before.

"Who's missing?" she asks. "There's someone else."

"Your dad left to watch Porter while Phil has a meeting. Your brother's in Philly. We'll call him in a bit. He'll be relieved to hear your voice."

"No, not Tom, someone else. I can almost remember." It's as if she has a word on the tip of her tongue. She looks down at her food.

Love and pain are two sides of the same coin.

She has no idea where that thought came from. She takes a bite. The food tastes like sand in her mouth. Suddenly she can't bear the thought of eating. Her sister and mom are so festive, like it's Christmas. Lucy wants to be part of their happiness. Neither of them seems to notice how quiet she's become. She's glad of that. She doesn't want her vague gloominess to drag them down.

Love and pain are two sides of the same coin. Why is that phrase repeating in her head?

"What happened in March?"

"You don't remember March?" asks Mollie

Lucy's mom appears uncomfortable. She turns to Mollie. "Sorry, I didn't mention it. I hoped by the time you got here her memory would be back. You do remember some things, right?"

"Some." Lucy fakes a smile. Since she woke, she has been pretending to remember much more than she really does. The good student in her wants to give the right answer, and the answer everyone seems to want is that her mind is intact and her memory is normal.

"I remember bits and pieces. But I thought maybe Mollie could remind me of stuff."

"I don't know, nothing much happened. You know how boring my life is now that I quit work. Each day blends into the next. I made dinners, wiped down the high chair, did some yoga, read Porter a million stories. You came every Thursday to do your laundry and Sundays for dinner."

"Did I ever mention Marco Han?" Both Mollie and her mom squirm when she says his name.

"Probably. You've had a crush on him for the longest time. But I don't remember any specific conversations. I don't remember much except it was lovely to have you around. It's funny how much we forget of everyday life, even those of us without any memory loss."

Her sister says this to try to comfort her, minimize her worry. But it doesn't work.

"What I do remember is when Mom called to let me know you were missing. She asked when I last saw you and I didn't know. It was that same sinking feeling when you realize your wallet is missing and you don't know when you last had it—but so much worse." Mollie tears up again.

What was it like for her family when she was missing? After being notified by Lucy's RA that no one had seen her for a few days, her parents caught a last-minute cross-country flight to help search. The worry, the wait, the uncertainty—it's obvious how relieved and happy they are now. Lucy wants to enjoy the fuss they are all making over her except for this nagging feeling that the danger hasn't passed.

"You came to my house twice a week. We texted almost every day. I don't know how I didn't notice you were missing."

"Don't be too hard on yourself." Mrs. Campbell hands Mollie a tissue. "We all have regrets. I should have noticed. I shouldn't have let you have your own room. I should have insisted that you wear Spex." Mollie looks meaningfully at her mom. "Then it would have been easy to find you."

Lucy tries to interpret their secret glances. They both color suddenly. For a moment she thinks they are blushing because she has caught them; but then she realizes it's because someone else has walked in the room.

"And here's the hero." Lucy's mom gives up her coveted spot to a clean-shaven young man with flaxen hair and earnest eyes. Lucy can't place the face of this stranger, but she knows she's seen him before. He has the sort of face that's hard to forget.

"Lucy, this is Nick Lethe. The guy who saved you."

He takes her hand gently. His touch alarms her. She pulls her hand away. He blinks, perhaps hurt by her gesture.

"Are you okay?"

Even his voice is familiar, thinks Lucy. *Maybe he's on TV.*

She nods. "Thanks to you, I hear."

This makes him uncomfortable. "Don't mention it."

"Sure, but you'll tell me what happened?"

"Later. I only wanted to see that you're okay. You should be with your family."

He steps away, giving his spot back to her mom. As soon as he leaves the room, probably before he is out of earshot, Mollie asks in a silly voice that should have been beneath her, "Sooo, what do you think?"

Her mom points out the pink peonies on the nightstand. "Those are from Nick. I should have mentioned that before so you could have thanked him."

Her mom and sister both look so expectant and eager.

"Um...he's nice, I think. But he's scary attractive."

"Isn't he?" says Mollie. "And he's smitten with you."

"You're kidding, right?" Lucy laughs a little and starts coughing again. They wait her coughing fit out. "You two can't be serious. For most of the forty-eight hours he's known me, I've been unconscious."

"You've always been a pretty sleeper." Her mom pats down a few hairs.

"Also, he's kinda old."

"He's just a college kid," counters Mollie. "He looks older because he's in a suit."

"Yeah, that's weird, right? Something about him makes me nervous."

"Of course he does," says her mom, who has now moved to the end of the bed to rub Lucy's feet. "He rescued you from drowning. Seeing him probably triggers those memories."

"But I don't remember a thing."

"Yeah, but you must somewhere deep down," says her mom. "I don't know how the mind works—that's Phil's thing. But it seems like even when we forget, we still remember. Like I'll find myself getting sad whenever I get out the Halloween decorations and then I remember, oh yeah, that's when I lost the baby. I was decorating for Halloween that day. Or my grandpa: His mom was French Canadian, and until he was two all he spoke was French. As an adult he didn't speak a lick of French, but my grandma said he spoke French in his sleep. Our minds hold more than we remember."

Her mom rubs lavender lotion on Lucy's feet. As the scent wafts up to her, she relaxes a little. She recalls something, something good. Pure relief and joy. Exactly how she should have felt waking up in the hospital. She also remembers brown eyes flecked with gold. Are they Marco Han's? Did he really try to kill her?

The sun sets. The tall trees turn to dark outlines against a burning pink sky and rose gold ocean. The view from her hospital bed is so lovely it makes Lucy sad and a little lonely. She knows exactly what Mollie means about that moment you realize your wallet is missing, that you've misplaced something important.

"Don't worry, you'll get your memory back." Mollie hands her the whole box of tissues. Lucy realizes her cheeks are wet with tears. "You'll see. Everything will be fine."

"Will it? Why am I so sad?"

"It's just your brain injury," her mom says, still rubbing her feet. "You heard what the doctors said. No need to worry. You're safe now."

She's too tired to talk. But her mom must be right. It will all come back to her. As she drifts to sleep, she seems to catch some almost-memories, unfinished sketches that could mean anything, like those brown eyes. Morning light seen through a tangle of branches. Yellow petals falling from the sky. An old man chanting nursery rhymes. And the ocean. She keeps seeing the ocean, glistening on the surface, murky underneath.

CHAPTER 28

A written word is the choicest of relics.
  Henry David Thoreau, *Walden*

I n the middle of the night someone's in Lucy's hospital room.

"Do you recognize this?" A teenage girl with straight black hair stands in the doorway. She holds a leather notebook.

"My notebook. Where'd you find it?"

"It's my brother's." She walks closer to the bed. "He didn't kidnap you. I know it."

"You're Marco Han's sister?" Lucy sits up.

"Yes, and you gave him this book. You were friends. He wasn't stalking you. I know it!" She places the open book on Lucy's lap. Sure enough, in her handwriting she reads:

Dear Marco,
  Can't wait to see all the wonderful ideas from your beautiful mind.
  I hope a memory or two will include me.

Lucy

She flips through the pages. All blank.

"Where did you get this?"

"What really happened on the boat?"

Lucy keeps turning the empty pages. "He didn't write in it?"

"What happened?"

"I don't know. I wish I did. But I don't remember!" She starts to cough. A head pops in. It's Nick.

"What's wrong?" He turns to Marco's sister. "Who are you?"

"She's Marco Han's sister. She says her brother's innocent."

The girl takes the book back and hands it to Nick.

"I have proof!"

He opens the book. He reads the inscription.

"Where did you find this?"

"He left it at home weeks ago. I kept meaning to give it back to him. It looked private, so I never opened it, not until he was missing."

"It's my handwriting," says Lucy, "and it looks just like mine."

"Yours?" asks Nick.

"Yeah, my sketchbook. I draw in it and write down stuff I don't want to forget. I wish I knew where it was. Then I'd know more about what happened."

Nick hands the book to the girl. "I know what happened. I saw it all." Marco's sister recoils. She didn't recognize him at first. How can that be? She must have avoided all news accounts of the kidnapping-suicide. "I'm sorry. But your brother...went crazy. He tried to kill Lucy. I saw him. I can't change what happened. I wish I could."

"You lie! My brother was a good guy. You lie! I know it!" Her face contorts with grief. "You lie!"

Her pain makes Nick uncomfortable.

Lucy stands up and tries to give the girl a hug; but she's trapped by her IV and oxygen tubes. The girl runs off. Nick comes over to assist Lucy. She's still trying to go after her. He puts his hands on her shoulders. "Let her go. Let her go," he says gently.

She sits down on the bed. "Maybe it's my fault. He was my friend, and I don't even remember."

"That book proves nothing."

"It's my handwriting. We must have been friends...at least."

Lucy's crying again. She pulls the oxygen tube out of her nose to let the tears flow freely. Nick sits on the edge of the bed and puts an arm around her. She cries into his shoulder, shaking. When she pulls away, she leaves snotty wet streaks on his expensive shirt. His face is now more striking by the real hurt in his eyes. Embarrassed that she has been sobbing on this stranger, she backs away.

"You're beautiful," he says solemnly. "You know that?" He kisses her. She slaps him.

Nick watches the kiss one more time before he deletes the memory.

In the morning Lucy does not remember the kiss or the slap or the teenage sister. Marco's notebook is gone.

CHAPTER 29

Rather than love, money and fame, give me truth.
  Henry David Thoreau, *Walden*

L ucy's running. Not in the woods, but in a grove of eucalyptus trees on campus. It's late afternoon, and she's moving fast. Pedestrians jump out of her way in alarm; bikes swerve to miss her. She looks back. Marco Han is chasing her.

Out loud she says a sharp little, "Oh!"

"What is it?" her mom asks.

"Nothing." Why does she protect Marco? Everyone thinks he guilty anyway, and he's dead.

"What do you think?" her dad asks. She has just tried on the new Spex he bought her when the memory resurfaced.

"Uh...they're just fine. What do I call them?"

"You get to decide that." Lucy feels the familiar twinge of annoyance she often has whenever her mom's more excited about something in her life than she is herself.

"First decide if you want a woman's voice or a man's voice."

She takes her new Spex off, classic frames in maple wood. "These look rather feminine, don't you think? Can I give them a Canadian accent and call them Anne Shirley?"

"Canadian accent we can do," says her dad. "Too bad you couldn't program them with a character's personality. I bet there's money in that. I'd name mine Gatsby and have him refer to me as Old Sport."

"I bet Mollie could do that," Lucy suggests as she hands the lenses to her dad. "She can do anything on a computer." She turns to her mom. "This is what you and Mollie were exchanging glances about yesterday. Dad was out buying me Spex, and you knew I couldn't say no to him."

"I hoped but didn't know. You can be very opinionated."

"I never understood what you had against Spex in the first place," says her dad, who is wearing Lucy's new Spex in order to program them with a name and an accent.

"It creeps me out a little, having a machine read my mind."

Nick laughs. Lucy had forgotten he was even in the room. He's been there since lunch sitting in a chair by the door reading *Paradise Lost*.

"I bet you read that just to look smart," she says.

"What? This?" He holds up the book.

"Yes. You read it to impress people." Her mom looks horrified. Lucy's being rude to the "hero."

"Are you impressed?" he asks.

"Depends. How long have you been reading it?"

"You want the truth?"

"What a silly question."

"Not at all. Most people don't want the truth."

"Consider me the exception. How long have you been reading it?"

"Three years. It was assigned in a class my sophomore year of college. I got an A on my paper, but I never finished it. I'm trying to make it right."

"Three years! That's persistence."

"One of my finest qualities. It will be longer if you keep interrupting me."

"I won't." Does he look disappointed? Lucy can't figure out what he is doing here in the first place. Sure, he came and brought her a beautiful leather-bound journal just like her old one except it feels more expensive. The paper's thicker. But why does he stay, and why are her mom and dad okay with that?

Lucy's not sure why she doesn't like Nick. He just makes her wary. He looks like the sort of guy who always has two or three supermodels on his arms. Why would he be interested in her? He can't be. She suspects he has some hidden agenda, but then she feels paranoid and crazy.

Only Karen seems to get why Nick makes her nervous. She came by this afternoon when he was still loitering in the hospital room half-heartedly reading his book.

"So, pink?" Lucy points to the streak in Karen's hair. Last time she saw it, it was blue. "I like it. It suits you."

"That's what you said when I changed it a month ago. You don't remember?"

"I've forgotten a lot. Maybe you could fill me in. I have this memory. It's my last memory, actually. We're waiting outside the computer science building and Marco Han was there. Did I meet him? Did we talk?"

Karen glances at Nick, his head now buried in his book. "Funny you should ask. Can you walk?"

"Sure, but I have to take all of this stuff with me." Karen helps untangle some tubes and refastens Lucy's hospital gown. She wheels the stand with her IVs and Karen carries her oxygen. Nick tries to assist with the oxygen.

"I got this," says Karen. "We need some girl time." He looks at her funny, with a mix of dislike and respect.

Lucy moves slowly, encumbered by the medical equipment.

"I don't know what to think of your Nick."

"Me either. My family is in love with him. But I don't know."

"Never trust anyone that good looking. That's why I took you for this stroll. I found something."

She hands Lucy a Polaroid. It's a picture of Lucy and Marco Han together in the common area of her dorm. She recognizes the couch and the picture on the wall behind them. His arm is around her. Lucy's looking at the camera; Marco's looking at her. The way he's looking at her with rapt delight, Lucy feels this ridiculous thrill. They look like a couple.

"Where did you get this?"

"It was on my bulletin board. I noticed it this morning. It's from your camera, I'm sure. Who else uses Polaroids and cassette tapes? But I can't remember you giving it to me. I must have taken the photo, but I don't remember anything about it. You'd think I'd remember if you and Marco were dating. That would have been huge, right? The police asked all about you and him. And I had nothing. I should give this photo to them, but I thought I'd show you first."

"I'm glad you did. Can I keep it?" Lucy thinks of that memory this morning, she was running from Marco. She was terrified. And then she looks at the Polaroid. She looks so, so happy. She feels this tug at her heart, a homesickness for a home she never knew. *Oh Marco, what went wrong?*

She keeps the photo under her pillow. Her mom and sister would be horrified to know she has a picture of Marco Han. She sneaks it home with her when she leaves the hospital the next day to stay at her sister's. Everyone thought going to Mollie's would be a better transition than moving straight back to her dorm room. But Lucy almost regrets this decision because all her sister ever wants to talk about is Nick. She's genuinely irritated that Lucy won't go out with him. He's asked her out twice. And she's said no twice. But on her third evening home the doorbell rings. Lucy answers it.

Nick stands there with a bouquet and a bottle of wine. Her

stomach lurches. She catches a bit of vomit in her hand and bolts to the bathroom. When she's finished, she leans against the cold ceramic toilet and cries. The more she cries, the more she wonders what is wrong with her.

Mollie taps on the door before entering.

"What was that?"

"You didn't tell me Nick was coming! I just wanted a family dinner."

"So, you threw up?" She hands Lucy some Clorox wipes. "Are you sick?"

"I don't think so. I just saw Nick at the door and freaked out." Lucy wipes the rim.

"I saw."

"I can't explain it. I don't know. He makes me uneasy. Please don't make me eat dinner with him!"

"Not with him but with our family. I can't very well make him leave."

"Have you noticed?" Lucy wipes her nose. "He's obscenely gorgeous and built. A freak of nature. It's too much."

"That's no reason to bolt out of the room."

"And now what will he think of me? I almost puked on his face. I can't see him again!"

"He doesn't care. Lucy, he's totally devoted to you. You know how rare that is. You should have seen him in the hospital. He slept there every night, keeping an eye on you. And those hospital chairs aren't comfortable. And he would buy us food. We were all so worried and excited and couldn't think straight, and somehow he'd bring exactly the right thing at the right moment. Give him a chance!"

"Fine! Give me a moment. I'm a hot mess."

As soon as Mollie leaves, Lucy indulges in one of her favorite pastimes—Googling Marco Han. She did this before the boating accident but Spex make it so much easier. She usually skips the articles about her kidnapping. She reads the older ones about his app and his company. He seems so nice, not at all like a kidnapper—and so cute in a disheveled nerdy way. It's hard to imagine that if he asked her out, she wouldn't have said, "Yes, please!"

Researching Marco Han calms her down enough to join the others. In the kitchen a flustered Mollie asks for a pasta fork. In a flash Nick hands it to her.

"I see you know your way around a kitchen," Mollie says with an approving look.

"I have a talent for finding things." Right then he notices Lucy. His smug expression evaporates. "Ah, Lucy! Now the fun can begin."

She appreciates that he doesn't mention her earlier behavior. And he seems genuinely happy to see her. Go figure.

Nick sits across from Lucy during dinner but spends most of the meal kissing up to Phil by asking him all about his work.

"It's like I have a free pass on jury duty." Phil speaks so fast spit lands on his beard. "They ask about my work, and when I tell them I specialize in memory, they ask if I've read certain studies on false memories and as soon as I say yes, they cross me off the list."

"Why?" asks Nick with such intense attention that Lucy's positive he's faking it.

"Because they know that I *know* that the testimony of an eyewitness is rubbish. We all remember lots of stuff that never happened and forget stuff that did."

Lucy considers Phil's words. She's been hoping for, waiting for her memory to come back. She's never considered that when she finally remembers what happened, her memory could be wrong.

"The second group was told to go with their gut feeling," says Phil. While she's been lost in thought, the table (or Phil, really) has moved on to something else, some study about how people purchase minivans. "Turns out those who went with their gut were significantly better at choosing the best vehicle than those who studied every variable."

"So there's data supporting following one's gut!" points out Mollie.

"Absolutely! Our conscious brain is limited in how much data it can process at once," explains Phil. "But our subconscious can and does analyze limitless factors."

This is all pretty cool. Maybe Nick isn't faking interest. But Lucy wants to get back to the idea of false memories. She looks up a few more articles about the topic on her Spex. What she finds confirms what Phil said about the worthlessness of eyewitness testimonies. There are lots of incidents in which a person convicted by the testimony of a single eyewitness is later proven innocent by irrefutable physical evidence. When she finishes reading, Nick is questioning Mollie about her old job. Lucy hates to interrupt. Those two are having so much fun flinging programming jargon back and forth, but she has to ask.

"Um...Nick?" It is almost (almost) endearing how pleased he appears. He turns toward her with a face as attentive and open as a kindergartner on the first day of school.

"So..." She falters suddenly, realizing this might be a rude question, but she's already begun and for some reason she doesn't care what Nick Lethe thinks of her. She half-suspects she could spit in his face and he'd still follow her with those pathetic eyes.

"Considering the unreliability of memory," she continues. "Is it possible that what you think happened when you rescued me from the boat isn't what really happened?" Did he flinch? Maybe, but he didn't seem offended. He jumps at the question. Of course he does; she's given him a chance to talk about his most heroic moment.

"Could be; the sun was low and there was some glare, but I know what I saw."

"But that's just it: everyone thinks they know what they saw," she says. "I just wish we had a video clip of it."

"Me too, but all I can do is give you my account. My boat swung close by yours. I recognized the name of it from news reports about the missing girl. And you waved your arms and yelled for help. I steered closer, but before I got there you were standing on the railing and that kid was trying to pull you down. The two of you struggled, and you jumped in the water. He followed after you. And the next part, I admit, I don't know what happened. Maybe he was trying to save you and just screwed up massively, or maybe he was blind with rage or drunk and didn't realize what he was doing. But he kept forcing your head under. He was going to kill you. I had to save you."

As he spoke Lucy tried to picture any of the events he described. He may as well have been telling her about a movie she'd never seen. But one bit resonated with her. When he mentioned jumping from the boat, she could see and feel that moment. She stood on the deck and leaped into gold speckled water.

"Does any of this sound familiar?" Nick searches her face.

"Nope, not a bit." She's not sure why she lied—to bug Nick, maybe? He does seem unnerved by the whole retelling. His eyes look distant as he tells the last bit about struggling to pull her unconscious body to safety, still searching the black waters for Marco. He never found him. The authorities have given up the search.

April 16, 2044

I dreamed about the boating accident. I drifted several feet under green waters, sinking, no longer sure which direction was up or down. Strong arms pulled me to the surface. I gasped for breath under a leaden sky. Nick pulled me through the water as I silently cried.

I woke feeling hollow, scared to go back to sleep. I didn't want to return to that cold water. So I took out this notebook. I wish I knew what happened to my old one. Then I'd know more about the past six weeks and why or if Marco Han actually kidnapped me.

Nick must have heard me asking about my journal because he brought me this one. It would have been the perfect gift except it came from him. Though, maybe he isn't so bad. The Nick in my dream— there was something I kind of liked about how he held me.

Was that dream what really happened or just my mind's reconstruction of events triggered by last night's conversation?

Lucy stays up for a bit and writes. When she finally drifts off to sleep, she dreams again. This time she's sitting on a warm rock bench next to Marco. His arm is around her and she's content. They are watching a movie in which they both star, an action adventure film. Car chases, gunshots and some kissing. Lucy quite likes the kissing scenes. She wants to kiss the dream Marco sitting next to her. She turns to him and he is gone. She sits alone. On the screen she can see Nick's face, larger than life, laughing.

CHAPTER 30

It's not what you look at that matters,
it's what you see.
Henry David Thoreau, *Walden*

"We look like a couple in that photograph, don't we?" Lucy and Karen eat lunch together outside the student union.

"What are you talking about?" Karen removes the tomato and mayo from her sandwich. Karen hates tomatoes. How can Lucy recall details like this but still can't remember a whole month of her life?

"The Polaroid you gave me last week. It's pretty memorable. I'm with Marco Han."

"That's huge! I've got to see it. Where did you find it?"

"*You* gave it to me."

"I did not!"

"You did! When you came to see me in the hospital."

"I'd remember that."

"One would think."

Karen is so confident, Lucy begins to doubt her own story. She has suffered some memory loss; maybe she's confused. She'll have to check her journal later today.

"Nick's coming to your party, right? You're not dating him?" Is there a hint of disapproval in her voice or is it interest?

"No, to my sister's chagrin. He's too old, don't you think?"

"He's not that old."

"Maybe not for you, but I'm just nineteen—today. But it's not only his age that bothers me. He's too perfect, don't you think? I mean he's so muscly."

"I don't mind muscles. But I hear ya. Something's off about that guy. His skin's flawless. I wonder if he wears makeup."

"I know, right?"

They have such a lovely lunch disparaging Nick that Lucy feels a twinge of guilt when she arrives at her sister's and finds him helping decorate for her birthday party. In order to hang paper lanterns across the back yard, he stands on top of a ladder, trying to tie a string to a branch just out of reach.

Lucy calls his name in greeting. He turns to wave, loses his balance and falls. Something about the windmill motion of his arms and the startled look on his face makes Lucy laugh out loud. Her mom and sister rush to him. But she can't stop laughing. She tries. It was a big fall. He could be hurt. A little late, she joins her mom and sister fussing over him.

"I promise I'm fine; give me a minute." He landed on the grass, his head missing a concrete paver by inches. As he lies there for a moment trying to get his bearings, Lucy's mind skips. Another figure lies on the ground. A big bearded man. Dead. Eyes staring at the sky. She no longer feels like laughing. She shudders, and reality returns to her. Nick is fine. He gets up, brushes the grass off his clothes. There are still a few stray pieces in his hair.

"What's on your ankle?" her mom asks Nick. "It looks bad." His right ankle has an ugly cluster of scabs and is a little swollen.

"A dog bite," he says automatically. "No big deal."

"What happened?" asks her mom. Why is her mom always so nosy about medical stuff?

"It's a boring story." He looks uncomfortable.

Lucy decides to save him and change the subject. "Thank you for the gifts. They're too much. But I like them. I really do."

"I'm glad." He looks away from her like he's embarrassed or maybe the sun is in his eyes. He smiles a real smile, not his calculated charming smile but a soppy smile that makes him a few degrees less handsome. She likes him better this way.

As soon as Nick leaves, her Mom and sister tell her how darling and adorable he was and why can't she be nicer to him.

"I can't help it. He's so easy to mock. I can't believe you guys didn't laugh. That fall was spectacular! And I was nice. I told him I liked his gifts. I wanted to throw them in his face. But I just simpered and said I liked them. Goodness, I'd think you guys would be freaking out that some old guy's interested in me."

"He's a kid," says her mom. "He's just twenty-three."

"And it's obvious how much he likes you," adds Mollie. "Do you know how Tom is flying here today? Nick paid for his tickets. He insisted. He paid for the whole family. It's hard not to root for the guy, and you're still so rude to him."

"I am not that rude." Lucy cuts another rose. She's arranging flowers from Mollie's yard in short vases running down the middle of the long tables. They are working with yellow roses, kumquats and nasturtiums. She plays with the foot-length nasturtium vines. The orange and yellow flowers pop out against the white tablecloth.

"It's just he's always around. And he's so free with his money and his compliments. I'm not sure what he's after."

"You're not, huh?" Mollie puts white napkins on the table. Lucy snips another cluster of flowered vines and stops to smell the bright orange bloom. Suddenly, she's on a hillside carpeted with flowers. She's standing with Marco Han. Is this a memory? But then she's on the same hillside with someone else—an old man with a white beard. The man's singing.

She puts her head in her hands.

"What is it?" Mollie asks.

"I'm not sure. A memory...maybe? Marco Han was in it. There were millions of these flowers and he was holding my hand. It felt like I liked him. But then I was with someone else, an old man. It doesn't make sense, does it?"

"No," says her mom. "Not at all. Why are you're pining after a dead guy who was stalking you—who tried to kill you, no less?"

"I'm not pining. I just don't think Marco kidnapped me. Maybe we were friends. Maybe I chose to go with him."

"You run away with a man?" Mollie raises her eyebrows in disbelief.

"Why not?"

"You have Mr. Perfect throwing himself at you, and you're not interested."

"I didn't say I was not interested."

This confession adds an extra bounce to her mom's step. "If you like him, you could give him some encouragement. You're always so cold and distant."

"I don't know... Nick just makes me...anxious."

"That's sexual attraction," says her mom. "You know that zing. It's a good thing. Goodness, he's so attractive he makes me a little nervous."

Lucy dresses for her party with care. She shaves her legs and paints her nails, although a couple nails smudge before she finishes. Nick's model girlfriends probably have immaculate nails. She had planned on wearing her white sundress but she can't find it. She takes everything out of her closet. Still, no white dress.

When she returned to the dorm after her hospital stay the room was eerily tidy. It felt like someone else's room. She wonders if whoever cleaned her room took her white dress. She immediately dismisses that thought. Why is she so crazy and suspicious all the time? She searches her closet again and every drawer until her room is comfortably messy. Still, no white dress.

This leaves her with Nick's gift, the blue dress, a soft cotton, the blue of an evening sky when the first stars appear. She tries it on. It matches her eyes exactly.

She puts on her Spex and makes a face. She can't get used to them. She pulls out the other gift from Nick: a long silver chain with a silver locket, a mini mindseye, the latest model. The locket can project images on the ground or the wall. The necklace is a custom piece with the computer built into an antique silver locket. She hates how much she loves it. How is Nick so good at choosing exactly what she wants? She puts in the earpiece and thinks, *Pippi, what time is it?*

And that's another thing Nick got right. She couldn't believe it when he told her the locket was programmed to respond to Pippi. How many times did she dress up as Pippi Longstocking for Halloween? She'd put a wire coat hanger in her braids so they would stand up. She's certain she's never told Nick about Pippi. But maybe while they were waiting for her to wake in the hospital, her mom mentioned it. Really, she shouldn't be surprised by Nick's thoughtfulness. He seems to know everything else. It's like he can read her mind.

Already on her way, Lucy sends a message to her sister, telling her she has decided to walk. She's in no hurry to get to the party, to be the center of attention. She takes the scenic route, a path that winds through groves of eucalyptus. The trees stand tall and straight in rows like soldiers. Thick honey light clings to each leaf, each flap of papery bark, each blade of grass.

"Your mom says you shouldn't walk that far," Pippi says. "Nick will pick you up."

Tell her I'm fine; I have you with me.

"She says a person is better than a piece of hardware."

Tell her...

"Wait, new message from Nick: Your mom asked me to pick you up. Are you good with that?"

Tell him I'd rather walk.

A few minutes later, "Nick says he will walk with you and he's glad you're wearing that dress."

Wait, how does he know?

She turns around.

Pippi whispers in her ear, "Nick says you're beautiful."

Where is he?

Nick's voice, not the computer voice inside Lucy's ear, answers, "Evening."

She jumps, letting out a screeching yell. Something about her own scream scares Lucy. The woods go from enchanting to threatening. She shivers and apologizes for her outburst. Nick doesn't laugh like most guys would on startling a girl. He looks desperately sorry. She feels guilty for not liking him more.

Pippi whispers in her ear, "Nick says, 'You're stunning.'"

Oh really? Pippi, tell him if he means something he should say it to my face.

He smiles and steps closer. Lucy wants to step back but doesn't.

"You are stunning and beautiful and breathtaking."

"You have some shining-knight syndrome. You believe you must fall for the girl you saved."

He takes her hand. "Something like that."

This is not the first time Nick has tried to hold Lucy's hand. Usually, at his touch she instinctively pulls away. This time she doesn't.

She can't explain it. All of a sudden she's panicked. The woods don't feel safe anymore. She wants a strong hand to hold. After a moment—long enough to realize she's not letting go—Nick looks down at her, pleased. He squeezes her hand. She doesn't feel any safer.

It's just that zing my mom was talking about.

Nick gives her his astonishing smile. Her stomach twists. *Yep, definitely scary attractive.*

They amble in a little before six, still holding hands. The party goers mingle around tables, nibbling on Mollie's clever appetizers, making small talk and shielding their eyes from the sun. Tom's family engulfs Lucy. She picks up her chubby nephew but keeps an eye on Nick, who excuses himself to look for drinks, Karen is talking to him—wait —is she flirting with him? And Nick, for the first time since Lucy has met him, has dropped his ever-present charm. He looks irritated. She edges closer. Tom and his wife are telling her all about their new pharmacy and gift shop. Lucy nods at all the appropriate times while trying to pick out what Karen says to Nick.

"She's a good girl. Sings in the church choir, visits the sick. Practically the Virgin Mary. How would she feel if she knew…?"

Lucy's sister-in-law, Nancy, asks her opinion about opening up a frozen yogurt shop in the store. Lucy supports the idea enthusiastically. She likes froyo. Who doesn't? Then she looks over at Nick. He's wearing a pleasant smile, but his voice has an edge. She can't quite catch what he's saying.

"That's just it," says Karen. "How does a college drop-out afford a penthouse in La Jolla? In just three years? Without ever being hired?"

Lucy knows the answer to that. Nick's a consultant, a very expensive IT consultant. She wants to defend him, but then she would have to admit to eavesdropping. Karen says something else, which Lucy misses. But the whole conversation annoys her. If Karen has serious concerns about Nick, why hadn't she mentioned them to her at lunch that day? The only real objection she made was that he waxes his brows.

Nick speaks so loudly that half the party can hear him.

"Can't you just say, Thank you for saving your friend?"

Still holding her nephew, Lucy joins them, breaking an awkward pause. "Nick, this is Trevor, Trevor this is the guy who saved my life."

Trevor, who's barely two says, "Nank You."

"Charming," says Karen. "You couldn't have orchestrated a better photo op. Don't worry, I got it all: video and still shots. I'm doing a fluff piece on you two. You don't mind?"

Lucy shrugs her shoulders. "I guess not. As long as Nick's okay with it." He puts his arm around her.

"So, it's official? You two are dating?" She raises her eyebrows at Lucy as if to say after-all-you-said-at-lunch today. Lucy wishes she knew how to raise her eyebrows to say after-all-you-didn't-say-at-lunch-today. But she doesn't. She just lets Nick put his arm around her. That hardly makes them a couple. She only lets him because she's annoyed with Karen.

Lucy answers the impertinent question with a "Perhaps." Nick appreciates her response. He catches her eye and smiles.

"How romantic!" Can everyone hear how sarcastic Karen sounds? "He saves your life; you fall in love. This could be a national story."

Karen excuses herself when Mollie announces dinner.

"Your hot little reporter friend is a pain."

"So, Karen's hot, huh?" Lucy squirms out of his arm.

"That's indisputable. It's also indisputable that she's irritating."

"Hmmm; well, she didn't have much good to say about you at lunch today."

"Really? What did she say?" He doesn't look too worried.

"Nothing much. I'm still trying to figure out who my friends are."

"And what about me?"

"Exactly." She walks away. She sits down at a table with her brother, purposefully choosing a spot without a free seat nearby. Over dinner Lucy has a good talk with Tom. He left for college when she was a year old; they've never been that close. She's taken aback by how concerned he is about her.

"It's so good to see you safe and sound," he says. "You don't know how much you love someone until you think you've lost them." A tear rolls down her cheek. Since the accident, the slightest things make her tear up.

She excuses herself and walks to the far end of the yard by the vegetable garden. She sits on the edge of a grow box. Yellow and red tomatoes cascade over the side. The light in the yard softens as the sun moves toward the horizon. The garden smells like tomatoes and the fresh lawn clippings used as mulch. Lucy picks a tomato and takes a bite. It explodes with sweetness. The juice runs down her chin. When she finishes, she picks more tomatoes in a hurry. She looks around for a bucket or something to put tomatoes in. *These will make a good breakfast.* She empties a plastic ice cream container partially filled with weeds and begins to fill it with red and gold tomatoes. Then stops. Why is she stockpiling tomatoes? She just walked away from an abundant dinner. Breakfast is provided in the dorms. She always has enough to eat. She contemplates the tomato in her hand, like Yorick's skull, when Karen sits down next to her.

"I'm not dating Nick."

"I know." She pats Lucy's knee. "I thought it would be better to tell you this away from the crowd. It's breaking news and all anyone can talk about." She gestures her head toward the party. "They've identified Marco Han's body."

CHAPTER 31

Our truest life is when we are in dreams awake.
Henry David Thoreau, *Walden*

A*pril 29, 2044*
I kissed a dead man, and I liked it.
I was biking down a river. I heard the thunder of an approaching waterfall. I tried the brakes, but they didn't work. Icy water sloshed in my shoes. The bike moved swiftly through a rocky canyon. I steered around jagged rocks the size of refrigerators, missing them by inches. The pounding water became deafening. I tried the brakes again, but they had no power over the pull of rushing water. I fell with my bike over a precipice. As I watched my body and the bike turn separate cartwheels in the sky, I realized I was dreaming.

I was certain of it when I landed on bouncy soft sand on a deserted island. The bike splashed in the water. Everything was bright—the beach, the ocean, the palm trees. They all seemed overexposed, almost white. And standing in a sun-bleached shirt and sand-colored shorts was Marco Han. And this is the interesting part: I was overjoyed to see him.

I said, "I thought you were dead."

He said, "Boo!"

I laughed and laughed and so did he. "You're not very scary."

"I'm not dead." He pulled me in his arms and kissed me.

And then I woke up. Someone was ranting about politics in the dorm hall. I checked the time. It was two a.m. I was relieved that there was so much night ahead of me, happy to go back to sleep, back to that dream. But I couldn't fall asleep. I kept thinking of that dream kiss and then something else—another kiss on the beach after dark, Marco's arms around me, my toes in sand, my hands in his hair and my whole body filled with blissful, delirious desire.

Was it a memory? The intense emotion felt so real. Did Marco kiss me on some dark beach? How could I forget? For a moment I'm thrilled that something so wonderful happened to me. And then I remember: He's dead. Some beautiful, brilliant boy is dead, and somehow it all feels like my fault. I can't believe that he kidnapped me. I'm certain he's innocent. It doesn't matter now that he's dead. All charges have been dropped. The police are no longer investigating. The whole incident is filed under a boating accident.

After lying in bed some time, examining every angle of the remembered kiss, I searched for articles on Marco. My locket projected onto the ceiling. After his body was discovered public opinion shifted. He went from "Crazed Cyber-Stalker" to a "Misunderstood Genius" who died under unusual circumstances. In most articles the boating accident was only given a couple sentences. I'm not even mentioned in some.

The bulk of the stories are all about how amazing Marco Han was, glowing tributes from mentors, students and leaders of the industry. I did find a couple conspiracy articles on fringe websites. One suggested that he's not dead but actually an alien that has returned to his planet. (The body found was his human disguise.)

His funeral was yesterday. That's probably why I dreamed about him. I watched a clip of his family following the coffin holding his remains out of the cathedral in Los Angeles. His mother walked out *into the sunlight, her head high, so beautiful and noble and tragic. I didn't know I was crying until a tear rolled off my cheek onto my pillow. That tear was the first raindrop in a torrential downpour. I sobbed, crying out loud. I tried to calm down mainly because I didn't want to wake anyone but the more I tried to calm myself the more the hurt inside of me forced its way out in terrible strangled howls. Tears streamed down my face and through my nose. I don't know why it hurt so much. And I mean real hurt. I finally understand the term broken heart. It feels like something inside me has shattered.*

I cried myself asleep. When I woke I realized I still had my mindseye in. I watched the clip from the funeral again. This time I cried silently. The tears were refreshing. When Marco's sister followed his mom out of the cathedral, I paused on her mascara-stained face, and something clicked.

Marco's sister.

A sketch book.

Nick kissed me!

How could I have forgotten? And the book. Nick's the one who gave it to me. I'd been so touched that he'd chosen a notebook exactly like my old one. I thought maybe he was right for me. Instead, it's only because he's seen the journal I'd bought Marco. Why hasn't he ever mentioned the sister's visit? I get why he might not mention the kiss. I slapped him pretty hard. This explains why he's always so hesitant with me. But he deserved that slap. What was he thinking, kissing me? I barely knew him. Though, I have to admit, replaying that kiss over and over in my head, I can't help but think kissing Nick Lethe might not be all bad.

CHAPTER 32

From his lips
   Not words alone pleased her.
   John Milton, *Paradise Lost*

"You kissed me."
   Nick stops at a green light. They are driving to dinner under a pink and gold sky.

"What are you doing? It's green."

"I made a mistake," he says with an edge.

"Doesn't this car have autodrive?"

"Autodrive is for wusses." He reverts back to his charming voice. "So... You remembered the kiss? And...?"

"Slapping you...and Marco's sister coming to visit. Funny you never mentioned that."

"I hoped you'd forgotten it, especially the kiss...and the slap." He tries to laugh but fails.

"I did forget, but it all came back last night." She glances at him. He grips the steering wheel with both hands. His face is stone.

"Are you okay?"

He tries to smile. "I was wondering. Now that you remember the kiss, what did you think of it?"

"It was fine."

"The kiss or the slap?"

"Both." He laughs, almost a real laugh, and relaxes a little. He looks at her with hungry eyes, and they both know that he's going to kiss her again.

Over dinner, Nick seems less grown up, less daunting. Sitting close to him, Lucy notices a blemish on his cheek, a red bump that would turn into a pimple. As soon as they order, she asks him,

"Why do you always wear a suit?"

"Because of my dad."

"Your dad wore suits?"

"Not in my memory. I mean, he probably did when he was younger and trimmer. He played football at a junior college. When he stopped, he gained a lot of weight. I'm not sure where he bought his clothes, where anyone buys clothes that size." Nick laughs an ugly laugh. "No, the first time I wore a suit was at his funeral."

"Oh! I didn't know. Sorry."

"Don't be. It was a long time ago. Ancient history. My grandma bought me a black suit for my dad's funeral. That day my whole world was buried in the ground. And I didn't cry. Probably should have, but I didn't. My grandma was upset, and I had to be there for her. In my nine-year-old mind I thought it had something to do with that suit, like it gave me super-powers. When my grandma died..."

"No! She didn't! That's terrible. I don't know what to say." She pats his hand on the table. "I didn't know any of this till now. You've met my entire family and I..."

"It's fine. Really. It's all in the past. I don't normally think about any of this. Only, you asked."

"Yes, and I am interested. So, the suit gave you powers."

"Or so I figured. I bought another suit for my grandma's funeral and I've been wearing them ever since. People treat you better when you dress sharp. Besides..." He makes a brooding male model face. "I look fabulous in one."

Despite herself, Lucy laughs, then stops. "You were wearing a suit when you saved me?"

"Yes, and I didn't have the sense to take off my shoes before I jumped in the water. You cost me a very expensive pair of shoes—hand-stitched Italian leather."

"Was it worth it?"

He doesn't nod or smile. He looks at her. That's answer enough.

"Do you remember any of it?"

"Maybe I do." Nick leans in closer and studies her face as she speaks. "I have dreams in which you're pulling me through the water."

He looks uncomfortable. She changes the subject. "What about your mom?"

"What about her?" He looks even more uncomfortable.

"Did she die too?"

"As far as I know she's still kickin'. Her name's Carol. I've never met her." He doesn't make eye contact. He looks out the window at some palm trees tossing in the wind. "I mean, not in my memory. She left my dad when I was a baby. In a way she killed him. He ate and drank to forget her. But he was a good dad."

A mask falls from Nick's face. It's suddenly easy to imagine him a scared, little boy. "For the longest time I totally thought she was dead. Dad talked about her being gone with such finality. He never said bad things about her. He'd say things like, 'You're a genius. You got that from your mama, you know. She was the smartest person I ever met.' I didn't find out she was alive till my dad's funeral."

Lucy offers another ineffectual "I'm sorry."

"I overheard my Grandma complaining to someone that my mom didn't even bother to send a note. That was a rough day." He tries to laugh. "Just as the impossible was sinking in, that my dad was gone, that he wouldn't be walking me to school anymore, and we wouldn't be spending the whole weekend watching Marvel movies, chowing down on popcorn and ice cream straight from the carton, I had to deal with the impossible truth that my mom was alive. And didn't want me."

"I don't know what to say."

He shrugs. "It is what it is. My grandma took me in. And she did her best. For years I would make up excuses for my mom. I had a wicked imagination. Maybe she was a secret agent working in a foreign country. I liked to think she teared up whenever she saw a little blond boy. Or her boyfriend was in the mob and was abusive and she couldn't get away. But whenever he beat her, she'd thank God that Nicky had been spared this life." He took a sip of his wine. "I was an idiot. The truth is she just couldn't be bothered with a kid. She never thought about me, not once."

"You can't know that!"

Nick makes a strange face. "Oh, I can. And I do."

"You should find her and meet her. I'm certain she'd be proud of you. If she saw how well you've turned out"–she takes a sip of her sparkling water–"and well...how, how successful you are–most mothers dream of having such a son."

"You don't know what you're talking about." He speaks in a harsh whisper. "My mom couldn't care less. I'm certain of that."

Lucy's speechless. Nick takes a few bites. Dabs his face with his napkin. When he speaks next his mask of charm returns. "Sorry to be so dramatic. My life's great—really! Have you seen my car? And my girlfriend." He reaches over and caresses her cheek. "I don't know why I told you all that."

"I'm glad you did. I mean, if we are ever going to have any relationship, we have to be open with each other."

"Oh, Lucy!" He looks at her like she's an angel with a broken wing. "You're so sweet and innocent. Yes, that's what I want."

They walk the long way from the car to the dorms. Nick pauses by a bench near a cluster of trees. "Let's sit." He draws patterns on her hands as they talk. Lucy's telling him about *Walden* and how much she loves that book and how she has this secret dream to live in the woods. Even in the dark, she can see him trying not to laugh.

"What's so funny?"

"You are. Normal girls don't want to live in the woods. Do you still?"

"What do you mean, do I still? I just said I wanted to."

He falters, "Uh... I'm not sure what I meant. Do you want to know what my greatest fear is?"

"Wearing Dockers?"

He laughs. "You're funny."

"Don't sound so surprised."

"I'm not surprised. I'm just saying the obvious. You're funny. You're beautiful. I like you."

She edges away from him. "Tell me about your last girlfriend."

"Hannah. She was a dental hygienist. Good hair, great teeth."

"How long did you date?"

"Two...no, three weeks."

"Does that even count as a girlfriend? So uh...this will be over in a week?"

"No, this is different."

"What? Because you haven't slept with me?"

"Yes—I mean—no. I mean I've never really let a girl into my head, before. I never tell them about my dad or my grandma, especially not my mom."

"How many other girlfriends are there?"

"A few."

"I see." Her eyes have adjusted to the dark. He has a sheepish smile. "You're right, this is different. You can kiss me and hold my hand but that's..."

"I can kiss you?"

"No, I mean, yes... I mean, that's not what..." But before she can explain herself Nick moves in. He kisses her lightly, like a breeze rippling the water, and pulls back. "No slap?"

"No slap," she murmurs, only kind of catching his reference. And then he really kisses her.

"Nooo! Don't kiss him!" But even as Marco yells at the screen, Nick pulls her in closer and kisses her some more.

CHAPTER 33

I never knew and never shall know
a worse man than myself.
Henry David Thoreau, *Walden*

Joe turns off the screen. "Stop it. Don't torture yourself watching
that over and over."

They sit in an odd assortment of chairs in the living room of
the abandoned house built on the cliffs between La Jolla Shores and
Torrey Pines.

"Why haven't I killed this guy yet?" Marco stands up. "Seriously!
Why? I'm sick of hiding."

"You're still recovering," says Joe.

"It would be self-defense. He meant to kill me. He thinks he
killed me."

Abuelita enters the room. "Maybe it's time."

"Yes, before that jerk..." Marco kicks over a metal folding chair
that clanks as it collapses onto the ground. "I had no idea I could hate
this much! I loathe him! Every night she dreams about me. Every
morning, he makes her forget."

"And then you get into her mind and make her remember," says Abuelita as she picks up the chair Marco knocked over. "I worry what all this forgetting and remembering is doing to Lucy. How do you know you won't cause permanent damage? She'll end up babbling poetry." She glances at the Poet, who stands nearby. "No offense."

He does not acknowledge her. He looks out the window and softly recites,

"The Sun now rose upon the right:
Out of the sea came he,
Still hid in mist, and on the left
Went down into the sea."

Abuelita turns to Marco. "Can't you help him?"

"We've been over this. There's nothing I wouldn't do for him. I owe him my life. But if you mean fix his brain, I'm not sure it needs fixing. I'm afraid I'd do more harm. He might know stuff we don't." Marco sits down. Abuelita brings her chair, a red café chair, her prize discovery from yesterday's dumpster raid, and sits down beside him.

"But it would be easier if we understood him. If everything he said wasn't a riddle. I mean, it's charming, and he says the sweetest things..."

"We all speak in riddles," says Joe, reclining in a green nylon beach chair. A red plastic cup sits in the armrest cup holder. Joe found this cup on the beach on a pre-dawn walk and has used it for the past three days. There's also a worn leather club chair, which remains empty. Marco insists that it's the Poet's chair, though he usually stands and stares out the window, aloof from the repeated discussions about what to do with Nick.

"There's only one option," says Marco.

"I have his place scouted out," says Joe. "We can definitely get in and since it appears he's working alone..."

"Old Nick is quick and slick. But we know a trick," says the Poet.

"Can you three really take him down? No offense, but, Marco, you've been sick, and Joe and Señor Poet, both of you have seen better days."

"Excuse me?" says Marco. "You and Joe were going to tie him up with just the two of you. We've got it."

"And Frankie will help," adds Joe. "We could strike tomorrow night."

"That's not soon enough!" Marco stands up. He paces the room like a caged tiger. "That guy chased her in the woods and now he's taking her to dinner and worse! Why? What's his game? He can't be doing this just to get to me. He thinks I'm dead."

"Maybe he likes her?" says Abuelita. "He could have let her drown, but he didn't. You have to give him that. Maybe he cares about her."

"Love requires respect, and there's no respect in wiping out a month of a person's life. He's probably trying to keep an eye on her sister. Last night Mollie tried to hack Phil's memories. She didn't succeed, but she will...soon."

"No es bueno," says Abuelita. "We can delete Nick's memories, but how long before he starts up his business again?"

"I don't care," says Marco. "I can't save the world. All I care is that he leaves me and Lucy alone."

"He won't forget Lucy."

"Won't he?"

"You already have enough to erase—important stuff," says Abuelita. "And too many people have memories of those two as a couple. There are national articles about the two of them. They're practically a celebrity couple. They don't have a couple name, but they have fans."

"Lick or Nucy would never catch on," Joe deadpans.

"The only viable option is killing him," says Marco. "Knock him out and leave him in the middle of the Pacific."

"You wouldn't!" says his grandma.

"I wouldn't? Why not? That's what he did to me."

"Marco, you're better than that. You have morals."

"Do I? I accessed and altered medical records to fake my own death. I've hacked major media outlets to create favorable reporting of my death, and my mother is picking out my headstone while I hide out here eating stale doughnuts."

"We all agreed it was for the best," says Abuelita.

"And now I plan to take a man by force, tie him up, steal his memories. How is it right for me to erase memories and wrong for him?" His voice grows louder. "Because I'm morally superior? Because I'm doing the right thing? Isn't that what Nick thought when he was deleting our memories?"

"The difference is we're right," says Joe matter-of-factly. He glances up from the tablet he's been closely attending. "What Nick's doing is wrong. End of story. We have to stop him. If you don't, I will."

"We don't have to decide anything right now," says Abuelita. "We all need a good night's sleep. Then we'll talk it over some more."

"No," says Marco. "What I need is food."

"The cupboards are empty," agrees Joe. "We should do another dumpster run. I'd like some bagels. I bet they throw away a lot of good bagels."

"What I wouldn't give for a fresh tomato," says Abuelita.

"I didn't realize that when I had myself killed off I was volunteering to be the delivery boy," says Marco.

"It was a genius idea, and now that no one's looking for you and you've grown that fine scruff, you're perfectly safe," says Joe. "As long as you don't run into Nick, which shouldn't be a problem because according to Mollie's Spex he and Lucy are at her house right now."

"What are they doing?" asks Marco.

"Watching home movies. Lucy's trying to refresh her memory."

"Put it on the big screen," commands Marco.

"I don't think that's such a good idea, mijo."

"*Do* it!"

The image flashes on the east wall. Three stray wires cut through the picture, remnants of a sconce looted from the house years ago.

The feed is live from Mollie's Spex. Mollie sits on an oversized chair kitty-corner to the couch, binding a quilt. Her hands and the edge of the quilt fill the screen.

"See, it's pretty boring," says Abuelita.

Right then Mollie looks up, giving a clear view of Nick and Lucy on the couch. He has his arm around her and is holding her other hand, their fingers entwined. He's not watching the movie; rather, he's watching Lucy watch the movie. She's laughing.

"He likes her," says Abuelita. "See how he looks at her. He definitely fancies her."

"Turn it off." Marco's voice goes quiet. "I've made up my mind."

CHAPTER 34

Long is the way and hard,
    that out of Hell leads up to light.
    John Milton, *Paradise Lost*

Lucy enjoys cuddling on the couch with Nick, even if she has this lingering feeling that they are both playing a part. Nick acts a little strange when he drops her off. Right as she is getting out of the car, he stops her.

"Lucy?" He looks worried. "Do you think people can change?"

"Sure. But most people don't. Good intentions are just that —intentions."

"She's lovely *and* wise." He gives her a sad smile. "You're more right than you know. Most people don't learn. They make the same mistakes over and over. I've seen plenty of that in my work. But I want to change." He stares straight ahead at the concrete side of the building. "There's a lot about me you don't know. I used to be a not-so-good person." He leans forward and rests his head on the steering wheel.

"Why are you telling me this?"

"Because you're right, we have to be open with each other. And this has to be different. I want it to be different. You're not like the other girls. Or maybe they are just like you and I never noticed."

They sit in silence for some time. It is not a comfortable silence, but Lucy can't think of what to say. She's warming up to Nick, but she's not that attached, not yet. She can walk away from this now. But she isn't quite ready to say something like that to him. She remains quiet and fidgets with the cuff of her sweater. The silence stretches. Finally, he looks up. For a moment he seems surprised to see her still sitting there.

"So, you're not dumping me after hearing what a scoundrel I am."

"Ummm... You never actually confessed to anything—except being a player, and I could tell that the moment I met you." She's done with the conversation. She gets out of the car. The eucalyptus trees in the damp night air smell like men's cologne.

He follows her to the dorm door.

"Can I still give you a kiss good night?" Without waiting for an answer, he kisses her.

She may have kissed back. She doesn't know. Something in her head screams, and she can't decide if it is the happy shrieks of a child riding a roller coaster or the frightened cries of a victim cornered by a predator. His breath is jagged. He pulls her in closer, so close she can feel his heart. She pulls away, surprised that she can pull away.

For a moment the only sound is the two of them trying to catch their breath.

"Any chance I can come up to your room?"

"Not a chance."

"I just want to talk. Don't you trust me?" He says this with his captivating smile. His teeth flash in the darkness.

She takes a moment to answer him. A white moth flutters around the security light. "Funny thing, I do trust you. But you still can't come up." She closes the heavy door behind her and runs up the stairs to her room. By the time she reaches her floor, she's panting and her heart's racing. She opens the door and locks it behind her before she realizes there's a dead man sitting on her bed.

CHAPTER 35

Any prospect of awakening or coming to life to a dead man
makes indifferent all times and places.
Henry David Thoreau, *Walden*

She doesn't scream or faint or say anything. She stands motionless, still gasping a little from the run up the stairs. Her mouth is open, she shuts it.

He looks like the Marco from her dreams, except he has the beginnings of a scruffy beard. He wears a dress shirt, untucked, the sleeves rolled up, the collar unbuttoned. He looks like he's been shipwrecked, but the look is good on him. Everything's good on him.

She can't take her eyes off him and not because he is supposed to be dead. All at once, she understands what people mean by love at first sight.

"Don't be afraid." He gets up, takes a small step toward her, and checks both of her ears for a mindseye. "I'd never hurt you."

"You're Marco Han?" This stranger stands so close to her but instead of it freaking Lucy out, she wants him closer. Without thinking she reaches out to touch him. For a moment, her hand rests on his shoulder. The warmth of his body radiates through his shirt. Her mind flashes to the memory of kissing him on the beach.

"You're not dead?"

"Nah... I switched some medical records."

"I dream about you."

"Yeah." He doesn't seem to know what to do with his hands. He keeps running them through his hair.

"But in my dreams, you don't have this." She moves her hand to his cheek, feeling the prickle of his stubble.

"No, that's not how you'd remember me." His eyes follow her every move. He steps back. She's crazy disappointed. She wants him to wrap his arms around her but that's ridiculous. To keep her longing in check, she avoids looking at him.

"I brought you something." Out of his backpack he pulls her leather journal.

"My notebook! I've been looking everywhere for this!"

He hands her the book. She makes herself comfortable on her bed and flips through it. The first few pages are sketches with random quotes, nature drawings and more than a few sketches of Marco on a bench. She remembers drawing these. The rest is crammed with words, line upon line of her own distinct handwriting, interspersed with drawings. The last dozen or so pages are written in another hand.

Her stomach knots as she turns the pages. More words, a sketch of a local canyon, details of a wildflower. Finally, a face she recognizes: a man with a goatee. On another page she reads:

To anyone who might find this book,

You should know that minds can be hacked by Spex. Memories erased. Lives rewritten.

To my future self,

If you don't remember kissing Marco, the mayor's memory or

*running to the woods, someone has deleted your memory. Read this.
This is what really happened.*

"Nick erased my memory?"

Marco nods.

"Mine too."

Her head hurts.

"I know it's hard to believe," he begins.

"No, it's not." It isn't. She's always been scared of Nick since the moment she woke in the hospital. She's avoided him, complained about him and pushed him away. But everyone insisted she was wrong. And she was beginning to think maybe they were right.

"I'm dating him," she blurts out.

"I know."

"I—I didn't know. I'm dating him! I kissed him!" She puts her head in her hands.

"I know."

"Is there anything you don't know?"

"I've been keeping a pretty close eye on you." He sits on the bed next to her, careful not to sit too close.

"You didn't kidnap me, did you?"

"It was more like you kidnapped me. You showed up in my room one night."

"I did?" Her cheeks burn. She's overwhelmed with what Marco's telling her, but also by how she feels about him. She wonders if he feels the same. With no memory of their past relationship—except that kiss—she's on uneven footing with him. It's obvious the way she keeps thinking about touching him and scooting closer, that she was (apparently still is) totally into him. But how does he feel about her? What if what he says (or she wrote) about Nick is true? Well, then she is already ensnared in one staggering relationship disaster. No need to rush into another. She tries to tamp down her feelings.

"How do I know you're not the bad guy?"

"You don't." His eyes are steady on her, brown with the gold flecks—one of the first things she remembered upon waking in the hospital. "But maybe if you read your journal...it's all in there."

She riffles through the book some more. She stops at a sketch of a tall bulky shrub. Underneath in her writing it reads, "Home Sweet Home."

"I lived in the woods?"

"You were hiding from Nick."

"That explains his comment the other night about living in the woods. He laughed at me." All her interactions with Nick shift, take on new meaning. He often had this knowing smile. How dare he wipe out her memories and then laugh at her?

"Okay, I'll read this, but please give me the abridged version now."

As he tells her the story, she listens for any clues that might confirm that they'd been dating. He gives all the facts about hacking memories and discovering Nick without any personal details.

"I actually don't remember any of this," he explains, "because Nick erased my memory first. So you told me all this stuff and of course I read your journal." He read her journal! Even if she doesn't remember the last month or so, she remembers perfectly well what a monumental crush she had on Marco. What silly nonsense had she written in there? He keeps talking in a calm deliberate, rehearsed voice. He seems worried she won't believe him.

When he gets to the events he actually remembers, the story takes longer. She doesn't ask many questions. She nods occasionally. She still can't remember any of it, but as he speaks, she has this sense of déjà vu. Something tells her it is true.

Lucy keeps thinking about the contrast between Marco and Nick. With Nick everything adds up. He is rich, attractive, attentive —not to mention that he saved her life—and yet she's always been wary of him. With Marco it is the opposite. Her supposedly dead, alleged kidnapper shows up in her dorm room in the middle of the night and she's at ease.

Her feelings make no sense. But maybe they do. She thinks of what Phil said about the minivan study. What people consider a gut decision is actually a logical conclusion based on info too vast for a conscious mind to comprehend. While her conscious mind felt okay about Nick, the rest of her mind recognized him for the creep he was. Something deep inside her remembered running from him. But why then was she feeling more comfortable with Nick and—if she's honest —more than a little attracted to him? Maybe if we persist too long with the wrong decision it begins to feel right? Or maybe sometimes physical desire trumps the wisdom of the subconscious? Lucy reminds herself of this as she listens to Marco's story. Maybe she wants to believe him because she has a weakness for tall, lean nerdy boys with shaggy hair and charming smiles.

"It was selfish of me to come here," he says. "The others didn't want me to, but if our plans don't work, I had to let you know the truth."

"And you, too. Right? You've been watching my memories."

"I have. I'm sorry. But I had to keep an eye on you. I haven't erased any of your memories. Trust me, I wanted to erase Nick."

"Why don't you erase his memories from a distance?"

"He doesn't wear a mindseye."

"He does too!" Lucy insists. "I never see him without Spex. He makes fun of me when I don't wear mine."

"He *must* have a mindseye. How else did he erase your memories before your parents bought you Spex? By the way, that was his idea. He told them you needed Spex to be safe."

"Ughh!"

"He's the worst. But he's cunning. He never wears a mindseye. He's altered his Spex so they're not thought-activated. Pay attention. He uses blinks and taps and discreet voice commands. And even then, he doesn't wear them when he's alone. We've hacked his Spex but still haven't seen the interior of his apartment. Tomorrow night we're going to take him hostage and erase his memory. Until then, you can't wear your mindseye. He can't suspect a thing."

"No mindseye. Act normal. Got it."

"And then um...after we take care of Nick," He bites his lip. "...then, well...maybe...we can start over?"

"So, we *were* dating?"

"Umm...yeah."

She can't meet his gaze. She doesn't trust herself. She keeps her eyes on her journal.

"You know, even though I don't remember you," she finally dares to look up, "I remember you."

Marco nods; his eyes catch hers. They both turn slightly and they are kissing. Kissing Marco is revelatory. He smells and tastes familiar, a mix of the ocean and citrus and a hint of spice. As they kiss Lucy relives a hundred perfect moments: cuddling Marco on a couch, standing close to him in the woods, arguing over something in the sunlight, talking comfortably in a dark car. She feels inexplicably happy and whole. And then just as quickly as they kissed, she remembers kissing Nick outside, only an hour or so before.

"Please go! I can't do this." She flops her head down on her pillow.

"I'm sorry." He stands up. "I shouldn't have tried. In my head you're still my girlfriend. I got carried away. I forgot that to you I'm a stranger...or worse."

"No, I believe you." She looks up from her pillow. "I do. I just need to be alone right now, to think."

"I don't want to leave you. It's been agony to watch you from a distance with Nick so close to you."

"It's just one day, right? As soon as you've taken care of him, you'll come back and tell me. Even if it's the middle of the night you'll come back to me and tell me, promise?"

"I will." He stands with his hand on the doorknob. "But Lucy, in case things don't go as planned, I'm glad you know." He opens the door and steps out. Before he shuts it, he leans his head back in. "And I'm glad I kissed you."

CHAPTER 36

Horror and doubt distract
His troubled thoughts
and from the bottom stir
The Hell within him...
John Milton, *Paradise Lost*

Nick returns to his apartment to find a note on his door from Karen, Lucy's sexy little reporter friend, cute but annoying, one of the few people who doesn't buy his story about rescuing Lucy. She's always asking questions, giving him extra memories to erase. And that picture– that infuriating picture of Lucy and Marco, one of the main reasons he's continued this charade. It's one more reason he's so eager to go up to Lucy's dorm room. He's scrubbed Karen's mind a dozen times. But it doesn't matter; she always reverts to the same state: an abiding distrust of him.

The note says, *Why Lethe?*

That girl doesn't give up. How did she find his place? How did she find his real name? She'd make an excellent detective or spy or whatever. He removes his Spex before opening his door, an old habit in case someone has hacked his mindseye, which has never seemed likely, but he wouldn't put it past Karen. Inside, he walks to the wall of windows. There's a faint reflection of his face on the glass, like the moon in the daylight. Marco Han is dead. It's over. And Lucy...sweet little Lucy is almost his. Everything's within his grasp. But he does not feel triumph or even relief; no, quite the opposite. He senses a growing burden, an emptiness that seems to be pulling him in.

On one of their many visits to his dad's grave his grandma remarked, "You don't seem afraid of death."

"I'm not." Nick was about eleven.

"That's healthy."

"I'm afraid of outer space."

She laughed.

"I'm serious."

"Of course, you are."

"It's so big and you can't breathe in space and it goes on and on."

"That is scary. I see your point."

Nick thinks of his grandma and his father, Marco and Rex and the woman in the canyon. Where are they now? Is death the end? There's a comfort in endings. He searches the unfathomable darkness. He thinks of outer space, planets, stars and galaxies unnumbered. His lungs tighten. He feels a misery he can't identify.

He turns to the wall of Lucy. On most nights this ritual calms his terror. He checks in on her, like a parent watching over a sleeping child. He's no longer searching for her, but he still scans other people's memories of her as well as her memories. Research, he tells himself. *I have to stay close, keep an eye on her. I have to win her over. My work is too important to be derailed by one silly girl.*

But who is he kidding? Does he really think he can save the world? His efforts to erase pain have backfired, big time. He saw Marco's family mourn for him. He watched Lucy crying on her dorm floor. And lately Mollie has been a nuisance. She's trying to mind-hack again, even as Nick tries to make her forget. Besides, he still hasn't found Abuelita and Joe. Everything's spinning out of control.

Maybe he should let go of his grand plan. Do something more realistic like mind-hack to play the stock market? That route always seemed so basic, not a bit heroic. What would Lucy think of that plan? Would she consider it dishonest or clever?

An image catches his eye. She's talking to Marco in her dorm room. So she lets *him* into her room, even if it's just a dream. Another stupid Marco dream. He can't hack dreams, but Lucy spends so much time contemplating these dreams, Nick has a good idea of what they contain. It's actually pretty blah for a Lucy dream. Usually there's fireworks or raining starlight. This is simply her dorm room. The lights aren't even dimmed. And now they're kissing.

And then Nick realizes that this is not the memory of a dream, this is the feed from the camera in her room. This is real time. Marco's alive.

CHAPTER 37

How many a man has dated a new era in his life from the reading
of a book.

    Henry David Thoreau, *Walden*

Lucy reads her notebook from cover to cover and then starts
again. She looks long and hard at the drawings of Marco and
those of Nick. In the book Nick has a goatee and Marco does not. In
her memory it's kind of the opposite. There's something endearing
about scruffy Marco. She's smitten with the Marco in her notebook,
this young man who has given up everything to find her. He seems
too good to be true; he probably is.

He added a few entries to her journal. The last entry in Lucy's
handwriting is about changing their plans to catch "the guy." The rest
is in Marco's writing.

*Lucy doesn't remember me. That man—he goes by Nick—has erased
me from her mind. To the rest of the world I'm an unhinged cyber-
stalker. They not only say I kidnapped Lucy, they blame me for my*

grandma's disappearance. And the testimonials! Everyone says I was such a nice guy—so brilliant and kind. But no one seems to doubt my guilt. No one's defending my innocence. Those from my lab, neighbors, teachers, childhood friends everyone's so quick to believe the worst. I suppose I should be grateful that I'm alive. I shouldn't be alive. I was knocked off the boat unconscious. I woke in dark waters gasping for air. I thought I was dying and my life didn't flash before my eyes. No, only Lucy. I wanted more time with her. Then everything went dark.

Later, I woke and I was out of the water. I could smell motor oil and dead fish. I was on a small motorboat with a man, singing above the buzz of the engine.

"Row, row, row your boat gently down the stream.
Merrily, merrily, merrily, merrily, life is but a dream."
"The Poet?" I asked.
"Marco...Polo; Marco...Polo."
He chanted as if he were playing the game, but I was positive he knew who I was.
"Is Lucy alive?"
"Merrily, merrily, merrily, merrily, life is but a dream."
I kind of went nuts. I asked over and over if she were alive. I yelled some. When I stopped, he recited a poem. (He's says it so often I have it memorized now.)

—Yet some maintain that to this day
She is a living child;
That you may see sweet Lucy Gray
Upon the lonesome wild.

"She's alive?"
He nodded. And then I remembered this book. If Lucy were alive, Nick would erase her memory. I knew I needed her journal. I told the Poet about it and how we had to go back to the boat to get it. I wasn't sure if he understood. And I wasn't sure if it was even possible. When I was knocked off the boat, the engine was still running.

He kept chanting, "Marco...Polo! Marco...Polo! Merrily, merrily, merrily, merrily life is but a dream."

But we were turning back to the boat. I'm not sure if he saw anyone when he climbed on board. It's hard to get anything out of the Poet. But he came back with the book and my portable computer. Then he took me to Joe and Abuelita. I have no idea where he got that pickup truck. It's so old it runs on gasoline. But the truck has come in handy. Abuelita took us to this house. She and Joe took care of me for a while. I had a bad case of pneumonia. Joe confirmed that, yes, Lucy is alive.

While I've been recovering, the Poet has shown Joe where Nick lives. From what I can gather, and it is a LOT of guesswork with the Poet, he has been trailing Nick ever since he showed up by the campfire in the canyon. That's how he was able to save me on the water. Now, we are all following Nick's every move, mainly through Lucy's memories. Every night she dreams about me. Every morning, he makes her forget.

There's a blank page after this entry. On the next page is a note.

Lucy,

What can I add to this strange tale of loving and forgetting? First, I want it on record that I love you. Those are loaded words, I know. And I haven't known you long. But I can't think of more accurate words, words big enough to describe how I feel. Honestly, "love" seems a flimsy word to describe this feeling, a positive energy too big for a body to hold, so big it must touch you somehow, which is crazy because you don't even know me—not anymore.

What is love when only one person remembers? Does it even matter? A part of me fears it doesn't. That's why I'm writing this, to document my one-sided love. But then even if you never know, if I die and you continue to forget, my love does matter...somehow. I want to believe love is more than chemicals and electrical signals. I want to

believe it can't ever really be erased. I hope so. Tomorrow I face Nick.
I'm not sure if I'll survive. But if I don't, my love will continue—even
if only in this note.

I love you.
Marco

She closes the book. The lavender light of approaching day floods her room. She's spent the entire night reading, but she still can't sleep. Her mind races. Marco's story is so strange, and yet she believes it. How to reconcile what she believed yesterday to what she believes now? But it isn't hard. Nick has always made her anxious. And it was so weird how he knew everything about her. Of course he did. He's been spying on her for weeks now.

She just needs to get through one day. She tries to sleep again but can't. She takes out her new notebook and writes. Only when she's written most of it down can she rest. She has complicated dreams with both Nick and Marco in them. A knock on her door wakes her.

Nick stands in the doorway, smiling relaxed. He's not wearing a suit; he's not even wearing a button-down shirt. He's wearing jeans and a t-shirt, which makes him look younger. Mollie was right; he's just a kid.

"I thought we'd get waffles."

A part of Lucy wants to believe that he actually cares about her. He looks like he does. But she knows better. She falters for a moment trying to find the right tone. Her dad used to say that the best liars build their lies around truth. She's mad at Nick. Furious. And though she can't let him know the real reason for her wrath; it would be much easier to be angry at him than pretending to like him.

"It's not okay to just walk into my room like that!"

"Sorry, I've been calling all morning, and it's a waffle emergency. Besides, the door was ajar."

Was it really? Lucy's certain she locked the door behind Marco after he left—after he said he liked kissing her.

"And I wanted to see you."

Don't give me that. You just wanted to spy on me.

All she says is, "I was sleeping. I had a rough night."

"Me too." He walks farther into the room, shutting the door behind him. "I kept thinking about you."

"I don't know about this, Nick. Don't you think we're moving too fast? You're so much older than I am." That is not what she'd planned to say. It just came out and she isn't at all sure if it is a good idea to break up, yet. She backpedals. "I mean, you're great; I just don't know. I'm so young." She looks convincingly confused, mainly because she is.

He puts his hand to his brow. If she didn't know better, Lucy would think he was actually hurt. He rubs his forehead like he's deep in thought. "Fine, so we don't date and I'll try not to kiss you or anything else. Though I'll be tempted. But can we still get waffles"—he gives her a small smile—"as friends?"

She is a little hungry, and it occurs to her that as long as she's with Nick he can't be searching for Abuelita or Joe, so she agrees. As she stands, her leather journal, the one Marco gave her last night, falls from her bed with a thud. Nick picks it up and sets it on her desk right next to her new journal, which is splayed open.

"You got another journal?"

She jumps out of bed and wedges herself between him and the desk. "Don't read that. It's private. I've had a lot to write about and sort out. You know, trying to find my memories?"

He reaches past her for the book. "May I?"

"You don't read people's journals!" She pushes him away. Her fury amuses him. "Now go downstairs while I change." She's still wearing the same outfit she wore the night before.

"Can't you change in the bathroom? Or out here? I'm okay with that."

"Ugh. No. I'm not changing in front of you, and if I go in my bathroom, you'll read my journals." No need for half-truths; that was the whole truth.

She waits till he leaves and locks the door. She takes both of her journals into the bathroom with her. There aren't too many hiding places in there: a shower, a toilet, a cabinet, a garbage can. She puts them in the bottom of the almost empty garbage can and piles lots of crumpled toilet paper on top. Then tops it off with makeup-smeared tissues. She looks in the mirror. She still has remnants of makeup from the night before and looks fine. And, really, why should she bother to look nice to go out with her ex-boyfriend/criminal mastermind?

In the lobby Nick chats with Karen and a couple other girls from the dorm. As soon as he sees her, he calls her name and puts his arm around her, as if the talk about breaking up never happened. She's annoyed but figures it's best to keep the peace for one more day.

At the waffle place Lucy realizes she's actually famished. She wants to order everything on the menu. Nick on the other hand only wants to talk. It's weird knowing what she now knows about him. It feels like they spend the entire meal exchanging charming lies, though perhaps that could be said of most new couples. As she polishes off her lemon drop waffle, Nick tells her how he once tried to create a waffle maker alarm clock. The idea was to wake him each morning with the smell of fresh waffles. The waffles always burned, and the overflowing batter messed up the mechanics of the alarm clock. It went off randomly, sometimes in the middle of the night.

She steals a bite of his chicken and waffles. Is this story true or is it just another enchanting deception? Probably that whole sob story he told the other night about his mom abandoning him and his dad dying was made up to get her sympathy. She hates how much it worked. If Marco's going to erase Nick's memories tonight, this is her last chance to understand him. What part of the half-truths he told her are true?

"Last night you said you've done some bad things." She sneaks another bite of his waffle. "So, you gonna fess up?"

He shakes his head no. "Serious lapse of judgment. I shouldn't have said that."

"How bad exactly? Are we talking traffic tickets or mass murder?"

"Somewhere in between. Most of what I've done is with work and it's *technically* not illegal, more like unethical. But I'm pretty sure *you'd* think it was wrong."

"Try me. How do you know what I think? You've only known me a few weeks, and a couple days I was unconscious."

"True, but I'm observant." He reaches across the table, takes a lock of her hair and twirls it in his fingers. To a bystander it might appear as if he is flirting with her, but to Lucy it feels threatening. "You never want to take advantage of anyone. Or intentionally mislead them." He raises his eyebrows slightly. "You're completely loyal and trustworthy." Her heart rate picks up. He knows.

Nick suggests a variety of ways they could spend the afternoon together, including showing her his apartment. Lucy politely declines. She's already agreed to go out with him again tonight, giving Marco and the others time to set their trap.

She waits for Nick in the lobby. Karen returns from a run wearing spandex and a sports bra, sporting some flashy athletic Spex. "Hot date? With Nick?"

"Turns out he's not that bad." Now that she knows he could be spying on her through Karen's Spex, Lucy intentionally says only nice things about Nick.

"Who ever said he wasn't?"

"You haven't always been so fond of him."

"What are you talking about? I'm probably too fond of him." Lucy's about to protest, remind her of their Nick-bashing lunch date. But then she realizes that Karen's mind has been erased. It's sort of creepy, especially, since the guy who erased those memories just walked in.

Nick kisses Lucy on the cheek. She stiffens a little. Does he notice? She reminds herself, just one more date, one more date for Marco. She's trembling.

Making an excuse about being cold Lucy runs upstairs to get her sweater, leaving Nick to flirt with Karen. After grabbing her sweater and saying a quick prayer, she looks under her pillow for the picture of her and Marco. It's gone. Maybe it slipped between the headboard and mattress. Heaving the mattress away from the wall, she frantically searches the floor, but she can't find it. A panicked idea crosses her mind. She rushes to the bathroom to the garbage can. Empty. The journals are missing.

Nick. But when? After getting waffles with him she spent most of the day in her room. The only time she left was to do her laundry. But she was gone only for a few minutes. How could he have broken in and left so fast? How much has he read? The last thing she wrote about was Marco giving her journal back. She hadn't written about his plan to erase Nick's memory. But it's still bad. It means that Nick knows that she knows. He knew she was pretending in the lobby. He was still pretending too, but why? If she can just keep him out of his apartment till eleven, Marco's plan might still work.

She's scared but knows what she has to do. She re-applies her lipstick and tries to smile. She speaks out loud to her reflection. "You can do this!" Her quavering voice isn't convincing.

Lucy's never been that great at small talk, and feeling that her life depends on it doesn't help. But Nick doesn't seem to notice or pretends not to. On the drive to dinner, he prattles on about how great this restaurant is that they are going to. An exclusive spot in La Jolla with an ocean view, his favorite place, really. She smiles and nods to everything he says without paying attention. She walks with him past several fancy restaurants with crowds of moneyed patrons. They enter a modern stylish lobby and take an elevator to the top floor. Nick types in a special code for the door to open. This must be some elite, private restaurant. Lucy feels ridiculously underdressed and provincial in her yellow sundress and sweater from Target. The door opens to a small lobby with a table with flowers but no maître d' or servers. Lucy catches a whiff of perfectly roasted meat. Nick types another code, and they enter a stylish room the whole west wall reveals a fiery orange sky.

"I thought I'd do something special for you tonight," Nick says as he pulls out her chair. "I made you dinner. How do you like my apartment?"

CHAPTER 38

In dealing with truth we are immortal
and need not fear change nor accident.
Henry David Thoreau, *Walden*

Lucy tries to find the words, any words. She can't let him see how scared she is. She walks over to the window, spouting mindless comments.

"This is some apartment, and you cook? You made dinner? How sweet." Her voice sounds fake and silly but she continues. If she can just get through the evening, Nick won't remember that she sounded like a blathering idiot. His mind will be erased—and this will all be over.

She's not sure how much this new development will interfere with Marco's plan. Maybe it doesn't matter. They might lose some element of surprise. They can no longer ambush Nick in his own apartment. But if Marco shows up with Frankie and Joe, they should still be able to overpower him. Maybe she can help. All Lucy has to do is keep Nick occupied. She sits down on the sleek sofa and asks how he learned to cook. He offers her a drink.

"You know I don't drink."

"That's why I bought all this." He wheels out a bar cart stocked with a variety of sodas from your standard Diet Coke to a Strawberry Rhubarb Pop. A gesture that yesterday she would have found totally sweet, but now feels calculated and conniving.

She selects a butterscotch soda. Nick takes a ginger beer and sits down beside her.

"I was hungry."

She looks at him, confused.

"That's how I learned to cook. I was hungry. Growing up it was just my dad and me. Since he worked late most nights, I took it upon myself to make the family dinner."

"How old were you?"

"In the second grade. I lived for cooking shows. I bought the ingredients on my walk home from school. I had some incredible failures. The first time I made pesto, I didn't know what basil looked like. I bought a bundle of herbs. It wasn't basil. For the record, tarragon pesto is a travesty. I had to throw out the whole dish and we had mac and cheese from a box again."

"Smells like we're having something fancier than mac-n-cheese tonight."

"Wine-braised short ribs." He puts his free arm around her. She tries not to go rigid. "I like cooking," he says. "It's like solving a puzzle."

"I bet you're good at puzzles."

"Oh..." He shifts his head slightly and stares her down. "I am."

The game is up.

He turns away from her. He talks while watching the burning sunset. "You're right, Lucy. I am too old for you. And as much as I don't want to"—he glances back at her—"and I really don't want to— we should break up."

She laughs, trying to sound unconcerned. "Break up? But we're hardly dating."

"That's right. It's odd that I even care." He looks back at the ocean. "Especially, since..." He pauses, turns back to her. "You're seeing someone else."

"I don't..."

"Marco's alive. I know. He should be here any minute."

"What?"

"He's hacked my Spex. I left them on so he could panic and come straight here to save you. From the description in your journal—and yes, I read all of it—I'd guess his hideout is twenty minutes tops from here. He's probably already on his way."

Lucy bolts off the couch and hurries to the entrance. Nick stands between her and the door.

"This is a trap, and I'm the bait!"

"So bright." Is he serious or sarcastic? "But it's not what you think, really." He removes his Spex and puts them in his suit coat pocket, which is draped over the couch.

"Trust me, I only want to talk."

"Trust you! Since I woke in the hospital, you've been lying to me, spying on me, and before that you hunted me down and made sure everyone forgot me. I'll never trust you!"

She pushes by him and tries opening the door. He steps aside, smiling a conceited smile. It's locked electronically. She stares him down. "Let me out."

"I can't. Sorry." He folds his arms across his chest like a bouncer. Lucy walks away from him, searching the apartment for another exit. He follows close behind, still talking. She doesn't listen to him. Most of what he says is more gibberish about being sorry and how she needs to trust him. She locates a side room full of exercise equipment. She picks up a kettlebell.

"What are you doing with that?" he asks, a sort of jeer in his voice.

She swings it at him. He avoids it easily.

"Lucy," he laughs, "Do I need to tie you up or something?"

"You wouldn't." She swings again and misses but only by a little. Panicked, Nick rushes out of the room. She goes to the window. Several feet below, there juts a narrow ledge. She takes a couple steps back, hefts the weight with both hands and throws it out the window. The sunset shatters with a crash.

She steps through the jagged hole avoiding the tall, sharp pieces. "Lucy! No! What are you doing?" He grabs her by the shoulders and pulls her back in. "You're going to hurt yourself!"

She screams. He puts his hand over her mouth and pulls her over to the couch. "You fool. You could have died." He covers her screams with a pillow. *Says the man who is smothering me!*

She struggles to free herself, but she can't move. He's so much stronger than she is. He's still talking, telling her to shush, but all she can hear is her own screaming.

"And you could have killed someone, anyone walking on the beach below. A kettlebell thrown from this height? That would be it."

He holds up the object he ran out of the room to get: duct tape. He tapes her mouth shut. Next, he tapes her to the chair.

"First, I have a couple memories I need to clean up."

Dozens of screens appear on the north and south walls. Lucy stops struggling for a moment. So many memories.

"I'm afraid a neighbor or two may have heard your fuss." He rolls up his shirt sleeves and zeroes in on a few screens. "Don't worry; it won't take long. I've got a direct line to all my neighbors' minds. I alter their memories often. This is Ms. Olson." On the screen is a yippy dog with a pink bow in its hair. "That's not her. That's her dog Frieda. Every time Ms. Olsen meets me she's amazed that Frieda doesn't bark at me. 'She always barks at strangers,' she says. 'You must be a dog whisperer.'" He laughs half-heartedly. "I am sorry about this, but you're dangerous. You could have killed someone."

Lucy tries to say, "You're one to talk." But it all comes out as mumbling.

The sunset fizzles out. As the light fades, the broken window turns dark, pointy shards of night against the twilight sky.

"What were you thinking? That's like a six-story drop."

She was thinking that there was a ledge a few feet below that she could climb to. All she wanted was to get out of the apartment, to keep Marco from danger. Now, she can only hope that he'll bring Frankie and Joe with him. She knows that Joe and Abuelita were going to San Pedro to pick up Frankie today while Marco waited for them at the cliff house. But she doesn't know their exact timetable. The plan was to be in Nick's apartment at eleven p.m. It is now a little past eight.

"Marco should be here any minute, but while we wait, I have something to show you."

Lucy's life literally flashes before her eyes.

"These are memories of you." He zooms in on one from last winter. She is skiing. "Do you remember that day?"

Every question Nick asks, whether he realizes it or not is a rhetorical one. Lucy can't answer. She's still gagged.

"This particular memory belongs to Fred Harville. You remember him? He remembers you. His memories have been most helpful in my search. Though I'd say he idealizes you. Your hair couldn't possibly look that good skiing. Your hair never looks that good."

She has to admit that he's right, even if he's being horrid. Her hair in the memory is a shade redder than it is in real life. It's smooth and wavy as if a stylist had spent hours fixing it.

"That's often the case with memories." Nick paces around her, avoiding eye contact with the real Lucy but wholly transfixed by the memories of her. The way he looks at her, she might have once thought she'd want a man to look at her with that much adoration. But considering that he has her bound and gagged, adoration seems overrated.

"People we like look better in our memories than they do in real life. People *like* you. Did you know that? When I first searched for you, I was confused by the difference between memories of you and footage of you in real life." He stops and watches a screen with Lucy decorating a Christmas tree last year. She's wearing twinkle lights loosely around her neck. None of the videos play sound but her lips move as if she's singing.

"Everyone who knows you thinks you're prettier than you really are." He turns away from the screens for a moment to look at her. "Even I do."

He focuses on another memory of her running a race. She could be the cover of a running magazine. No one looks that good when they run.

Marco bursts into the apartment. "Where is she?" For the briefest moment his face registers astonishment on seeing Lucy bound and surrounded by memories of herself. Nick approaches him.

"Marco, I'm way glad you came..."

Marco punches him hard in the face. Nick stumbles back, wiping the blood from his cheek on to his white shirtsleeve.

"Listen, I don't want a fight."

Marco hits him again, and again. He kicks and punches with fury. There's a grace to Marco's fighting. He's younger and slighter than Nick but seems to be winning.

Nick keeps backing up, saying, "You don't understand." He isn't hitting back. He protects his face with his fists and ducks to miss most blows but not all. His eye is swelling, his nose bleeding. Blood stains his shirt. He curses and yells for Marco to stop, but he doesn't hit back. With each punch and kick he edges back. They cross the room knocking over the sand and rocks from the Zen garden on the coffee table.

Soon Nick is backed against the window, the not-broken section. Marco is so consumed with rage, he doesn't seem to notice a portion of the window is smashed. He keeps hitting Nick over and over and over.

"Enough!" Nick yells as he pushes his whole body against Marco. Marco leaps back. Nick starts fighting. He hits hard. Marco turns a little and takes a backward step.

Lucy can see the danger, but she can't warn anyone. Her screams are gagged. Marco stands perfectly framed by the broken window, as if surrounded by the jaws of night. Nick jabs him hard, moving forward. Marco jumps back and falls out the window.

CHAPTER 39

The mind is its own place, and in itself
   Can make a 'eav'n of hell,
   a hell of 'eav'n.
   John Milton, *Paradise Lost*

"Nooooo!" It takes Lucy a moment to realize the scream is Nick's, not hers. Her yells are still muffled by duct tape. Nick kneels at the window's ledge, cursing softly and reaches down. Lucy wants to know what he can see and at the same time doesn't. Is Marco's broken body lying on the ground below? But maybe he made it to the ledge several feet below. The ledge is only a hand-span wide. It was a stretch to think she could make it if she'd carefully lowered herself down. And Marco jumped not knowing it was there. It's too much to hope for.

Nick lowers his upper body out the broken window. A piece of glass scrapes his arm. Fresh blood spreads like a flower blooming on his white shirt. He strains and groans and pulls Marco up through the window.

For a moment, both rest on the glass-littered floor, gasping. After catching his breath, Nick stands up and offers Marco a hand.

"Why?" Marco asks still on the floor not taking the offered hand. "Why save me?"

"I need your help." Nick walks to Lucy's chair and starts removing the duct tape from her legs. She wishes he'd get to her mouth. She has so much to say. She can tell he's trying to be careful, but it still smarts as it rips off skin and hair.

Marco stands, brushing off bits of glass. "My help?"

"Trust me, you'll like this. Give me a minute." Lucy's legs are now free, and she stands.

He puts his hand on the tape over her mouth. "I'm going to take this off. But I need you to be quiet and listen—for once." He gestures toward the broken window. "This wouldn't have happened if you'd listened to me."

She tries to scream, "None of this would have happened if you hadn't erased our memories!" It just comes out as "Nom, mon, nom, mon!"

He laughs. "Maybe I leave this on."

"Take it off!" Marco's voice rings with righteous indignation. Nick rips the tape off her mouth. The sting makes Lucy's eyes tear.

Marco approaches her and gently helps her take the tape off her wrists. Nick wipes the blood dripping from his nose, with the back of his hand, leaving a gruesome smear on his face. He plops down on the couch. "Have a seat. It makes me nervous with you two glowering above me."

Lucy remains standing. Marco sits on the edge of the coffee table. He looks down at his own blood-splattered hands and back up at Nick, whose nose is still trickling blood. Nick lifts his suit coat, which had been draped neatly over the couch the entire fight, and removes a white handkerchief from the breast pocket. He puts the handkerchief to his nose. "I brought you here because I want something only Marco can give me."

He pulls his Spex out of the jacket's inside pocket and puts a mindseye in his ear. "Erase my memory. That's all I ask. I want to forget knocking you off the boat. Forget about Rex falling, the homeless lady bleeding in the woods. Make me forget that I ever knew how to erase people's memories."

Marco sits stunned.

Silent.

"Well?" asks an impatient Nick. "Will you do it?"

Marco picks up some bits of broken glass off the table, gingerly placing them in his hand. "I don't know."

"Of course you can," says Lucy. "That's the plan, isn't it?"

"And Lucy." Nick lets his eyes flit to her and then looks away. "Make me forget her."

"You love her?"

"I want to forget her...forget all of this.... Erase the pain, please."

"I can't."

"You can!" Nick stands. His voice is loud on the verge of yelling. "I've seen your work. You're good!"

"That was, may I point out, before you wiped out my memory. I'll try to erase your memories. But I can't take the pain away, not really. When I'd forgotten Lucy, I still felt the ache of losing her. I didn't know what it was. But I had this constant tightness in my chest. And the moment she was beside me, it was like I could breathe again."

"You'd have gotten over her; all of my clients do. Everyone forgets."

"Do they? Don't you have a lot of repeat customers? Aren't they doing the same things over and over trying to mask the pain? The only way to begin to heal is to go through the pain and make things right."

"That's what I'm doing. I'm returning you to Lucy. Now she knows. She knows the truth about me. She won't forgive me."

Lucy resents how Nick talks like she isn't even there. She hates how he won't even look at her.

"I might." She walks around him and the couch slowly. "You don't deserve it, but I might. You used me. You erased my memories. You erased a part of me. And then you pretended to...pretended to...well.... And then you tie me up and gag me, like a hostage." She stops pacing. "There's no...no...no..." She searches for a word strong enough but can't find one.

"You're right," says Nick. "I was wrong. I didn't want to hurt either of you. I never did. I wanted to run my business in peace. I only wanted you two to forget me and my work. I never meant for anyone to die. Then that homeless woman..."

"Her name was Penny," Lucy corrects.

"Yes. So then Penny died and Rex was shot and I thought I killed Marco. Trust me, hell is real. I'm living it."

"Good." She sits down at the table still set for dinner.

"Now, if Marco will just erase my memory."

"Fine, I'll try."

It doesn't take long to set everything up. Both Nick and Marco wash the blood off their hands and faces. Nick shows Marco his computer equipment. It's strange how fast those two are talking like colleagues. Nick's setup impresses Marco. And Nick seems pleased to show someone his work, someone who can truly appreciate it.

Lucy is sweeping broken glass when he approaches her. She stops her work.

"We're almost ready," he says. It's a little past nine p.m., Frankie and Joe will be showing up in an hour or so. Nick knows they are coming but asked Marco not to wait. "And um...yeah... I had a couple things I wanted to say to you before...you know."

She brushes the last bits of glass into the dustpan. "I have nothing to say to you."

"I get it... I do." He takes the dustpan out of her hand, sets it down, steps forward and kisses her. He says a lot with that kiss. And though at first Lucy is nothing but surprised, her body takes over. She answers back. People have all sorts of latent and confusing desires in their hearts, and it turns out she cares for Nick more than she wants to admit. She kisses him and all the best parts of him goodbye. He steps back and smiles a satisfied smile. She looks across the room at Marco who watches them with his eyes wide open.

Nick speaks first. "Now I'm ready."

CHAPTER 40

What is dark within me, illumine.
John Milton, *Paradise Lost*

"Don't erase too far back, okay? I want to remember my dad and my grandma," says Nick. He is lying on the couch with a mindseye in. They are waiting for his sleeping pill to take effect.

"I'll only delete the memories related to mind-hacking," Marco assures him. "They should all be interconnected—right?"

"Yeah. Sometimes I find by breaking a few key moments you can wipe out large swaths of memories."

"Like one small interruption in the power grid can knock out the lights in an entire city," suggests Lucy.

"So bright," Nick says, looking at her all sappy. Marco balls his hands into fists and reminds himself that there's no reason to punch the guy again.

"Yes, so you'll only need to go back a few years at most. I stumbled into mind-hacking working with Dr. Wells three years ago."

"Dr. Wells?" asks Marco. "Someone else knows this stuff?"

Nick takes a while to answer and when he does speak it's with much effort and long pauses. "I...don't think...he remembers..." He fights against the drugs. "We're good...right? I was trying to make people happy. I didn't want...to hurt...anyone. Lucy...you happy?"

Sleeping Nick looks younger, sweeter, harmless. Marco still wants to hit him.

"How are we going to do this?" asks Lucy. A lens from the ceiling already projects a three-dimensional mind. Marco walks to the middle of the image. He waves his hands like a conductor leading a symphony. The multi-colored brain zooms into a galaxy of stars. He picks out the brightest one.

"This must be an important memory. Let's check it out. He makes a hand movement that looks as if he were throwing the light against the wall. An image appears. Lucy is sweeping glass. She bends over. Nick looks down her shirt.

Real Lucy self-consciously puts her hand on her shirt as she watches. Marco is glad they're watching Nick's memories and not his. Truth be told, he has a few memories of looking down her shirt.

The memory plays on. Nick approaches Lucy, and her eyes projected on the wall are as big as saucers; they're eager.

She clears her throat. "Um, that's not what it was like. His memory's tainted."

"I know," says Marco. "Obviously, he kissed you with his eyes closed. We remember things we never saw." The memory soon pans back and reveals Lucy's hands on Nick's back and in his hair. Something he couldn't have seen but could remember. It's uncomfortable sitting in the dark with his once and (hopefully) future girlfriend watching her kiss another guy. In a lame attempt to make the moment less awkward Marco keeps talking. "As soon as we file memories away, we reconfigure them into something we understand. He must have thought of that kiss a lot for it to shine so brightly."

"It wasn't like that, really."

"I know. I saw. But it was closer to that than you want to think." He sighs, snaps his fingers and the memory's gone. "I have no problem deleting that one. What's next?"

He picks another cluster of light, much larger if not brighter than the memory of the kiss. He tosses it on the screen.

Lucy gasps. Nick's working in a lab with a well-dressed older man. "The Poet!" The old man is clean and well-spoken. He's showing Nick his most recent discovery: accessing memories. It's not with Spex but with a similar device. At the Poet's request, Nick searches the old man's memories—running barefoot as a boy on the ocean's edge, studying at Oxford, dancing with a beautiful woman with big brown eyes.

"I bet that's Clara Lou," says Marco. "He was always singing about her."

Now it's another memory. Nick is alone in the lab. He logs onto the Poet's computer. He's searching for someone, a middle-aged woman named Carol Smith.

"Wait a minute!" says Lucy. "I bet that's his mom."

He hacks into her Spex and then into her memories. He's jubilant. He dances round the room! This must be the first time he's accessed a person's memories via Spex. He then starts sorting through the brightest memories. The woman, a platinum blonde who wears tights shirts and short skirts, works as a receptionist in a dentist's office. She has a crush on the dentist, a balding, married man. The highlights of her life seem to be traveling to Vegas with friends, taking a lone trip to the Grand Canyon and appearing once on a game show.

"This lady can't be his mom. She has no memory of a son," says Marco.

"It's his mom. I know it. He said her name is Carol. Don't you see? She doesn't ever think of him. He told me—I thought he was trying to get my sympathy—he told me. He said his mom never thinks of him, and I said he couldn't know that."

Carol sits in a restaurant booth across from an older man who wears his shirt unbuttoned, revealing graying chest hair and a gold chain. The two start making out. Nick switches off the computer, puts his head on his desk and sobs.

"He wasn't lying," says Lucy. "I had no idea."

"Seems like we're doing him a favor deleting that one." Marco sets to work.

"Yeah, he's better off without that." Lucy fixes Marco a plate of the short ribs Nick had made her for dinner. They're lukewarm but still delicious.

He opens another bright memory. It's on Joe's boat. Lucy's driving with impossibly perfect hair. Nick laughs and the two look up.

He speaks to Marco in a calm voice. "Please buddy, I really need to talk to you."

"He didn't say that! Did he?" says Lucy.

"Yeah, and where's the gun? I distinctly remember a gun pointed at my chest."

"There it is." Lucy gestures to the gun Nick's carrying half-heartedly. It doesn't look like he's pointing it at Marco as much as he's giving it to him.

Marco watches himself in the memory go down to the deck with Nick right behind him. At the bottom of the steps he pivots and roundhouse kicks Nick, knocking the gun out of his hand. As Nick tries to get up, Marco launches at him with a strong right hook. As Nick falls back, Marco picks up the dropped gun.

He points it a Nick's head. "I will kill you! I swear!"

"No, don't!" Lucy screams. She's running down the steps. Marco hesitates. Nick seizes the moment. He punches Marco hard and wrests the gun out of his hand. The two fight across the deck.

Watching the memory, Marco is amused. All of his jumps and kicks appear higher than humanly possible. He must have impressed Nick. In the tussle they knock over a bucket of bait, and slick fish splatter across the deck. That detail is right. Marco remembers fighting in the fish.

To avoid the slippery mess, the two jump onto the back bench of the boat. Marco throws a high kick to Nick's head, Nick ducks and delivers a punishing upper cut. Marco keels over backward and careens into the water.

Nick jumps after him. He swims to Marco, who's floating face first in the water with his arms and legs sprawled out as if he were making a snow angel. Nick flips him over and checks to make sure he's breathing and starts pulling him toward the boat, which is moving away since the engine is still running. He has almost reached the boat when Lucy jumps into the water.

"Wait, why did I do that?" she says out loud.

"I don't know. I was unconscious. I thought he must have pushed you from the boat. He was telling the truth when he said he saved you." Marco shakes his head. "Go figure."

It was true. Nick, still pulling Marco's dead weight, starts swimming out toward Lucy and her splash. She thrashes in the water. She coughs and gasps, choking on water. Her head slips below the surface. Nick curses and screams and lets go of Marco.

He dives down in the dark water searching for Lucy. He pulls her up to the surface. She coughs and howls and scratches at his arms. Treading water furiously, Nick holds her shoulders and shakes her.

"Stop it! Stop it! Or you'll get us all killed. I'm trying to save you and your stupid boyfriend." Lucy deflates. She becomes pliable and lets him pull her back to where he thought Marco should be. But he isn't there. "No, no, no, no!" Nick swims and screams. Lucy whimpers in his arms. "Marco? Where's Marco?"

The light in the memory is golden, the light prior to sunset, but when he can't find Marco it darkens. They skip the sunset. It must have happened. But in this memory the ocean goes from gold to murky gray and dark shadows. Nick swims for a long time looking for Marco. The boat's gone. He treads water in the middle of the ocean, supporting a barely conscious girl. There's no moon or stars. The only light is the slight glow emanating from Lucy's pale face. In a choked voice Nick mutters, "Don't die, Lucy! Oh please, God, don't die!" His face is wet. It's hard to tell with the darkness and all the ocean water, but it looks like he's crying.

"You can't delete that," says Lucy.

"I know."

CHAPTER 41

Awake, arise or be for ever fall'n.
John Milton, *Paradise Lost*

Nick wakes on his living room couch in the bright light of late morning. A girl sits nearby, back-lit by the window. As his eyes adjust, he recognizes her freckled face. He murmurs her name. "Lucy?"

He sits up, "Lucy!" He stands up. "I remember you!"

Marco walks in. "You're up. Good. About time."

"Marco! I remember you. I remember Lucy. It didn't work!" He sinks back down on the couch. "You're not surprised."

"Sorry," begins Lucy. "I mean, we deleted a memory or two." She blushes. *Why is she blushing?*

"I wanted to." Marco stands behind Lucy framed by the broken window. A fishy breeze wafts through. "Believe me, I wanted to. But when it came down to it, it felt wrong. I can't play God. I can't erase your memories. Somehow that seems worse than killing you."

"Lucy! Convince him. He'll listen to you."

She looks at Marco her eyes asking a question. Watching those two, Nick feels a pang. Barely back together, and they seem to have an unspoken language.

"Don't you get it?" she says. "Your memories are you. Sure, we looked through your memories and some were...um...not so flattering."

"I'd say!" Marco chimes in.

"But in the end, we decided we don't want to delete you."

Nick puts his head in his hands. "My head's pounding."

Abuelita pushes a tray with coffee, toast and eggs in front of him. "Eat and you'll feel better."

Nick didn't realize anyone else was there. He looks around the room. All these people he'd only seen in memories are now living and breathing and offering him food in his living room, like apparitions come to life. He says their names one by one. "Abuelita, Joe, Frankie... You all saw?"

"Don't forget the Poet," says Abuelita. "He's asleep now, but he watched too. It was very..." She pauses to think of a polite word. "...engaging."

"Even though Abuelita had us skip all the best parts," says Frankie with a smirk. "But we got the general idea. Farmers' markets! And to think I've been wasting all my time at bars."

Nick glances up and catches Lucy's gentle gaze. His face burns. What did she see? What does she know?

"You watched my memories."

"You begged us to," says Marco.

"You were supposed to delete them!"

"I wanted to, believe me, I wanted to." Marco shakes his head. "But I couldn't, or rather...I won't. It wouldn't be right."

"What do you mean, it wouldn't be right? It's justice." Nick stands up again. "I almost killed you!" His voice rises. "I made my fortune blackmailing public officials. I drove Lucy into the woods for fear of her life. I'm vain, selfish and controlling!" He bangs his mug down on the coffee table. The black liquid laps over the sides. "You have the chance to be rid of me, and you won't take it! Why?"

"You've changed," says Marco. "You've learned something. I can't take that from you."

"He's right," says Lucy. "If he erased your memory, you'd be back to square one. You could do all the same terrible things, or worse, over again."

"You're cruel! You know that? I'm miserable. Two people are dead because of me. I don't want to remember!"

"Are you saying you don't deserve this?"

He can't bear Lucy's gaze, and yet he can't look away.

He nods. "I deserve this. I know. And every punishment you throw at me. But don't you see, erasing my memory, it's the only way. It's the most elegant solution. You can't trust me. *I wouldn't trust me.* You definitely shouldn't. But erase my mind and you'll be free. You live your lives; I'll live mine."

Marco wipes up the spilled coffee. "If only it were that simple."

Nick gets in his face. "It is that simple. Erase. My. Memory!"

"I can't. If I did, I'd risk wiping out every good thing you've learned from your mistakes. I'm not smart enough to play God."

"Marco's right," says Lucy. "We spent the whole night talking it over, and we see only three ways forward."

Nick opens his mouth as if to speak. "No." Lucy holds up the roll of duct tape. "Do I need to use this?"

"I shouldn't have done that."

"Yes, and...?"

Nick looks at her, confused.

"This is when you apologize."

"Right, I'm sorry. I really am."

Lucy continued, "Fine, that'll do for now. Okay, first, we could tell the police or someone in the government that minds can be hacked via mindseyes. Frankie doesn't like that idea..."

"Let me guess." Nick turns to Frankie. "You know too many corrupt government officials?"

"Some of my best customers."

"Mine too." Nick shrugs. "Probably right about that."

258 | RUTH MITCHELL

"Then, we could go public," continues Lucy. "Tell the whole world that minds can be hacked. Eventually, this is what we have to do. The truth always comes out."

"But before we let the cat out of the bag it would be preferable," Marco interjects, "if we had a decent way to prevent mind-hacking."

"Preferable and profitable," says Nick, stroking his chin. "You have my attention."

"I suppose we could make some money," says Marco. "But mainly I want to prevent bad things from happening. I don't trust the public to protect themselves. People either won't believe or won't care. No one wants to believe there's anything negative about the technology that makes their lives convenient. The only ones who will take the threat seriously are those who will use the vulnerability to their advantage."

"True that," says Nick. "What's option three?"

"Vigilantes." Marco stands up. "We protect people from the danger they don't know exists. Maybe there's no one else who can mind-hack, but just in case, we need to be ready. I can't do it alone. You're smart. Possibly smarter than me. What do you say? Will you join us?"

CHAPTER 42

All change is a miracle to contemplate,
   but it is a miracle which is taking place every instant.
   Henry David Thoreau, *Walden*

Theresa can't sleep. It's two a.m. She gets out of bed. Her husband's peaceful sleep irritates her. Grief knocks him out while it leaves her painfully awake—awake but so tired. The more exhausted she becomes the less she can sleep. She walks in a trance. She has been cut off both root and branch. In one week, she's lost both her mother and her son. Her sorrow's so heavy she feels it will crush her. She puts her right hand on her sternum, a counter pressure to her heartache. With her hand holding her heart, she steps out on the back patio and watches the moon on the water, trying to think of anything but Marco and her mother. There's nothing else to think of.

"Mom."

She does not turn her head. "I'm fine, Rachel. Go back to bed. You need your sleep."

"Mom." The voice, though familiar, is lower than her daughter's.

260 | RUTH MITCHELL

A hand touches her shoulder. She knows that hand. She turns around and her living son embraces her.

When Theresa finally lets go of Marco, she sees her mother. Abuelita has watched the mother-son reunion with silent tears. "Oh, Mama!" She falls into her mother's arms and weeps. Abuelita holds her daughter a long time, stroking her hair, saying soft words. Marco leaves them. He goes around the house, turning on lights, waking his family, spreading joy.

Eventually, they all gather in the kitchen. Grandma Han sets out food. Marco takes a large bite from a chocolate-layered cake left over from his own funeral.

"This is what heaven must be like," says Rachel. "Except this is better."

"No mija," says Abuelita. "This is glorious, but heaven will be better. Wait and see. You forget I have a son and a husband there. And then there's God—I can't wait to see Him."

"You'd better wait," says Theresa, reaching across the counter and squeezing her mother's hand. "I still need you here." They talk and cry and laugh until the darkness is replaced with morning light. Mostly Abuelita tells their story with Marco giving occasional commentary. "Shouldn't you tell the police or someone in the government?" suggests Theresa.

Marco shakes his head no. "According to Nick, that's the worst idea possible."

"Frankie agrees," says Abuelita as she cuts another slice of cake.

"Frankie?" asks Rachel. "Frankie knew about all this and you didn't tell me?"

"We couldn't; we had to keep you safe from Nick," says Marco.

"Frankie's been a big help. Remember, he saved us on the roof," says Abuelita. "He also helped us fake Marco's death."

"I was wondering how you did that," Marco's dad says as he slathers some kimchi on his potato salad. Theresa's too overjoyed to notice he smuggled the forbidden condiment into the house.

"He knows a few tricks to decompose a body beyond recognition.

We dropped Rex's body in the ocean, and I switched his dental records for mine as well as DNA samples. I'm not proud of that."

"I knew those weren't your bones. I just knew it," says Theresa.

"Yeah, you kept me busy for a while. You kept making them retest the bones and double-check the records. Faking my death was a nightmare, and it didn't work how I hoped. I was hoping Rex's bullet wound would make the police reexamine the case and suspect Nick. I overlooked, of course, who I was up against. I'm pretty sure Nick was doing his best to make the police forget all possible leads that conflicted with his story."

"And now you're going to work with him?" asks Rachel.

"He has outrageous skills. And until I can design a safer mindseye, we need to keep an eye out for anyone else mind-hacking. We spent most of today theorizing on how to secure memories. I think we can do it."

"I don't like it; I don't trust him," says Rachel.

"I don't completely trust him either." Marco sits down on the empty barstool next to his sister. "But I'd rather work with him and keep tabs on him, than wonder what he's up to. And after looking into his memories...I don't know. He's not the monster I thought he was yesterday."

Rachel continues muttering. To appease her, Marco gives her the rest of his cake. He inspects the leftovers from his funeral. He fills his plate with bulgogi, rice and kimchi.

"What about this Lucy?" asks his dad. "How are things working out with you two?"

"Yeah," says Rachel. "She doesn't remember you as her boyfriend. That's got to be weird for her."

"I think it is." He recalls kissing her in the dorms and then that last kiss between Nick and her. "I want to pick up where we left off but...I don't think she can. Any advice?"

"Give her time, give her space," says Rachel. "She'll come around. You know what Mom always says. 'The things we love most return to us.' You and Abby returned to us—from the dead, even. She'll return to you." Marco looks over at his mom, who had been listening on the couch but now has fallen fast asleep.

Nick enters his living room dressed in his workout clothes. He watches his north wall, his wall of Lucy. One by one he turns the memories off. The last screen is the feed from her dorm room. She's sleeping, her hair spread on her pillow, the morning sun shining on it like light through maple syrup. Her face soft and untroubled. He once wondered why so many people considered her so much prettier than she actually is. What is closer to the truth: perception or reality? He cuts the feed and deletes all the footage taken from her room.

He gets on his treadmill facing the opposite wall, his constant scan through the rich and the powerful. He will continue inspecting them but now with a different purpose. He'll be searching for other mind-hackers. He starts running, watching the various screens. This morning, the images of shame and intrigue make him sick. He speaks the command to turn them off. His walls go blank. He turns off the treadmill and walks to the window, the broken hole now boarded up with plywood. A soft blue sky fills the rest of the window, shimmering with the promise of a hot day. The water is clear, steady waves edged with frothy white surf. The sand on the beach is smooth and clean, all footprints and debris washed away. Nick decides to do something he hasn't done in a long time. He goes outside and runs on the beach.

After running north a few miles, he stops. His thoughts are too heavy to run. He sits on a large, flat chunk of fallen rock, so deep in thought he doesn't notice the surf creeping up higher, splashing around his ankles. The salt water cleanses the bite marks on his ankle, leaving a slight burning sensation.

"You've changed," Marco had said. "You've learned something. I won't take that from you."

Have I changed? He thinks of the Poet, or Dr. Wells, as he knew him. It's hard to describe how Nick feels when he thinks of Isaiah Wells. Regret, mainly, and that alone is a change. It's a change for the better, but it doesn't feel like it. It was so simple when he believed everything he did was justified.

For the last few years Isaiah's fate has been an uneasy question at the back of Nick's mind. With more discoveries and a growing business, he'd almost forgotten all about his mentor until he saw his face out the restaurant window.

When Nick first met Dr. Wells three years before, he was an energetic, eloquent, dedicated scientist. He was good to Nick. He gave the young undergrad great freedom and responsibility in the lab. They were trying to access the memories of stroke patients—a cause dear to Isaiah because at seventy he'd already suffered a series of small strokes.

One night they got into fight about how to best use their discoveries. The professor started spouting gibberish. He reverted from his crisp Oxford English to the Caribbean lilt of his childhood. "Eenie meenie miney mo, Catch a tiger by a toe!" The next day he was back to normal. But two days later he suffered a major stroke. Nick was the one who called the paramedics.

Dr. Wells was recovering in a neurological rehab center when he disappeared. The nurses said he simply walked out the door. The old man had made two previous escapes, each time showing up at the lab, getting right back to work. He may have tried to go back to the lab the third time. Nick doesn't know. By then he had cleared all their research off the computers, left the lab, and set off on his own. When he should have been looking for Dr. Wells, he did his best to hide from him.

Was Dr. Well's brain damage Nick's fault? Probably not. But he knew the doctor was experimenting on himself. He suspected the danger and never said a word. And when the old man went missing, Nick didn't look for him. He was happy to keep their discoveries to himself.

Yesterday when the Poet walked into his living room, Nick

recognized him immediately. "Dr. Wells?" The old man didn't say a word. Everyone watched him stare Nick down, none of them certain what was going on in his jumbled head. But Nick felt sure that he recognized him and that he remembered. He suffered under Isaiah's gaze. He thought he saw pain and betrayal. He wanted to apologize, but words seemed empty. What could he say? I'm sorry your mind's messed up and that it's partly my fault. I'm sorry I didn't look for you when you went missing. Sorry I moved and hid from you. Sorry I hoped you were dead. The only sound in the room was the distant crash of the waves below. Finally, Nick took a step toward Isaiah and said, "I'm sorry."

The old man closed his eyes, and in a raspy voice sang,

> *"I once was lost, but now I'm found.*
> *Was blind, but now I see....*
> *Through many dangers, toils and snares*
> *I have already come;*
> *'Tis grace hath brought me safe thus far*
> *And grace will lead me home."*

He opened his eyes and embraced Nick. When he stepped away, some of Nick's dried blood flaked off onto the Poet's shirt.

CHAPTER 43

If one advances confidently in the direction of his dreams,
   and endeavors to live the life which he has imagined,
   he will meet with a success.
   Henry David Thoreau, *Walden*

Thursday when Lucy goes to her sister's to do laundry, she finds Marco and Nick there, sitting with Mollie at her desk. Joe's there, too, lounging on the couch, reading. He follows Nick everywhere and considers himself his warden.

If only Mollie had warned her, she would have worn something different—maybe put on mascara. As it is, she's wearing sweats with her hair up in a messy bun.

"Why hello, my pretty." Nick greets her with his signature smile.

Marco looks irritated. He gives the slightest nod and mumbles something.

He walks out the front door.

"What's his deal?" asks Nick.

Lucy gives him her best death stare and hurries to the laundry room.

She has no idea where things went wrong with Marco. She read over and over what he wrote in her sketchbook. He said he loved her, and she believed him. He hoped that love would last after death. But it hasn't even survived a week. She stuffs her dirty clothes into the washing machine with undue violence.

Except she does love Marco, or, at least watching him from a distance, she thinks she could. He's assembled this odd group of vigilantes, leading with unflagging optimism and patience. Not surprisingly, Nick rubs some people the wrong way. He's used to working alone and always thinking he's right. But Marco has a real knack for talking him down. Mollie says that Marco's the only one Nick completely respects.

Mollie was a little shocked when Lucy asked if she would help her ex-boyfriend and dead kidnapper work together to prevent mind-hacking. But she wasn't one bit surprised to discover that people could mind-hack. She was already at it again. She'd run into a fire hydrant sometime during Lucy's sojourn in the wilderness and didn't want Phil to tease her about it. The same day they accessed Nick's memories, Mollie successfully deleted the fire hydrant incident. This development made them all more confident in their decision not to delete Nick's memories. If Mollie was back at it so soon, he would be, too.

Mollie was a smidge disappointed she had to confess to Phil that she had altered his memories. But Phil proved to be remarkably understanding. Turned out he was more proud of his wife than angry, said he always knew she was brilliant. He and Mollie, who have no memory of Nick as a bad guy, have adjusted the quickest to working with him. Mollie's been helping Nick develop an alert system that detects when a memory has been breached. Phil's working with Marco to figure out how to retrieve lost memories. Nick's apartment is home base for their operation, which is the main reason Lucy hasn't spoken to Marco. She's not ready to face Nick, not yet. If Marco wants to see her, he knows where to find her. And now her worst fears are confirmed. He's avoiding her. He darted out of the house at the sight of her.

Tears roll down her cheeks as she puts in the detergent. She reminds herself that it is silly to cry over a boy she doesn't even remember dating.

There's a tap at the door. She wipes her eyes.

Another tap and Marco's voice, "Lucy? Are you in there?"

She opens the door. He's holding a shopping bag.

"Can I come in?"

"Sure." He steps in the laundry room, which is not big enough for two people.

"I got this for you." He hands her the bag.

"My quilt!" She hugs it. It has a faint whiff of Marco. It's funny that she recognizes his scent.

"I suppose it's time I gave it back to you."

"Yeah..." She pulls herself up so she's sitting on the washer, making her eye level with him "So this is it? You're breaking up with me? I mean, not that we're really dating or anything..."

"No, the opposite." He smiles, and something about his smile makes her whole body smile back. "I was thinking we could start over." He nervously rakes his fingers through his hair. "I mean...if that's okay with you."

"It's more than okay."

"Then no time like the present. Let's get dinner."

"Aren't you supposed to be saving the world or something?"

"The world can wait." He offers her a hand down from her perch on the washing machine—a totally unnecessary act of chivalry that she loves. Back on the ground they stand uncomfortably close. Both enjoy the discomfort.

Marco speaks first. "I thought you were avoiding me."

"I was avoiding Nick."

"That's reasonable."

"I thought *you* were avoiding *me*."

"I was giving you space. I saw that kiss. And whatever you say..."

"You thought I liked Nick?"

"He does give you a saintly glow in all of his memories. What girl wouldn't want that? I don't want you to feel obliged to date me because you did once—or twice—before."

"Is that why you didn't want to erase his memories?"

"One of many reasons. You deserve a choice."

"He taped me to a chair with duct tape! He's not a choice. I don't like Nick, promise." She reaches up and brushes his hair out of his eyes. "I like someone else."

They walk out hand in hand, Marco carrying the rolled-up quilt under one arm.

"Where are you two going?" Mollie asks.

"Out," she answers. "Don't wait up. We have some catching up to do."

"About time," says Mollie. "Have fun."

"Hey, Nick," says Marco. "If you have time, see if you can break into my bank account. I'm running low on funds. You have all the info, right?"

Nick does not turn to look at Marco or Lucy. He keeps his back to them with his eyes on the display. He answers with a bite of sarcasm. "Sure thing, lovebirds."

Marco spreads the quilt on tufts of dry weeds and dirt near the edge of a cliff above the ocean, while they argue about whether this picnic spot is where they went on their first, first date, which is ridiculous since neither of them actually remembers. They're relying on an account from Lucy's journal. This spot seems to match her description: a grassy bluff overlooking the ocean. The sky is dark gray with random streaks of light seeping through. The water shines silver where the light hits it.

After he brings her up to date on some of the small things they did together on Joe's boat, Lucy mentions that she's thinking of changing her major.

"What? Why?"

"Isn't it obvious? I've been reading my journal. I was so helpless hiding in the woods. I mean, it worked out because you helped me nicely. But I don't ever want to be so clueless again. I'm thinking I'll study computer science so I can help you guys."

"Don't underestimate the power of philosophy. If it weren't for all your high ideals and courage, none of us would've ever known what really happened."

"Except for what was in my journal."

"No, Nick would have destroyed that."

"It's embarrassing knowing that you read it. There's some pretty silly things in there."

"Not at all; I loved it. I read every good thing you wrote about me. Especially when it looked like you were falling for Nick. I can't say how hard that was to watch. That's why when I saw him face to face I lost it. Sorry you had to see that. I worried that after seeing me fight Nick and hold the gun to his head in that memory, I thought maybe I scared you away."

"I wanted to beat Nick up, too. I was just waiting for some sign from you."

"And I was waiting for some sign from you. But I was done with waiting. That's why this morning I brought your quilt with me. I went out to the car to get it."

"That's why you left? I've been so confused. I didn't know what was up with you. I kept reading and rereading what you wrote."

"Now it's my turn to be embarrassed." He fixes his eyes on a fishing boat in the distance.

"Don't be. I loved every word, especially the last part." Their legs touch while their feet dangle off a three-foot ledge. "Did you mean what you wrote?" she asks.

He looks at her. He knows exactly which part she's talking about.

"Every word." He leans in and brushes her lips. She returns the kiss. Kissing Marco is delicious déjà vu. His hands, his lips, seem inevitable and right. Images of him, fragments of memories or details taken from reading her journal all swirl through her head. Marco laughing in the sun. His eyes full of hurt the moment after Nick last kissed her. Marco nervous or excited always brushing his hands through his hair. Marco concentrating on his work, his mouth serious, his eyes dazzling. Gentle, considerate Marco helping his grandma. Marco fighting Nick, full of fury and power.

Who is this boy kissing her? This person that she knows and doesn't know. Remembers and doesn't remember. She knows that she doesn't really know him. Can't possibly ever know everything about him. But kissing him she feels something, something like coming home.

As they kiss, the world feels brighter and warmer as if the sun has moved out of the clouds and settled on the two of them. But when they open their eyes, the sky's still gray. White caps stir the water. A chill wind sweeps up, spitting out an occasional rain drop. They huddle together.

"Maybe next year I'll take your class."

"If I return to the living. Can't teach if you're dead."

"Yeah, right. What are you going to do about that?"

"For now, be a ghost."

"That sucks."

"Nah, I have plenty of money. Abuelita will inherit most of it. And there's lots of benefits to being dead. No taxes, no jury duty. And it's a plus for you, too." He puts his arm around her. "Ghosts don't have much opportunity to date. Not that I'll be looking."

"When you put it that way...but still. I feel terrible about putting you in this situation. Abandoning your work and school."

"Why? You didn't erase my memory or frame me for kidnapping."

"Yeah, but I'm the reason you got involved in the first place, remember?"

"No." He brushes a raindrop off her cheek. "I don't remember, and neither do you."

They find this so funny that they laugh and kiss and laugh some more. Holding hands, they scurry along the muddy trail. They keep looking at each other, smiling and laughing, turning their faces to the sky, letting the rain wash their tears away.

EPILOGUE

If you have built castles in the air, your work need not be lost;
that is where they should be. Now put the foundations under
them.

Henry David Thoreau, *Walden*

"Whose party is this?" Karen asks as they enter the cable car built in the cliff.

"Abuelita's," says Nick.

"She's your grandma?"

"No, my friend's."

"But she's your cook?"

"Don't call her that. She does cook most of our meals, and she's an amazing cook. But it's her house and we're her guests."

The cable starts moving with a shudder. The car drops at a sharp angle. The passengers face the ocean as they plummet.

"Whoa! It feels like we're falling off a cliff."

"Yeah, this ride makes bringing the groceries a thrill."

The sun's setting. Billowy castle-like clouds light up in various shades of pink and orange and blue.

Nick says, "Lucy Campbell will be here. You two are friends, right?"

"Lucy? Did you bring me to make her jealous?"

"No, Lucy has a boyfriend."

"What? Who? How come I've never heard of him? Boyfriend?

Why wouldn't she mention that?" The car stops with a jerk and a loud clank.

"Are you ready to meet a lot of strangers?" asks Nick.

"I've got my *Good with Names* app."

"Um no—before you come in, you'll have to take your Spex off." He removes her glasses.

"Oh, that kind of party. I didn't think Lucy would..."

"No, quite the opposite. Has anyone told you that you have the prettiest eyes?"

"You've tried that before, Nick. It won't work. Why can't I wear my Spex?"

He puts her lenses in his suit pocket.

"My friend is extremely private."

"Is he hiding from the law?" she says jokingly.

"Technically, no." Nick opens the cable car door.

Marco's waiting for them. "You took forever; where..."

Nick steps out, "Sorry, I ran into an old friend and..."

Karen walks out of the tram carrying an armload of almond blossoms. She recognizes Marco the instant he recognizes her.

"Marco Han!"

"Karen Burns! She's a reporter! Nick, what were you thinking?"

"I thought he was dead! I thought you killed him!"

"I didn't kill him. Obviously!"

"A reporter, seriously?"

"This is the story of a lifetime!"

"You thought I killed him?"

"And she remembers me. You were supposed to take care of that."

"You thought I killed a man and you still went out with me? You're using me!"

"It's my job. Anything for the truth."

"Yeah, well—the truth sucks." Nick pushes by her, retrieves the twenty-pound bag of ice from the cable car and storms off, leaving Karen with Marco. Nick practically knocks Lucy over as she comes out the door.

"What's...?"

"Nick brought a date. The worst possible date." Marco turns to Karen. "Don't take that personally."

"It's hard to take any other way."

Lucy shoots him a disapproving look. "Why don't you go help Abuelita, and I'll show Karen around." She turns to Karen. "Nick shouldn't have invited you. But he did. So, either he's a complete moron..."

Marco interjects. "I'll take that option."

"Go on; be good." Marco leaves, closing the blue door behind him.

"Anyhow, either he's a complete moron, or..." Lucy glances at Karen. "He really likes you."

Karen avoids Lucy's eyes. She studies the potted succulents. A lizard scurries across the biggest pot. "Nick doesn't care about anyone."

"Not true. He adores Abuelita. He must; he got her this house and even helped her paint it pink."

"It really is pink? I thought it was reflecting the sunset."

"No, it's always pink or blush. Hey, don't worry about Nick and Marco. They'll come around. They always do. It's actually a relief to let you in on the secret. I wanted to tell you so many times. It's especially good since you are always trying to set me up. But we just didn't know how to bring Marco back to life without the whole story going public and we aren't ready for that yet."

"What story?"

"Remember how I used to spy on him? Do you remember any of that? Or did Nick erase it?"

"I remember plenty. That's why I've been pestering Nick. Though lately, it's been more like he's pestering me. I never thought Marco kidnapped you."

"Stay for dinner. We'll tell you the whole story. Abuelita's making tortillas, and Marco's grandma is bringing bulgogi, and Nick made Abuelita's famous key lime bars."

Inside the house is pink, too. Not actually; the walls are painted white, but the entire west wall is windows and the colors of the sunset flood the room. Abuelita and Nick work in the kitchen. Abuelita rolls out tortillas. Nick slices lemons. Abuelita, intent on her cooking, doesn't notice the newcomer. Nick sees them and hastily turns away to look in the cupboards for nothing in particular. Karen thinks he's mad, but Lucy seems amused at his reaction.

A teenage girl with thick black hair and world-weary eyes washes equations off the windows. "My brother loves to do all his thinking on these windows."

"Well, you can't beat the view," says Karen.

It's a clear day in February. The horizon is far away, and the sky is layered in colors.

"You're Marco's sister, right?"

"Yes, this is Rachel," says Lucy.

"We've met before."

"Really?" asks Rachel, only mildly surprised. "When?"

"Last spring you came to me when Marco was missing. You told me he was innocent."

"Sounds like me. I always knew he was innocent, but I've never met you. Or at least I don't remember meeting you. Your face is sort of familiar. Someday I'm going to have to have Marco fill me in on all that was erased."

"Erased?"

"She doesn't know?" Rachel looks at Lucy, perplexed. "I thought only those who know are invited. We didn't even invite my uncles."

"I know, I know," says Lucy. She tries to give Rachel a please-stop-talking-about-this look. She doesn't want Karen to feel anymore awkward than she already does. "Nick invited her. Let's make her feel welcome."

"That explains it. Probably did that to annoy Marco."

"I'm certain he enjoys her company, and annoying Marco is just an added benefit."

"Who exactly lives here?" asks Karen.

"It's Abuelita's house. Marco and the Poet also live here. Joe and Nick have their own places, but they're here so much they might as well live here. They've spent the last six months remodeling it. This is their housewarming party but the guest list is limited because most people think Marco's dead."

Rachel says, "My parents are coming, and my other grandparents."

"And my sister Mollie and her husband Phil and my nephew Porter. It's nice that my sister's family knows about Marco. And now you do. All my other friends think I'm crazy for breaking up with Nick."

"I never did." Karen raises her voice. "I never trusted him."

Nick looks up from the island in the kitchen.

"I don't trust Nick, either," says Rachel.

"Smart girl." Karen glances over to see if Nick's still listening in. He's busy slicing lemons.

The brass bell at the door rings with a loud clang. Lucy answers it. She and Marco arrive in the entryway at the same time. They welcome Mollie and Phil and Porter. Rachel hurries off to put away her cleaning supplies. Karen stands by herself looking out the window. The Poet approaches her. He looks out the window, not at her. He speaks slowly,

> "In the peaceful west
> Many the sails at rest—
> The anchors fast—
> Thither I pilot thee—
> Land Ho! Eternity!
> Ashore at last!"

"You must be the Poet."

Still watching the pink-fringed waves crashing, he answers, "I'm the Mad Scientist."

A woman with silver hair joins them. "His name's Isaiah. He speaks only in poems and songs."

"Stroke?"

"Something like that. He's lovely. He remembers more poems and songs than I have read in my many years."

"You must be Abuelita." Karen hands her the flowers. "These are for you. Nick bought them."

"Almond blossoms, such a sweet scent, sí? So, you're Nick's girl?"

"Oh no, barely acquaintances."

"And he *invited* you here?" Abuelita raises her eyebrows.

"He seems to be the only one who doesn't think it was a terrible idea."

"Well, he must have his reasons." Abuelita gives her a comforting smile. "Mi casa es tu casa."

"Thank you; this place is fantastic."

"Isn't it? It's like living in a daydream. I've wanted this house for many years, and everyone told me it would never happen, and here I am. Nick got it for me. I'm not sure what he did to get it, probably don't want to know."

"This is why she's so quick to overlook Nick's faults," says Lucy as she joins the tête-à-tête with Porter in her arms.

"He's also a terrific help in the kitchen," adds Abuelita. "I thought it would be difficult to leave my old neighborhood, my old life. But it's been invigorating. I feel like I'm seventy all over again. Nick dotes on me. Marco—well, Marco's Marco. His optimism is boundless. And the Poet—he's always saying the most beautiful things."

The bell clangs again. Marco's parents and grandparents arrive. Lucy leaves to greet them.

Marco's mom embraces him. She ruffles his hair and asks if he's growing it out. "No, just busy; I haven't had time."

"Nick always keeps his hair immaculate."

Marco shrugs and puts his arm around Lucy. "I guess we make time for what matters most to us."

Theresa greets Lucy warmly. Marco jokes with his dad and talks to his grandparents in Korean. His grandparents and father fuss over the couple. Soon they sit down to eat.

Over dinner Phil tells Joe a new joke he heard. "There was this admiral who was famous for winning every battle." Mollie looks at Lucy; they both smirk.

"Before every battle he would take a folded paper out of his locket, unfold it, read it silently, and then go on to win. He never lost a battle, not a one. Everyone wants to know what is on his paper." Marco listens intently. He doesn't realize that Phil has already told him this joke.

"The admiral never lets anyone see what's in his locket. He even sleeps with it to protect it from prying eyes. Finally, he dies. Everyone can't wait to find out what's in the locket. What is the secret to this great admiral's success?" Phil lowers his voice to a whisper. "They open it. They unfold the paper." He moves his hands as if he's opening a locket and unfolding a paper. "Finally, they have the answer. The paper read: Left=Port and Right=Starboard."

Some laugh, some groan. Mollie rolls her eyes. She says to Lucy, "Don't you think there are special exceptions to mind-hacking?"

"Yeah," says Marco who's sitting between his sister and Lucy. "It's perfectly reasonable for me to hack into the minds of any boys Rachel might date."

"I'll do that for you," says Mollie. "Especially if you delete a certain joke."

"Deal," says Marco.

The Poet sits next to Grandma and Grandpa Han. He speaks poems to them: They speak Korean to him. Somehow, they seem to understand each other. Nick makes pleasant conversation with Karen. Both pretend the awkward moment at the door never happened. The meal is delicious. Karen takes one more bite of her kimchi rice. The west window turns lavender. Stars appear. Porter falls asleep at the table.

Later, Karen helps Nick with the dishes while Abuelita says goodbye to her guests.

The sink is built into the kitchen island so that one can enjoy the ocean view while washing dishes. Lucy and Marco have stepped out on the narrow balcony that runs along the west window. The two are shadows against an indigo sky.

"Does it bother you watching them together?" Karen asks Nick.

"Marco deserves Lucy."

"And you deserve...?"

"Not this; Abuelita spoils me, the Poet forgives me, Marco trusts me. They're all so good to me. They've made me soft. I guess that's why I invited you here. I would have never taken such a risk in the past. But that's what happens when you hang around good people; you get into the habit of trusting. And I want to trust you. Tell me, Karen Burns, if I tell you the most outrageous story, could you keep it secret?"

"And if I attempt to broadcast it, you'll erase my memory?'

"You've been paying attention."

She nods.

"Yeah, I might do that."

She laughs, "Then what choice do I have?"

"I might not steal your memories. I haven't yet, have I?"

"I wanted to ask you about that. Why not?"

"It didn't work. I tried, but you kept writing about me in your notebooks. And you kept rereading them. I first asked you out to get a hold of your notebooks. I never got very far with you. I could always tell you didn't like me much."

"I could always tell you were hiding something."

"Is that why tonight you seem to like me more?"

"Perhaps." Karen hands him a glass to dry and then says, "But going from deep distrust, to mild distrust isn't much of an upgrade."

She has a sweet round face with a small but well-formed mouth. Her signature red lip stain is beginning to fade; underneath, her lips are pink and childish. Her eyes are large and blue, not the soft twilight blue of Lucy's eyes, but a brisk blue, like cold mountain water.

"Your eyes are the most striking blue."

"You can't help but talk pretty to girls, can you?"

"Sometimes I might mean it."

"Sometimes." Karen turns from Nick's searching gaze. She looks out the window to the couple on the deck. Nick's eyes follow hers. To their surprise, it has grown too dark to see outside. Instead, they see a reflection of the large room and the two of them doing dishes together.

"You can trust me," she says,

"It's a long story."

"There are a lot of dishes."

Nick tells Karen the whole story, starting way back when he knew the Poet as Isaiah Wells and they worked in a computer lab together. Marco and Lucy come in at about the point where he erased Mollie's and Marco's memories. At times Lucy or Marco interrupt with a correction. At other times one of them has a moment of clarity: "So that's how you found me?" Karen realizes she's no longer drying the large pot she's holding. She stands with a limp dishtowel, lost in the story.

Much later, when Nick returns from walking Karen to the gate, he finds Abuelita waiting for him in the kitchen. He's genuinely happy to see her. He never had parents wait for him after a date. She tells him to sit at the bar while she serves him cocoa.

"You like this girl?"

"Perhaps."

"You risked a lot for a perhaps. You could have brought any number of girls without compromising security. But Karen Burns..."

"I know, I know, I shouldn't have done it. But I don't know..." He takes a sip of his cocoa. It has cinnamon and a hint of cayenne in it. "The thing is—she didn't forget me."

"Ah, of course. That makes sense. In the end, that's what we're fighting for, isn't it?" Abuelita has a far-off look. Nick searches her brown eyes, full of eighty years of joy and sorrow. After a pause she adds, "You cannot love unless you remember."

ACKNOWLEDGMENTS

I finished my first draft of this book in the fall of 2013, so it should come as no surprise that I have a lot of people to thank.

First, I must thank you, my friend, for picking up this book and reading it all the way to the acknowledgments. I hope this means you are looking forward to the next installment in Lucy, Marco and Nick's story.

Rachel Huffmire, you are the acquisitions editor who made my dreams come true. Thank you for your instantaneous love of this story and continued support in so many areas. You always send an email with advice or encouragement right when I need it.

John M. Olsen, you are a magician of an editor. With a few elegant solutions, you untangled my narrative and made it shine. Thanks also for tidying up a fair amount of run-on sentences and creative punctuation.

Ashley Literski, if I didn't know you better, I'd think you can mind-hack because you got the cover just right. In one intriguing image, you captured the essence of a rather complicated story. And as a bonus, you used my three favorite colors. Thank you! I love it!

A big thank you to everyone at Immortal Works Publishing. You have all been so friendly, accommodating and pleasant to work with. I feel like I've joined a large, supportive and wonderfully quirky family.

Now to my loyal beta readers: Lara Alder, Rebecca Barney, Josie Crittenden, Anna Farnsworth, Ken Farnsworth, Monique Fraser, Carrie Hamilton, Brandan Hull, Rebecca Hunt, Diedra Jardine, Melissa Kwapich, Becky Lawlor, Ben Lehnardt, Hans Lehnardt, Michelle Lehnardt, Sammie Lehnardt, Collette Mitchell, Sam

Mitchell, Mollie Payne, Sam Payne, Lynn Reeves, Christy Robinson, Colleen Sanders, Jordan Smurthwaite, Matthew Teynor, Gina Thompson and Jenn Winn. If it weren't for you guys, this book would still be languishing in a harddrive. Thank you for reading and rereading my book, pointing out typos and plot holes. Thank you for sending random texts— sometimes more than a year after reading— just to ask how my book is coming along and to tell me, one more time, how much you love it. Thank you for designing covers for me, just for fun. Thank you for telling everyone you meet how much you love this book. Thank you for reading it to your families on road trips. Most of all, thank you for believing in this story even when I wanted to give up on it.

My two most devoted beta readers deserve special mention. Harrison Payne, you started copyediting for me when you were eleven. Even then you were better at it than I am. I was beyond flattered when you asked to do a book report on my unpublished book. Your longstanding loyalty kept me motivated to find a publisher.

Besides me, Becky Hull has read and edited the most variations of this book. I could always count on you when I needed a meticulous edit on a tight deadline. I don't know how you do it; you are truly Superwoman. And even after the umpteenth read, you still gush about my book. A true gift to an aspiring writer.

A big thanks to my writing group: Jeanne Becijos, Danielle Thompson, Alyssa Cannon, and Jessica Kim. You deserve a medal for enduring all the variations of "Chapter One." Thank you for cheering me on. And thank you more for telling me hard truths when my book was not working. A special thank you to Jessica, you gave me much needed cultural coaching to make the Korean side of Marco's family more realistic. Muchas gracias to Diana Trefflich. You were so generous supplying me with details and suggestions from your own family to flesh out Marco's Mexican relatives.

A big shout out to Professor Brock Kirwan who teaches neuroscience at Brigham Young University. Thank you for answering my many questions about the brain and memory. One of my all-time favorite dinner conversations was with you and your graduate students from the Memory and Decision Making Lab. It was so much fun discussing the nature and fallibility of memory. You deserve credit for all the science I got right in this book. As for the bits I may have gotten wrong, well, as we know, memory is faulty. ;)

Finally, thank you to my family. My four marvelous children: Lizzy, Zoey, John and Will. You humored me as I repeatedly read my manuscript out loud, tried your best to comfort me after each rejection and often had to fend for yourselves when I faced a deadline.

My deepest thanks to my husband, Bill. You have always been ridiculously supportive of my writing. Even when I thought I was wasting my time with this project, I knew *you* didn't think so. Thank you for working hard and paying the bills while I neglected the laundry and chased my dreams. Each day you reconfirm my belief in true love. Thank you.

ABOUT THE AUTHOR

Ruth grew up in Salt Lake City writing plays for the neighborhood kids and "exploring" the woods near her home. She met her husband, Bill, on her first day of school at the University of Utah where she graduated with a degree in journalism. She worked as a reporter for the Deseret News before they moved their young family to Texas for Bill's medical training. After three years in Dallas, they relocated to San Diego, welcomed their fourth child and put down roots. Ruth enjoys long rambling conversations, baking (she makes the best pies), party-planning, road trips and running (slowly) along the coasts and canyons of Southern California.

This has been an
Immortal Production

CPSIA information can be obtained
at www.ICGtesting.com
Printed in the USA
LVHW111621070220
646226LV00002B/296